9/16

P9-DHP-902

THE
MONSTER
ON THE
ROAD
IS
ME

THE MONSTER ON THE ROAD IS ME

J. P. ROMNEY

FARRAR STRAUS GIROUX

New York

Farrar Straus Giroux Books for Young Readers
175 Fifth Avenue, New York 10010

Printed in the United States of America
Designed by Kristie Radwilowicz
First edition, 2016
1   3   5   7   9   10   8   6   4   2

fiercereads.com

Library of Congress Cataloging-in-Publication Data

Names: Romney, J. P., author.
Title: The monster on the road is me / J. P. Romney.
Description: First edition. | New York : Farrar, Straus, Giroux, 2016. | Summary:
   "In Japan, a teenage boy with narcolepsy is able to steal the thoughts of supernatural
   beings in his sleep, and uses this ability to defeat a mountain demon that's causing
   a string of suicides at his school"—Provided by publisher.
Identifiers: LCCN 2015036280 | ISBN 9780374316549 (hardback) |
   ISBN 9780374316556 (e-book)
Subjects: | CYAC: Supernatural—Fiction. | Demonology—Fiction. | Narcolepsy—
   Fiction. | Japan—Fiction. | BISAC: JUVENILE FICTION / Fantasy & Magic. |
   JUVENILE FICTION / Social Issues / Adolescence. | JUVENILE FICTION /
   Humorous Stories. | JUVENILE FICTION / People & Places / Asia.
Classification: LCC PZ7.1.R6685 Mo 2016 | DDC [Fic]—dc23
LC record available at http://lccn.loc.gov/2015036280

Our books may be purchased in bulk for promotional, educational, or business use. Please
contact your local bookseller or the Macmillan Corporate and Premium Sales Department at
(800) 221-7945 ext. 5442 or by e-mail at MacmillanSpecialMarkets@macmillan.com.

For Rebecca, who made this road possible

THE
MONSTER
ON THE
ROAD
IS
ME

Aiko was the first. Nothing about her was that different, really. She liked things any fifteen-year-old girl in Japan likes. Flowers, I guess. Hair accessories—bows and stuff. Hello Kitty, maybe? I have no idea what girls like. Which is why I've been on exactly one . . . two . . . oh, wait, no dates ever. I sat behind Aiko for two years and in all that time I only managed to have two real conversations with her. One of them was in homeroom. The last was at her funeral.

It was the crows. Aiko started seeing them at the beginning of first year. A few weeks later she died. Coincidence? Could be—there are crows all over Japan. But the crows of Kusaka Town are not normal crows. They watch you, clicking their beaks and flicking their wings, hungry to break into your mind. They'll push their way into the deepest tunnels of your thoughts, and once they're inside, you can never get them out.

WELCOME TO KUSAKA!
LOVELY BAMBOO FORESTS, MISTY MOUNTAINS,

RICE FIELDS AS FAR AS THE EYE CAN SEE.
WELCOME TO THIS TOTALLY NORMAL
JAPANESE TOWN!

If our town had a sign, it would read something like that. And you might believe it because, you know, it's a sign. But I've got news for you: that sign is a liar. Not a single word about crows, or mountain demons, or river trolls. And it's never good when someone has to promise that they're normal. If you meet a person and the first thing she does is tell you that she's "totally normal," you can be one hundred percent sure that she is not. Kusaka Town is like that.

On the day the crows took Aiko away, I was standing in front of my homeroom class, a neatly written piece of paper in hand.

"In the year Hōan 4, Prince Akihito became emperor of all of Japan. He was a generous ruler," I recited, "but when he was twenty-seven his brother tried to steal the throne."

I glanced back at my teacher, Shimizu-*sensei*. "I added that part about him being generous. I mean, who really knows, right? His brother was probably jealous that Akihito-*tenno* was getting all the ladies and, like, drinking all the *sake* or whatever."

"Koda."

"I mean, I don't have a brother, but if I did and he was emperor and drinking all the rice wine, I would probably hate his guts, too."

"Koda."

"I wouldn't care if I had a brother now, obviously. Not much to be jealous of when your family owns a *shiitake* farm. Well, joke's on you, brother I don't have—I hate *shiitake* mushrooms. The farm's all yours."

"Koda!"

"What?"

"Gods above, can you focus on something for five minutes? Look at me. Look right here. Okay. Now, finish your report."

"And so—"

"Not to me. To your classmates."

As I turned back to the class, Shimizu-*sensei* buried his face in his hands.

"And so began the Hōgen Rebellion, which eventually forced Emperor Akihito from the Chrysanthemum Throne. After being exiled, Emperor Akihito became obsessed. He searched out ancient Chinese texts that told of eternal life and the revenge of the damned. The emperor supposedly died in the year Chōkan 2, but most historians believe he entered the Tengu Road."

"Most historians?" broke in Kenji, whom I hate.

"Many historians," I shot back.

"Liar. How many exactly?"

"One hundred and seventeen. You smart-ass." I mumbled that last part.

"Koda, just finish your report," Shimizu-*sensei* said.

"And start with 'I read on the Internet that,'" Kenji helpfully interjected.

I tried to ignore him. "Most, or some, or one historian

believes Akihito-*tenno* entered the Tengu Road and was transformed into a mountain demon of immense power. As a *tengu*,
he could change himself into a giant condor. He flew all over
Japan starting civil wars and *samurai* rebellions, causing earthquakes and monsoons—he even brought about the fall of the
imperial throne itself."

When I stopped and looked up, two kids in my class waited
a moment and then clapped. Weakly. Kenji hissed, *"Usotsuki,"*
and threw a pencil at me.

"Baka," I shot back at him.

Shimizu-*sensei* leaned forward in his seat. "Stop it. Both of
you. Just . . . Koda, go sit down."

I squeezed along the aisle to my seat, avoiding Kenji's stupid face. When I dropped into my chair, Aiko turned back just
a bit.

"You're not a liar," she whispered.

"Yeah, well, some people don't believe in mountain demons,
I guess. Their mothers probably don't love them enough to
teach them important things."

"I believe in *tengu*," Aiko whispered. "My mother left my
family to live with a salaryman named Hiroshi, though. So
maybe I don't believe in them after all."

"Oh," I started, "I didn't mean . . ." but then trailed off and
sat there in silence.

Aiko slowly turned back to the front. Which is pretty much
how all our interactions began and ended: with awkward
silence.

Shimizu-*sensei* walked up to the chalkboard and wrote down our next assignment. "You're first-year students in high school now," he said. "I expect your compositions to be at least ten pages. This will be due next Friday, and your topic will be as follows."

He wrote on the chalkboard:

Something I Regret

"And it has to be real. Something you actually experienced. I'm talking to you, Koda. Koda, did you hear me?"

"Yes."

"What did I just say?"

"Write a report."

"On?"

"On, let's say, airplanes?"

"Not even close. Look at the board, Koda."

"Huh. Question: Can we write about airplanes if we want to? I'd like to be a pilot someday, so I think I could do a really good job on this report—if it was about airplanes."

Kenji raised his hand. "Koda probably hit his head and doesn't understand the assignment. Maybe it would help if he put his bicycle helmet on. Then he could hear what you're saying better."

I glared at him. "That doesn't even make sense. I'd hear worse with the helmet on. Besides I only need it when I'm riding my bike . . . or if my head feels, you know, sleepy or whatever."

"Weirdo," Kenji said.

The bell rang.

"Thank the gods," our teacher said. "Dismissed."

Aiko walked up the aisle before I could say something like, *Sorry for insulting the fabric of your broken family life. My bad.* She stopped in front of Shimizu-*sensei*'s desk while most of our class filed out into the hallway.

"I regret something," she said. "I regret not freeing the black birds."

Shimizu-*sensei* looked up from his papers.

"Sooner, that is. For not freeing the black birds sooner."

"Sure thing. Birds," our teacher said, returning to his papers.

"They're crying," Aiko continued.

"Sorry to hear that."

"No," she whispered, leaning in close. "*I'm* sorry to hear that."

Aiko Fujiwara was smart, despite how that last conversation made her sound. She'd started saying increasingly strange things in those weeks, the weeks before she died, but she was usually quiet, so no one really noticed. Even on good days Aiko floated along in her own little world. Which can be attractive to a guy like me. In an isolated and bizarre sort of way.

Aiko was prettier than a lot of the other girls in our class. She had bright black hair that fell down to her waist and she always wore this silver barrette pinned above her bangs. Her eyes were brown and huge, and she had long, delicate fingers. She was the kind of girl who makes the words in your mouth start wrestling to see which will come out first. Of course, when I opened my mouth, all those words usually ran off like a bunch of cowards. But that's how it'd always been with Aiko.

She turned without looking back and left the room.

"Until we meet again," I blurted out from my desk. Because apparently I turn into a forty-year-old with a monocle when I try to say goodbye to girls I like. Shimizu-*sensei* looked up from his desk, shook his head, and then went back to his papers.

Aiko: five hundred points. My words: zero.

The students of Kusaka High School made their way downstairs to the first floor. They stepped out of their school slippers. They laughed and shoved each other while pulling on their street shoes in the *genkan* entrance, then turned and walked out into the sunlight.

Most of the students unlocked their back tires and rode their bicycles home, but a few lived far enough into the mountains that the school hired a bus driver to take them back and forth. Yori, the driver, swung the doors open.

"Everybody on," he called out at the top of his voice. "If you get left behind, a water troll will suck out your life-energy."

The students laughed and pushed their way into the empty seats.

"I'm serious," Yori said. "You will be a dry and bitter husk.

And we're off!" Yori cheerfully folded the door shut, and the bus pulled away from Kusaka High School. The kids on bicycles rode out like a flock of birds into the rice fields and the neighborhoods below.

I ran back inside the school and returned my copy of *The Hōgen Rebellion* to the library, but I wasn't fast enough. Ino-*sensei*, the school counselor, caught me on the stairs.

"Koda."

I looked up, still fishing through the front pocket of my slacks for my bicycle key. *"Konnichiwa,"* I said.

Ino-*sensei* smiled and replied, *"Konnichiwa, Koda-kun."* And then stood there. Still smiling.

Okay. Now it was my turn to talk? "I was returning a book," I said.

She nodded. Even the creases in her eyes were smiling.

Ino-*sensei* and I had these interactions once in a while. I didn't really mind meeting with a counselor, considering my . . . personal issue, but there was an awful lot of smiling that went on. And I am not a good smiler. Picture a bullfrog getting choked, and that's pretty much what my smile looks like. So I shifted a bit, forced my signature froggy grin, and realized my hand was still pretty deep in my pocket. Ino-*sensei* suddenly noticed it, too.

"Sorry," I said, yanking my hand out. Ino-*sensei* was twenty-three years old, and other guys in class talked about how pretty she was. That's a nice way of putting what they said about her. I didn't talk like that. I didn't even think like that. Most of the time I honestly didn't understand the words they were using.

When I pulled my hand out of my pocket, my bike key, along with a huge Pikachu bobblehead keychain, popped out. Listen, just about every businessman in Japan walks around with a cutesy charm dangling off his cell phone. It's not that weird. But as I stood there grinning, Pikachu bouncing back and forth against my leg, the following thought passed through my mind: *Maybe boys in high school shouldn't be carrying these around.*

Ino-*sensei* motioned to the counseling room. "Do you have a minute, Koda-*kun*?"

"*Hai*," I said. Anything to stop the grinning and the bobbling.

"You did well today," she said, sliding the counseling door behind me. "Very well. I'm proud of you."

"Proud that I didn't fall asleep during my report today?"

She knelt down at the low table on the *tatami* mat floor. "Reports can be stressful."

"You must be proud of almost everyone in first-year Class B. Only two people fell asleep. Neither of them was me."

She smiled. "Would you like some *o-cha*?" she asked, twisting the cap from a bottle of green tea.

"*Arigatō gozaimasu.*"

As she poured a glass she asked if I'd considered wearing my helmet during the report.

"It's funny you say that, because I did consider it," I said.

"But then I remembered it's autumn and indoor bicycle helmets aren't really in fashion right now."

"Did you feel stress?" she asked, sliding the tea forward on a coaster.

She meant the kind of stress that makes a kid in my condition fall asleep and smack his head on a desk corner. "Nope. Kenji even said he couldn't believe how good my report was."

"He said that, did he?"

"Or he said he couldn't believe my report. It's hard to remember."

"Was he right?" she asked.

"About what?"

"Were you fibbing on your report?"

"Not at all. I mean, mostly not. A little. There was one part. It's called dramatic irony."

"Do you know what 'irony' means, Koda?"

"I do not."

"And how did you respond to Kenji?"

"Well, first I bowed. Then I thanked him for his razor-sharp wit and slowly backed out of the room so that my presence wouldn't offend his ancestors any further." I sipped from the glass. "Or I may have called him a stupid idiot."

"Probably the second one?"

"Probably."

She nodded. "Well, I don't want to keep you long. I'm sure you have fifteen-year-old things to do. I just want to remind you that this is a safe place to talk. You understand that, don't you?"

I finished the last of my tea and nodded. "Uh-huh."

She crossed her hands in her lap and said, "Thank you for coming, Koda-*kun*. I'm very proud of you. Well, mostly proud of you. Be careful out there." She smiled and then bowed.

I bowed lower and said, *"Iro iro arigatō gozaimashita."*

I walked down the concrete steps of Kusaka High School and made my way toward the bicycle awning tucked back from the street. I didn't have a clue what I was going to write for my composition assignment. "Something I Regret"? I regret not punching Kenji in his fat left eye.

Pikachu's head bobbled back and forth from the lock on my tire as I walked my bike toward the street. I lifted the enormous helmet out of my bicycle basket and latched it under my chin. Picture half a watermelon strapped to a broomstick and you get the general idea of what this thing looked like on me. Thankfully, it stayed in my basket. Most of the day.

My last "incident" had been more than two months ago. Before that time, I hadn't really had an attack for a year and a half. People like my parents and Ino-*sensei* were making too big a deal of this. If I was falling asleep every other day, fine, stick a giant helmet on my head. But once or twice a year? I'll risk cracking my head on the floor. Believe it or not, helmets are not one of the socially accepted forms of high school headgear.

I turned my front tire in the direction of my family's mushroom farm and set my foot on the pedal. Then I heard the front door to the school open behind me. I looked back and saw Aiko walking down the concrete steps.

She was carrying a few books in her arms, and as she made her way down the stairs she started mumbling to herself. I couldn't make out what she was saying. The sounds just dripped off her lips and evaporated into the mountain air. When she reached the bottom, she tripped and fell. It was a strange fall. Like she hadn't realized she was falling until just before she hit the ground. One of the few times a soccer-ball-sized helmet would have done someone some good.

I should have rushed forward and helped her pick up the books. I should have sprinted over and offered her my hand. I could have at least called out, *"Daijōbu?* Are you all right?" But I didn't do that. I couldn't do that. Like so many times before, when it came to Aiko I couldn't say anything at all.

This time was different, though. Aiko pulled herself up from the pavement. Her eyes were glossy and faded. She looked like she'd been crying. Not from the fall. From before that. She left her books on the ground and walked over to me. My muscles seized.

Aiko Fujiwara looked me straight in the eye, confused, like she didn't recognize me. She pushed my helmet back and took my face in her hand. That was when the world went cold. Ice cold. Middle-of-space, pitch-black, sinking cold. I could feel it on my breath, in my hair, beneath my skin. I knew exactly what it meant. I was having another attack. And for the first time, I was glad I had that stupid helmet on.

In my dream Aiko was bleeding from a cut on her knee. It

was so cold that the blood should have frozen solid, but it seeped down into her wool sock and stained her leg bright red. The stain looked like a *sakura* flower—a cherry blossom in May. It made me think of picnic festivals and music and shrines.

"I have to free the black birds," Aiko said in my direction. "I have to do it by myself. There's nowhere left to hide."

"What are you hiding from?" I asked the frigid air between us.

"You won't arrive, Yatagarasu," Aiko whispered past me. "You won't arrive in time." Her lip trembled.

> *"Crows fly.*
> *A traveler on the road*
> *Is lost."*

That was new. Aiko was always a little odd, but I sure don't remember her talking in *haiku* before.

That's when my vision flickered back. That's when the air felt warm again. That's when I saw my legs tangled up in my overturned bike frame. It had been two months since I'd fallen asleep like that, and now it'd happened in the parking lot of the school. In front of Aiko Fujiwara, of all people.

Aiko left me on the ground. She picked up her fallen textbooks and loosely stacked them in her arms. She stared off into the mountains behind the school, chattering to herself, bleeding down the outside of her leg. She didn't look at me again. Her feet shuffled forward, and I lay there watching as she walked up an old tea farmer's footpath. From somewhere behind the school, a flock of crows lifted up like a black wave and stormed after her. Their cries were deafening, but Aiko didn't even notice.

The next morning they found Aiko's body in the school gymnasium. She had drunk a liter of cleaning fluid. I was the last person to see her alive. I should have gone after her.

Something I Regret

2

The day before Aiko's funeral I steered my bicycle down the backstreets to the Lawson's convenience store. Of course, the easiest way to get to Lawson's is riding straight down Route 33, but my folks are afraid I'll fall asleep and drift out into traffic. So I take the backstreets. And always wear my special helmet.

Sometimes I pretend my bicycle is a Yokosuka seaplane. And instead of riding down dusty old backstreets, I'm flying along the coast of Japan, delivering *shiitake* to all those people who can eat mushrooms without throwing up.

For as long as I can remember, I've wanted to fly. To be a pilot who could soar above the clouds and leave the tiny roads and the mountain villages behind. Sometimes I even pretend I was alive during the Pacific War. *You should totally be a pilot, Koda,* someone would say. *You never suddenly fall asleep. In fact, I've never seen you sleep for even a single moment. You could fly to America and back without ever getting tired.*

And I'd say, *Yeah, I pretty much never sleep. Got too many things to do.*

This would get back to the admiral of the Imperial Navy, who would give me my own Zero-*sen* fighter plane.

Fly like the god wind and crash your plane into the enemies of our beloved emperor, the admiral would say.

Or, I'd interrupt, *instead of doing that—and this is just a thought—I could fly around the world. Which would also be good for the emperor and all that other stuff.*

The admiral would step back and size me up. *I don't like it. I do not like it one bit. But you are the boy who never sleeps, so here are the keys. Make the emperor proud. And by the way, take off that helmet, boy. There are no helmets allowed in the Imperial Navy.*

Yes, sir! Gladly, sir! I'd say, punting my stupid helmet off the side of the aircraft carrier.

But then I get to the convenience store and remember I'm just a high school kid with a secondhand bike and a sleeping disorder. Oh well, there's always the ride home.

"I'll take a bowl of *oden,*" I told Haru as I walked into the store.

"What do you want in it?" he asked.

"I don't know. *Konyaku, tamago,* a little *daikon.*"

"Broth?"

"Sure." I slid Haru two *go-hyaku* coins.

"Nah, take it. On the house."

Even though he was three years older than me, Haru was my only friend in Kusaka. That makes it sound like I had friends outside of Kusaka. Nope, he was my only friend, period.

Haru lived with his uncle in a broken-down house at the

end of our street. His uncle was the kind of man who would push a shrine maiden down a flight of stairs for a warm glass of *sake*. Or for anything really: a coin, an old boot, a bit of tinfoil. The man was simpleminded, and a bastard. Not a good combination.

Haru didn't graduate from high school. He dropped out, stayed in Kusaka, and eventually picked up a job at Lawson's. I usually stopped in after school or when I was in the area delivering *shiitake* to the vegetable stands behind Route 33.

"How's your paper?" he asked, sliding a pair of chopsticks across the counter.

"The one from homeroom?"

"Sure. The one about the robot."

"Robot?"

He pulled a cigarette out of his shirt pocket. "It's not about a robot?" he asked.

"No. When did you ever have robot homework?"

He shrugged.

"And that is why you didn't graduate," I said.

"Let's go outside," Haru said, walking around the counter.

"Can you just take a break like that?"

"I don't know. There's no one here anyway."

We sat down on the curb and Haru lit his cigarette. He held it out to me, but I ignored him. I might be the only fifteen-year-old in Japan who doesn't have a fascination with smoking. Just not that interested in it. I did try it once. My face got all puffy and my skin turned bright red. It was like my body was somehow allergic to breathing in poison.

And really, none of the other fifteen-year-olds should be smoking either. It's obviously against the law. But no one takes that seriously when you can just walk down the street and drop a couple of coins into a *jidōhanbaiki*.

In Japan we love our vending machines. We'll put anything in them: cigarettes, batteries, TV dinners, raincoats, pornography, used underwear. Think of almost anything, and I'll bet you can find a *jidōhanbaiki* somewhere in Japan that's selling it. I've seen a six-year-old kid buy a two-liter bottle of *sake* from the vending machine down the road. I guess his father was too lazy to get up and buy it himself. At least, I hope that's what was happening.

"People like robots, you know," Haru said.

"Hmm."

"Maybe it's a girl robot. She could wear this sexy outfit and fly around rescuing people."

"You remember what homework is, right?"

"Vaguely."

"The paper is on something we regret," I said.

"Shimizu-*sensei*?"

I nodded.

Haru took another drag. "I bet he regrets assigning that now."

"Yeah," I said.

"Didn't you say that girl talked to birds?"

"Aiko talked *about* birds. There's a difference."

"But they were birds that weren't there?"

"A bird," I said. "It was mostly this one bird. Yatagarasu. But yes, he wasn't there."

If Aiko was crazy for talking to something no one else could see, then a lot of people in Japan are crazy. The ghosts of ancestors, gods and goddesses, spirits from local shrines—most people worship things they've never actually seen. I didn't care if Aiko was a little too quiet or spent her breaks on the balcony looking for a three-legged crow. Crows are cool enough, or so I used to think.

"Who drinks bathroom cleaner?" Haru asked. "Who wants to die like that?"

"It was a message," I said.

Haru snubbed his cigarette and flicked the butt into the parking lot. "How do you figure?" he asked.

"Well, they closed the school after Aiko's body was found, right? They washed down the doors and the *genkan* and the stairs. They polished and mopped everything to get the school back to the way it was. But now the building just reeks of cleaning fluid. They didn't remove Aiko from the school at all. They just scrubbed her deeper into the walls."

"That's pretty sick."

"They realized it, but only after it was too late. You should see the place now. No one messes around in the halls or plays badminton in the courtyard during break anymore. Everyone just stays inside with the windows open and the fans on," I said.

"And I thought this *mimonai* Lawson's job was bad."

"It was a message, Haru. No one can ignore her now."

"I bet it was a message about that driver—what's his name?"

"Yori-*san?*"

"Yeah, the crazy guy who drives the bus."

"Yori."

"I bet the message was: *He finally did it.* The creepy little driver finally killed one of us."

I pushed up from the curb. "Whatever. I gotta go."

"Seriously? Are you mad? It was a joke, Koda. Not a good joke, I see that now. But c'mon."

I kicked out the stand on my bike and steadied the box of mushrooms tied down to the back. "I've got deliveries to make, Haru. See you tomorrow."

"Whatever," he said.

I fastened my helmet and pushed off down the street behind Lawson's. The sliding door dinged softly behind me.

Forget Haru. I didn't know why, but Aiko had chosen me just before she died. She had walked up to me and whispered in my ear. All I'd ever done was stare at her from the back of our homeroom class, but for some reason she stepped into my dream and told me she had nowhere left to hide. Her death wasn't random. It meant something. It had to. I just couldn't see it yet.

3

Aiko's family lived in a house that must have been two hundred years old. Latticed wood and paper doors. *Bonsai* trees. A small pond for *koi*. All tucked into a mountainside covered with bamboo and scrubby trees and ferns twisting over the ground. An ideal Japanese house in an ideal Japanese town, right?

Instead of traveling to Kōchi City, Aiko's father decided to hold the funeral inside their home. The front doors were pulled open, the family shrine was moved to the sitting room, and the yard was flooded with flowers and lanterns and *ihai* spirit tablets.

I wound my way through the maze of men and women in black suits and dark *kimono*. I saw classmates in pressed uniforms, eyes stained, holding on to their handkerchiefs like they were tiny pieces of Aiko herself. They never thought twice about her before, but after she died she suddenly became the most important person in the entire world.

Ino-*sensei* stood near the entrance to the house, placing a hand on the shoulders of the students walking by. At times she would cross her arms and hold her elbows as if trying to physically hold herself together. Headmaster Sato walked up the front stairs with his wife and nodded to the school counselor without looking her in the eyes.

I put my foot on the first step.

"Hello, Koda," Ino-*sensei* whispered. "Did you come alone?"

I nodded. Someone in the sitting room was crying loudly. Now that I was standing here, I wasn't sure I could actually go inside. I couldn't keep the images of Aiko's family from running wild through my head. I knew that tomorrow morning Aiko's father would dress in his black suit and drive his daughter's remains to the crematorium. He would return home and wait while a Buddhist priest laid her body on a metal tray and closed the oven door. In time, her father would get a call from that priest telling him to return. Aiko's father would stand over the ashes of his daughter. He would pick out her bones with a special pair of chopsticks and place them carefully in an urn.

"Start at the feet and end at the neck," the priest would say. "That way she'll be upright in the tomb."

Aiko's father would nod and concentrate on keeping his hands steady. He'd wipe at his eyes, trying not to spill his tears on what remained of his only child.

"Please, come in," said a woman sitting at a thin table at the top of the stairs.

I shook away the images, bowed to Ino-*sensei*, and walked inside Aiko's home. I set a silver-and-black envelope of condolence money on the table. The woman took the envelope and said, "Thank you, Okita-*san*. Please sign your name here."

I picked up the pen and wrote *Okita Koda* into the guest registry. The woman bowed and motioned for me to enter the sitting room.

I turned the corner to see Aiko staring at me. She was wearing her school uniform, a silver barrette pinned in her hair. She looked pretty but serious. Not a corner of a smile. No sadness in her eyes. She looked like she was thinking. Thinking of how she could escape the golden frame keeping her trapped inside that huge portrait.

Guests were seated on either side of Aiko's shrine. I walked up the center aisle and bowed to her family on the left and then again to the right. Her father was there, his face red and stony. Her mother was missing. Maybe she and Hiroshi the Salaryman couldn't be bothered to return to Kusaka.

I stepped closer to Aiko's portrait, which was drowning in a sea of flowers and fruit, *mochi* rice balls, and leafy green branches. I draped a string of *juzu* prayer beads over my hands and bowed to her. Standing there, I didn't know what to whisper to Aiko. I wasn't very good at talking to things that weren't there. After a few moments I bowed again. I guess our last conversation wasn't really a conversation at all. I hoped if Aiko was watching, or listening, or whatever, I hoped she knew the things I couldn't say out loud.

I reached out and took a pinch of incense. I dropped it into the copper burner set up in front of the shrine and watched the smoke drift up over her portrait. The wisps hung in the air and then disappeared completely. I started to leave, but stopped when I caught sight of a three-legged crow.

To the side of Aiko's portrait sat another shrine. This one belonged not to an ancestor, but to the absent Yatagarasu. In the most ancient historical records, this large three-legged crow led Jimmu, the first emperor, to what would become the first capital of Japan. The small shrine was decorated with paper lanterns and statuettes and reliefs showing how Yatagarasu swept down from the heavens and saved Jimmu, leading him safely to his new home. Maybe the shrine was there so that Yatagarasu would find Aiko, too.

I turned and bowed quickly again to her family so that they wouldn't see my face. I hurried through the room and out the front door. The woman seated at the thin table handed me a decorated bag full of tea and small chocolates. I thanked her and quickly walked away from Aiko's used-to-be home. I held my hand over my eyes and stepped down into the crowd of mourners, winding my way toward the front gate.

I thought I could make it through Aiko's yard. I thought I could get on my bike and push away from that place where three-legged crows look for lost girls and words hang in the air like threads of smoke. But before I could reach my bike I collided with another girl, this one dressed in gray.

I looked up and for a fraction of a second I thought I'd run into Aiko. The girl was about Aiko's height and her eyes looked almost identical. She even had a silver barrette in her hair.

I wanted to bow and say *Sumimasen*, but the words froze solid in my mouth.

"Get up," the girl in gray said.

I tried to answer, but the world had become so cold that my lips could barely move.

"Get up, Seimei! Please!" she screamed, looking past me as if I weren't even there.

Icy air swirled around my limbs, stiffening my muscles, locking my face and eyes onto hers. This wasn't real. I'd fallen asleep. *Not here. Please, don't let me lose my mind here.*

The girl in gray reached out, and the tips of her fingers began to smoke. "You'll wish you were dead," she barked. Smoke swirled up out of her sleeves and through the neck of her dress. "By the fire of Inari, you'll wish you had died with the rest of them!" Through the freezing fog her eyes burned like broken shards of brimstone.

I forced the funeral bag in front of my face, shielding myself with tea and small chocolates. The girl screamed and the world around us exploded in flames.

"Koda. Koda, open your eyes. Look at me, Koda."

Ino-*sensei* lifted my neck and pressed a damp handkerchief to my forehead.

"I'm sorry," I said. The words dribbled out of my mouth and down the side of my face. I tried to stand up.

"Slowly," she said, helping me to my feet.

All around me stood classmates and teachers and people I'd never seen before. People who should have been paying their respects to Aiko but now looked on in utter confusion

at the fifteen-year-old who had just passed out in her front
garden.

I pushed past Ino-*sensei* and steadied myself. They weren't
saying it, but I knew they were thinking it. *At a classmate's
funeral? How could he do such a thing? Has he no shame?*

"I'll drive you home," Ino-*sensei* said.

"I'm fine," I shot back.

"Koda, I'll put your bike in the back and drive you away
from here."

My knees felt weak. "Okay," I whispered, because getting
away was the only thing I wanted.

The girl in gray, who was never smoking and was never on
fire, stood off to the side. She watched me as Ino-*sensei* and
I stumbled through the crowd of silent mourners. When I
looked back from the front gate, she was still staring at me,
leaning between the black suits and dark *kimono*, keeping her
eyes firmly locked on mine.

4

It's called *suiminhossa*. Sleep attacks. It mostly happens when . . . How did the doctor put it? When the area of my brain that regulates stress dominates the motor control centers of the brain itself. In other words, my feelings sucker-punch my head and I black out. It's only really dangerous when I'm riding my bike. Or attending funerals, apparently.

It didn't always used to be like this. Before Aiko, I'd only had two attacks in my whole life. The first time was when I was thirteen. It was embarrassing. Also, it happened at a public bathhouse—so I was as nude as a *sumō* wrestler's left butt cheek.

I'd soaped myself clean in the showers and then stepped outside to the public bath. Steam was rising from the water and drifting up into the open mountainside. There were other men on our side of the partition, mostly old, lounging around in the hot water with their arms folded neatly across their bellies.

I sat in the water next to my father. He leaned back, closed his eyes, and let out a long sigh of relief. Soon, though, I got this uneasy feeling. Not the feeling of being surrounded by old, naked guys—I had gotten used to that feeling a while ago—but the feeling I was being watched. And I was. I turned to see a stumpy man crouching in the water on the opposite side of the bath.

I was going to say something like *Hello* or *Good evening* or *Maybe you shouldn't stare at nude boys in a bathhouse*, but he had this look in his eyes. He seemed annoyed by me being there. Like I was seeing something I shouldn't be seeing.

My father shifted and brought handfuls of hot water up over his head and neck. Is it strange to be sitting in a public bathhouse staring at a naked man who is staring back at you? Probably. Probably, yes. But no matter how upset the squinty man appeared to get, I just couldn't look away. The fear bubbling up inside wouldn't let me tear my eyes from his. He had this *tanuki-gao*. A raccoon-face. You know, kind of squished in the middle. Awful, beady little eyes. A face that makes you think he's hiding a whole mouthful of razor teeth.

The man tilted his head to the side, the way a dog does when it looks confused. He raised his hands from the water and shook his palms at me. *"Dete ike, suri. Dete ike."*

Why was he calling me a pickpocket? The words sounded muddled and confused. It took me a few seconds to work through what he was saying, but by then it was too late. The stubby man had pushed up from the water. He was walking at me and shaking his hands.

Now, when a naked man starts calling you a thief and waving his fat fingers in your face, that is probably the best time to leave the bathhouse. I looked at my father, whose head was half submerged, and when I turned back, the raccoon-faced man grabbed my hair and shoved me beneath the water. I pushed up, gasping for air, frantically searching for a reason in his crazy eyes. That was the first time I had a cold dream.

I'd never been that freezing before. This wasn't "winter without your coat on," this was "winter exploding out of every pore in your body." The bathhouse had become a glacier. It was so cold that the water should have been a single sheet of ice, but it kept flowing as if it weren't affected by the temperature at all. The raccoon-faced man—the one who had just been attacking me—was now squatting with me on the banks of Kusaka River.

Reaching down into the water, the stubby man pulled up a handful of leaves. He rolled them in the palm of his hand and set the wad on the earth beside him. When he took his hands away, the leaves weren't leaves anymore. They were crumpled *ichi man* bills. Dripping wet, mashed together—there must have been fifty thousand yen just sitting on the edge of the river. A small fortune. Especially to a thirteen-year-old.

The raccoon-faced man reached down and pulled up another handful of leaves and set down another handful of cash. He narrowed his eyes and clicked his tongue and said into the air, "Men don't want wishes anymore. All they want is this." He held up a hairy fist dripping with paper bills. "With enough money a man can make anything he wants appear. No need for wishes anymore. No need for *tanuki*." He threw the bills into the air, but only leaves came tumbling down.

"They're wrong," he cried. "Money won't save them. Money won't save any of us. Not against the Tengu Road and the monster that lives there." He dropped his hands into the water. "They are infected with it," the *tanuki*-man said. "They will bring destruction on us all."

The next thing I remember was my father kneeling over me, shaking my shoulders. I tried to breathe in, but my lungs were paralyzed. I screamed and only water gurgled out. When I sucked in, it was like inhaling through a coffee stirrer.

The doctors later said that the stress of the stubby man's attack kicked off my narcolepsy. I'd fallen asleep and slipped below the surface of the water. My father pushed away the strange man and dragged me out of the bath. My attacker disappeared from the bathhouse, though nobody could say in what direction he ran. I never saw him again, but it didn't matter that much—my life had already changed forever.

"*Suiminhossa,*" the doctor from the hospital said.

"Narcolepsy? My boy will never sleep again," my mother said, beginning to cry.

"No," the doctor said. "No, just the opposite."

My mother cried some more. "My boy will never wake again."

"Okay, not the opposite. It just means he might fall asleep in inappropriate places."

My mother sobbed even louder. "My boy will never be appropriate again."

My father took my mother by the arm and led her out of the small examination room. And then I was all alone. A thirteen-year-old sitting across from a doctor and three nurses. One of them coughed.

"Do . . . do you have any questions?" the doctor asked.

I thought for a minute and then said, "Can I still fly airplanes?"

"That's cute," the doctor said, smiling to the nurses, who smiled right back. "Sure, you can still fly on airplanes. You can even take a nap on an airplane if your head is feeling especially sleepy."

"No," I said. "Not can I *ride* on an airplane—can I *fly* the airplane? Can I still be a pilot?"

Everyone laughed, but when they saw I wasn't laughing, they stopped. One of them coughed again.

"No," the doctor said. "No, I'm afraid that wouldn't be safe."

A year and a half went by before my second attack. Well, attacks. Very small attacks. Like three of them. In a single day. I really think that should just count as one, though.

Haru and I were sitting in front of Lawson's watching the cars speed by on Route 33 when this guy on a scooter lost control and jerked into an oncoming truck. I don't remember exactly what it looked like because it happened so fast, but I do remember the sound. The horrible crumpling of metal and popping of plastic. By the time the police and the paramedics arrived there wasn't much left. The handlebars were in a rice field nearby. A tire was found in someone's garden.

As the police cars and the ambulance were pulling away, I saw the scooter's rearview mirror lying in the parking lot. I wrapped it in a *furoshiki* to take home. Haru said it was morbid to keep the mirror because the driver was going to die on the way to the hospital.

"I could use it, though," I told him.

"Use it for what?"

"I could keep it in my bathroom. Make sure the back of my hair is straight."

Haru kicked a piece of broken glass. "Somewhere that guy's ancestors are crying because you said that."

"I'd think of him every time I walk into the bathroom."

"You don't even know who 'him' is."

"It doesn't matter," I said. "The important thing is that as long as I have this mirror, he isn't really gone. Someone remembers that he was alive and driving down Route 33."

"Not driving particularly well."

I ignored him. "And isn't that what we all want in the end? Someone to remember us? Doesn't that keep us alive in some small way?"

"I'll tell you what, Koda. If I die, keep a picture of me somewhere. Don't make a comb out of my hand. If that's my only choice, I'd rather not be remembered for running my dead fingers through your hair each morning."

"Gross," I said. "And you won't die. At least not anytime soon."

I smiled, but Haru wasn't looking at me. He was staring off

in the direction of his uncle's house. "Just keep a picture of me somewhere," he said again.

When I got home, I unwrapped the rearview mirror and set it on my bathroom sink. Tried to, anyway. As soon as I touched the plastic my world went ice cold. I dreamed of the accident Haru and I had just seen, only this time from the scooter driver's point of view. Because I didn't know what really happened, my imagination filled in all sorts of details. The man lost control of the scooter because he'd been drinking. He'd been drinking because he knew he was going to get fired from his job at Daimaru Department Store in Kōchi City and he didn't know how to tell his elderly mother. He lost his balance and swerved into the oncoming truck. That's where the dream stopped. I woke up with a mean bruise on my head from the edge of the bathroom sink.

I pushed myself up from the floor. My face was throbbing. I picked up the rearview mirror and the world went ice cold again. The dream was the same as before. Drinking. Going to get fired. Shame. Losing balance. Oncoming truck.

I opened my eyes. There was blood on the floor. I must have split that bruise when I fell for the second time.

"Koda," my mother called upstairs. "Koda, are you all right? Do you want me to come up there? I'll get my cane and walk up there if you need me."

"No," I called back. "Don't do that. I just . . . I just dropped something." I propped myself up against the side of the door and made it carefully to my feet. *Head wounds bleed way more than they need to,* I remember thinking. Having learned absolutely nothing, I reached down for the rearview mirror and blacked out a third time. My mother sent my father upstairs after me.

"It's just a nick on his forehead," my father said.

"It's a giant gash! He could have died!" my mother cried. "He could have fainted, stumbled into the toilet, and drowned."

Which seems like the absolute worst way to go, if you ask me.

"He'd just seen a bad accident," my father said. "He was stressed. Our boy is not strong in the conventional use of the term."

Hey.

"We should be watching him every day," my mother said, continuing her freak-out. "He should never leave our sight. We'll get the old truck running and take him to school every single day."

"And who's going to do the driving?" my father asked. "You haven't driven that truck in thirty years. The boy just needs a bicycle helmet or something."

"What if he falls asleep and a car hits him?" my mother shot back.

"Give him a helmet and forbid him from riding on Route 33. He'll be fine."

My father and I don't usually see eye to eye on, like, anything, but I'm glad he was there that day.

"Fine." My mother surrendered, tossing the rearview mirror into the trash can. "But only if the helmet is custom-made.

None of those stylish motorcycle helmets for my son, no. It has to be three times the size of a normal helmet. With ear protection. Like a batter's helmet that covers his entire skull. It's very important that any person in the same town as our child instantly sees that he poses a danger to himself and everyone around him. Also, this will make sure no girl ever dates him. Ever."

I may be adding a little bit to that last part. Anyway, that's when I was supposed to start wearing my helmet during "high-risk" situations like bike riding, combing the back of my hair, and talking to girls.

"He can't wear the helmet everywhere. You'll make an outcast of him," my father said. "Besides, he'll probably do something odd like decorate it with Pokémon stickers."

"I won't do that," I protested.

But yes, I did.

The day after the funeral I was standing in the parking lot of Lawson's, downing the last of an energy drink and waiting for Haru's shift to end. Tomorrow all the students would return to Kusaka High School and try not to talk about Aiko. There was nothing left to say. We'd exhausted the hows and the whys. No one really knew what Aiko was thinking that night. She never told us. Sometimes terrible things just happen. Isn't that what they say? The only thing we can do is try to stop those terrible things from happening again.

But guess what? We'd already failed.

I threw the empty can into the recycling bin and looked through the window. Haru was ringing someone up at the counter. When I turned back to Route 33, I thought I saw a white cat dart across the street and disappear under a parked van.

No, it wasn't a cat. Too big to be a cat. I took a few steps forward. It might have been a fox.

Foxes are rare in Japan. I guess. I've only seen a couple of them in Kusaka, so I suppose that means they're rare. I think people say it's good luck to see a fox. Don't they? Well, if they do, they're wrong. I bent over and peered under the van. Nothing. Foxes are not good luck. You can see it in their eyes. And their sharp little teeth. Never trust an animal that can bite off your kneecap. *That's* what people should really say.

Ichiro, star pitcher of the baseball team, walked to school, jimmied open the window to the teachers' lounge, and made his way to the math teacher's classroom. He apparently knocked over a can of pencils on Ikeda-*sensei*'s desk. People made a big deal out of that. I don't know why. Especially considering what he was about to do. "Ichiro was the kind of student who would pick up a friend if he accidentally knocked him down," they'd say. "It's strange he left the pencils on the floor like that."

No, it's strange that he was upstairs in Ikeda-*sensei*'s classroom, kneeling in the dark with a kitchen knife. That was strange.

The next morning, Kusaka High School locked and chained its doors. Most of the teachers and staff stood outside with their faces in their hands. They told the kids to ride their bikes back home. They flagged the drivers to turn around. They sat on the steps, close to one another, and waited for the sirens to come.

Again.

5

Kusaka High School closed for the last week of September. Eventually the cars and the trucks and the flashing lights pulled away, leaving the building chained up and draped in shadow. As I rode by on my way to deliver mushrooms, the school rose slowly from the rice fields. Yes, Kusaka is that kind of Japanese mountain town. The kind where we have to build our schools in the middle of rice fields. It always reminded me of a *daimyō* castle surrounded by bridges and moats and narrow dirt paths.

And just like a real *daimyō* castle, the school was built to last centuries. There were heavy metal doors and thick panes of glass with iron-plated storm shutters. Every surface was painted white to reflect the sun and keep out the salty sea air. For eighty years the school had stood up against everything Japan could throw at it: earthquakes, typhoons, flash floods, mudslides. But it couldn't keep Aiko out. And five days later it couldn't keep Ichiro out either.

Oddly enough, things were quieter at school after the

second suicide. We'd spent all the words we carried around when Aiko died.

Ichiro Kobayashi had moved to Kusaka late last year to live with his uncle. He transferred from a school in Matsuyama and no one really knew why. Some kids on the baseball team said his parents died in a car accident. Others said he woke up one morning and they were just gone. Whatever happened, Ichiro was quiet about it. He was nice to the kids who asked, but you knew he couldn't say anything. Not *wouldn't* say anything. *Couldn't.*

After the transfer to Kusaka, Ichiro was immediately promoted to starting pitcher on the baseball team. He made the other students look like the idea of hitting a ball with a bat was so difficult that we should all just give up and do something easier, like calculus or astrophysics. That was Ichiro. Tall, fit, popular. But then he broke into the high school at night and went all feudal Japan on us.

Back in the olden days, long before we settled our differences with celebrity game shows, insane obstacle courses, and Dance Dance Revolution, *hara-kiri* was how a *samurai* purged himself of a great dishonor. The warrior would dress up in a ceremonial *kimono* and cut open his stomach with a short sword. I guess they figured his shame would spill out onto the floor. I don't know who first came up with the idea that shame is something that can actually be cut from your insides, but I bet it was a process of trial and error. Is this the shame? Nope. Okay, how about this squiggly thing? Still feeling shame.

Well, this thing is beating, how about this? Yep. Yep. Feeling less shame already. Feeling less of everything, actually.

The disgraced *samurai* could choose a friend to stand over him with a long *katana* blade. When the *samurai* finished cutting himself, the friend would bring down his sword and end the *samurai's* suffering with a single stroke to his neck. That was considered an act of mercy, by the way. I'd sure hate to be that one *samurai* who had no friends in the village. Who am I kidding? I *would* have been that one *samurai*.

But Ichiro wouldn't have. He had plenty of friends at Kusaka High School. None were with him that night, though. He knelt on the math room floor, alone, a kitchen knife in hand, and bled out in the darkness.

Using his hand as a *shodō* brush, Ichiro had painted a *kanji* symbol on the floor. The only ink he had was draining out between his fingers.

烏

Karasu.

Crow.

The blood seeped into the floor. So deep, in fact, that the more the teachers scrubbed the strokes, the more permanently they etched the *kanji* into the tile. When they stood back and saw what they'd done—how the ghostly word would not be removed—they just abandoned the room. They turned off the lights and shut the math room door and tried to keep Ichiro's last *kanji* a secret from the rest of us.

The school remained chained and bolted during the next week. Teachers were assigned to drive by at night to check for broken windows. That probably wouldn't have stopped any-thing, but it made everyone feel a little safer.

"Name seven things that make people in this town feel safe." Haru took a drag on his cigarette and blew out the smoke. Somewhere behind us the television in Lawson's blared colorful commercials at no one.

"Seven things?" I said, leaning back on the curb.

"Yep."

"Disposable face masks. That would have to be number one."

"Of course."

"*Kōban* police boxes."

"Easy."

"Crossing guards."

"Okay."

"Delicately wrapped fruit, a bowl of *miso* soup, braided rope."

"From a shrine?"

"Yes."

"And the last one?"

"I'll go with a *bā-chan* pushing a baby carriage."

"What?" Haru laughed. "No way, that's totally creepy, and not safe. Seriously, why would a little old lady buy a baby carriage in the first place? Where's the baby that should be inside? What exactly is inside it now? Is it a doll? A broken picture frame? A human head?"

"*Baka*," I said, kicking Haru's shoe. "You know why they push them around. Some women work in fields and get their spines jacked up from sporing mushrooms all day. Some women lean on baby carriages for proper back support. Some women fill those carriages with groceries because they don't drive anymore, and when they finally push the stupid thing home again, some women have treats for their sons if they've finished their homework."

Haru crushed his cigarette butt on the asphalt. "Right. Sorry about that. Your parents are old."

"They're freakishly old! And my mother pushes around an empty baby carriage. So what? You work at an empty convenience store!"

"Okay, okay," Haru said. "You know what absolutely makes no one feel safe, though? Bus drivers. At least not the ones who have the brain of a fifteen-year-old."

"Yori-*san*? That's not fair. They fired him and he hadn't done anything wrong."

"Of course he did." Haru lit another cigarette. "He was standing in the parking lot shouting about river trolls tricking the students into killing themselves. He absolutely should have been fired. That is the exact opposite of making people feel safe."

"He was a nice guy."

"Who told the school board a *kappa* was murdering children."

"I didn't say I believed him."

"Well, I'm glad we cleared that up," Haru said, taking another drag. "He got what was coming to him."

Haru and I sat on the curb as the evening grew darker around us. It's true that not many adults liked Yori. He didn't wear a blue blazer or white gloves like the other drivers who took us around on field trips. He didn't sit quietly in his chair, face forward, bowing and waving from the wrist like some pageant queen. He wanted to talk to us. He wanted to laugh and have conversations with people who thought the same way he did. For Yori, that was a bus full of high school students.

And we liked him. When he drove us on field trips or other school outings, he always talked to us like we were people, not kids who should be disciplined or ignored. He knew how to drive a bus—sort of—but where he truly shone was in details. Small, intricate, mind-spinning details. He could chat about your favorite food one minute and then *manga* the next. You could ask him what his favorite Pokémon was and he wouldn't say "the cute green one with the hat." Yori could go on and on about Hasuburero and how he evolves for a second time into Runpappa after being exposed to a Water Stone. If you're an adult and have any clue what that last sentence means, congratulations, you are an *otaku* nerd. But for us, Yori the Bus Driver always had answers. Even if the questions were silly. Or weird. Or just plain stupid.

"You shouldn't breathe in the smoke, you know."

Haru and I flipped around. It was hard to see her at first. She was standing near the far corner of the building. When she walked into the light of the front window, though, I instantly recognized her face.

"Why do you put the smoke in your mouth?" she asked. "Mouths aren't made for that." And she would know because the last time I saw her she was on fire in Aiko's front garden.

"Who are you?" I said.

"Who do I look like to you?" she replied.

"A girl in a gray hoodie."

"Then that is who I will be."

"What's your name, girl in a gray hoodie?" Haru asked.

"Moya."

She walked over to the curb. She was wearing a pair of jeans and a gray zip-up with ears on the hood. She looked like any other fifteen-year-old who had never been on fire before.

"Moya?" Haru said. "That's not a normal name."

"Of course it's normal. It's totally normal," she said, pulling the cigarette from Haru's mouth and pinching the embers.

"Hey," Haru said.

"And I didn't come to talk to you, anyway, smoke-mouth. I came to talk to your friend." Moya sat down on the curb next to me, knees pointed in, lips cartoonishly pouty.

"Me?" I said. "Why?"

"Because sometimes it can be hard when you're the new girl at school."

"Are you . . . I didn't know you went to our school," I said.

"Just moved in. Down the street."

"What street?" I asked.

"The one over there."

"I have no idea what you're pointing at."

"It's called . . . Mountain Street."

"Mountain Street?"

"Something like that."

"Did you just make up a street name?" Haru asked, poking his head forward.

"No."

"You looked up at the mountains and then said Mountain Street."

Moya leaned in to me and said, "That guy's rude."

Haru laughed. "There are, like, ten streets in Kusaka, and none of them are Mountain Street."

Moya shrugged. "I was kind of hoping a cute boy could help me out with a teensy little problem."

"What cute boy?" Haru said. "You mean Koda?"

"Let's just hear her out on this one," I said. "Also, you're an awful friend."

Moya smiled.

"I'm sorry," Haru said to me. "It's just, you're so young, and you wear that giant helmet all the time."

"What?" I said, looking back at Moya. "No . . . I . . . it's just a regular bicycle helmet."

"A comically large bicycle helmet."

"It's because of the padding, Haru. There's nothing funny about responsible headgear!"

I looked back at Moya. She wasn't smiling anymore.

"Gods, you two," she whispered. "Look, Koda, I need you to steal something for me."

"Okay, she's all yours," Haru said.

"You want me to steal something?" I said. "That's your teensy problem?"

"Well, you are a thief, aren't you?"

"What? No."

"Sure you are," Moya said. "Look at me. Let me see your eyes. Don't touch me, though."

"I wasn't going to."

"I'm serious, kid."

"I wouldn't."

"I will punch you right in the boy bits if you lay one finger on me."

"I don't touch girls!" I blurted out.

"Smooth," Haru whispered.

Moya leaned in close to my face. "Yep, you're one of them," she said.

"One of what?"

"A *suri*. A pickpocket. A cutpurse. You know, a thief."

"Um, no. I'm fifteen and I've never stolen anything in my life."

"Normally, kid, this is not a good thing. Everybody hates a thief, especially *suri*. Also, you're kind of small. And Haru's right—you have a ridiculous helmet. But for now, I need something stolen and you're the only one who can do it. Here's the address."

Moya handed me a piece of paper.

"Seriously, who are you?" I asked.

"Have you seen the crows, Koda?" Moya said.

Haru leaned forward. "What crows?"

"I'm having a private conversation with your weird little cutpurse friend here, thank you very much."

"That's insulting," I said.

"Your *handsome* cutpurse friend," she corrected.

"Well, all right, then."

"Have you seen the crows?" Moya repeated.

I looked over at Haru.

"This isn't an abstract question, Koda," Moya said. "These aren't normal crows. They watch you back. Either you've seen them or you haven't."

I didn't want to say it, but . . .

"Yes."

"Then this is the one time in the history of the world when being a dirty little thief is the best thing you could be. Go to the address. It's the only way to stop what's happening to this town."

"What exactly am I supposed to steal?" I said. Because *that* was obviously the sanest question to ask.

"A memory," Moya said, pushing up from the curb.

"A memory? You want me to steal a memory?"

"Of course," she said, looking down at me like *I* was the moron. "It will be attached to something you'd find in a river. Maybe a rock. Or a stick. An arrowhead! Arrowheads would be an excellent place to start. Very traumatic. If you see an arrowhead, definitely steal its memory."

"Steal the memory from an arrowhead? What does that even mean?"

"*You're* the *suri*. Go to that address and steal the memory that's there. Don't wait, kid. The Road is spreading."

With no other explanation whatsoever, the strange girl turned and walked back the way she came.

Haru slowly pulled another cigarette from his shirt pocket. "Well, she is fired."

"What?"

"I'm firing her."

"From what?"

"I don't know. From being a person? She's cute and all, but she is broken in the head and I am firing her from being a person like the rest of us. What the hell was that about crows?"

"She asked if I'd seen crows."

"Everybody's seen a crow before."

"Then everybody would have said yes."

I folded the piece of paper and slipped it into my slacks.

"You're not seriously going to that address, are you? I guarantee it leads to a graveyard. A graveyard for kittens. That she made herself."

"Actually go there?" I scoffed. "No, I wouldn't do something like that."

But yes, I would.

6

School reopened during the first week of October. When third hour ended the next day, Shimizu-*sensei* set down his chalk and excused us from homeroom. The rest of the students filed downstairs to change for gym class, but I stayed behind. What was an arrowhead memory anyway? And what made a new girl from "Mountain Street" think I could steal it? The last time I'd tried to steal something was when I was eight. It was a pack of strawberry Hi-Chew. I dropped it down my pants when my father was at the register at Lawson's. The candy slipped right down my leg and hit the floor. Everyone turned around. "I'll take that as well," my father said, shaking his head. The cashier raised an eyebrow and added it to the receipt. That was the beginning and end of my grand criminal endeavors. I'm thinking Moya might have me mixed up with some other teenage thief from Kusaka.

"Hurry, Koda, go," Shimizu-*sensei* said.

I got up from my desk. I started to walk out of the room, but something stopped me. It was Shimizu-*sensei*. He was just staring out the window. It wasn't like he was bored or even sad. It was something else. He looked afraid.

I almost minded my own business and left the room, but then I remembered Aiko and turned around. *"Daijōbu desu ka?"* I asked. "Is everything all right?"

Shimizu-*sensei* reached out and touched the windowpane. "Do you ever feel like someone could be watching you?"

Yes. She has a name, wears a gray hoodie, and is sometimes on fire.

"Um, no," I quickly said.

"I mean, a ghost, Koda. Do you ever feel like a ghost is watching you?" He turned and smiled. Not a normal smile. More like a my-house-just-burned-down-and-all-I've-got-left-is-this-smile smile. "I'm kidding," he said. "Totally kidding. But seriously, we make these shrines and pray to our ancestors hoping they'll hear us, right? But what if they really are listening? What if they're watching us back? That isn't comforting, Koda. That isn't comforting at all. It's terrifying."

Interesting point. Hadn't thought of that before. I wanted to say something intelligent, but instead I just opened my mouth and said, "Uh."

"Go on to gym class, Koda." Shimizu-*sensei* turned to the window again.

"Are you going to be all right?"

He didn't look back.

I stepped out of the room and walked down the hall. People were definitely not feeling safe. Students, teachers, office ladies—it didn't matter. The two suicides had broken each of us in different ways. Sometimes you caught people crying in the halls. Sometimes teachers took smoke breaks too far from the school. Other people, like the headmaster, stayed in their office all day with the door shut. Shimizu-*sensei* was afraid of ghosts. That's not so strange, right? Just another kind of fracture.

I stopped in front of the glass door to the mathematics room. That was where they'd found Ichiro last week. Inside. Alone. Twisted at the foot of Ikeda-*sensei*'s desk.

I reached out to try the door. It was unlocked. The room was empty and the lights were off. The windows should have lit up the walls, but they didn't. It was hard to see. The room was deeply dark and deeply empty.

I walked inside the math room and closed the door. Stupid? Maybe. Creepier than dead ancestors? Probably. Better than doing basketball drills in gym class? Definitely.

The smell of the room stung my eyes. No one had been in here since they'd cleaned it. The chairs were still piled in the corner. The teacher's desk was pushed back against the wall. Near the front of the room, Ichiro's last word was rubbed raw into the floor.

I knelt down over the faded lines. I could almost feel Ichiro in the strokes he'd left behind. The floor was cold beneath my feet. I reached out to touch the last place Ichiro had touched.

The searing freeze shot up my fingers and under my sleeves. It wrapped around my neck and mouth and eyes. The entire universe was suddenly frosty and still as the carvings on a grave.

Then the chairs in the corner shifted. I knew I'd fallen asleep, but knowing you're dreaming somehow doesn't stop the panic. I heard someone straining to tear apart a piece of fabric. I tried to say something. Tried to ask who was there. But when I opened my mouth, only cold air came out.

I stood up, turned, and reached for the door, but then the moaning came. Softly. A whisper of a moan, really. A voice lost in a winter's fog. "Don't go," it said. "Please. Don't leave me here with them."

The voices of a hundred crows filled the room, drowning out the floating voice. I let go of the door but didn't turn around. I could feel a shadow swaying back and forth behind me, rising up from the pile of chairs. "They told me it was my fault," the voice cried. "They told me I could have stopped it." The voice was now screaming to be heard over the wings and the screeching. "How would the birds know that? How would cutting myself bring my parents home?"

Through the reflection in the glass door, I recognized his face. The birds fell silent.

"Crows fly.
A traveler on the road
Is lost."

Ichiro recited the words. The bloody knife fell from his fingers, clanging to the floor.

7

The room was still dark and abandoned when I woke up. I gripped the door frame, slowly pulled myself to my feet, and stepped into the hall. Somewhere below me I could hear balls hitting floors and walls and old backboards.

"Were you in Ikeda-*sensei*'s room?"

I turned, my head still feeling swimmy. It was my best friend, Kenji. Great.

"No," I said. "The door was open, so I came over to close it."

"I'm going to tell," he said.

"Do it, Kenji. But make sure you wipe the cookie crumbs off the front of your shirt first."

I guess I wasn't the only one who was going to be late to gym class.

"*Baka*," he hissed, and scurried off down the hall.

I rubbed my head where I'd smacked it on the floor.

By the time I got changed into my white shirt and blue shorts and slipped into the gymnasium, the boys were on one half of the court throwing basketballs at an uncooperative hoop and the girls were practicing proper volleyball form by hitting a ball over an imaginary net. Ikeda-*sensei* was sitting on the lowest bleachers.

No one liked Ikeda-*sensei*. He was an ex–*sumō* wrestler teaching math and physical education at a high school. If that sounds like a demotion, you'd be thinking the same way he does. The doctors couldn't explain it, but Ikeda-*sensei*'s eyesight went from eagle perfect to mole-man blind in less than a year. He had to get these superthick glasses, drop out of his *sumō* stable in Ōsaka, and return home to this dinky town. As you can guess, he was a very large, very angry, very blind man. Students didn't like him, parents didn't like him, fellow teachers didn't like him. He was as big and mean as an ox. And like any ox, Ikeda-*sensei* was to be avoided at all times.

"Koda, over here!" called out Kenji, apparently still on a sugar high from his secret cookie break. "You want to shoot a basket?"

He asked that last question with a demonic grin crawling across his face. He knew I didn't want to shoot a basket. He knew I couldn't make a basket if I was standing on a ladder clutching the rim with one hand. But all the other guys had stopped and everyone was staring at me.

"That sounds like fun," I said through clenched teeth.

Kenji hurled the ball at me. I grabbed my head and dropped to the floor. Which seemed like a totally reasonable thing to do when someone was trying to murder you with a rubber ball. No one saw the potential danger in this, so they all just laughed instead.

I picked myself up and smiled at Kenji. "Tossed it a little hard there, didn't we?"

"*Gomen*," he said back. "Forgot who I was throwing it to." He grabbed another ball and gently rolled it along the ground. Fifteen seconds later the ball bumped against my toe like an infant's kiss. I kept my eyes locked on Kenji and snatched it off the ground.

I walked up to the orange line and bounced the ball with both hands.

"Gods," someone whispered.

Well, if this was the one time the gods were looking down on me, I hoped they'd guide the ball through the air and help me slam that hooping net—if that's a thing people say. I shot the ball. And missed. Not the hoop part, I missed the backboard. And the pole. And the wall behind it. I did hit the bleachers, though, which, considering how all of my other gym classes have gone, was a record.

"Ooh, so close," Kenji said gleefully. "All you have to do is aim higher. And throw the ball a little harder. Well, a whole lot harder. Just pretend you're a normal boy and not a five-year-old *shōgakusei*. Then shoot the basket. It's my fault really, I should have clarified that."

"Oh, yeah?" I said. "Like this?" I grabbed another ball and threw it. Hard. I don't think I've ever thrown anything in my life as hard as I threw that ball. And I didn't miss! Did I make

a basket? Of course not. But I did hit the hoop. *Take that, Kenji!*
The basketball zinged off the rim like a stray cannon shot.
Over the heads of the boys standing by. Over the divider
line. Over the imaginary volleyball net.

"*Yabai!*" the girls screamed.

Oh. That's not good.

It was like the ball was drawn straight to the side of some
random girl's head. She never had a chance.

"Koda!" she screamed. "Are you serious?"

"That's enough!" Ikeda-*sensei* barked from the corner.
"Everyone shut your awful little mouths!"

"But Koda threw that ball at my head!"

Technically the ball was chucked at the basket, and somehow in
all the bouncing that ensued her head got in the way.

Good point, brain.

"Quiet, all of you," Ikeda-*sensei* shot back.

"Koda hates me," the random girl cried.

Not true, not true. I don't hate you. I barely know you.

It's the gods that hate her, my brain said.

Obviously.

"Stop fooling around," Ikeda-*sensei* bellowed, lifting his
huge frame from the bleachers. "Get back to your drills."

The girl with the basketball head wound receded into a
gang of her supporters. Kenji walked up behind me and
slapped me on the back. "Couldn't have done it better myself."

He's going to choke on a salmon bone one day and pee himself
in front of the whole class, said my brain.

I laughed. If you've ever seen Kenji maul his food at lunchtime, you'd know he was bound to choke on something sooner or later. And after he does, I'm going to slap him on the back and say, *Couldn't have done it better myself.*

Good one, my brain said.

I rode my bike slower than normal along the backstreets after school. I'd been lucky that no one important was on the second floor when I took my little tumble in the math room. That was three sleep attacks in just a couple of weeks. My narcolepsy was definitely getting worse.

Moya had asked if I'd seen the crows. Aiko had been searching for a three-legged crow named Yatagarasu, and Ichiro wrote *karasu* on the floor before he died. Maybe the crows had been following other kids at Kusaka High. Maybe they'd been following me. If I could do something to stop them, then it was definitely worth a ride to Moya's mysterious address.

I jerked my bike to a stop in front of an old, abandoned house. Not a kitten graveyard, exactly, but not a place you'd want to be walking around at night. I took off my helmet and unfolded the piece of paper Moya had given me. Yep. This was it. I swung my foot over the seat and walked through the front gate, which was almost welded shut with rust. I stepped up to the front door and slid it back with a loud, metallic scrape.

"*Gomen kudasai*," I called inside. My voice echoed through the musty *genkan*.

Nothing.

"Gomen kudasai," I called again.

No one answered. I was about to shut the door when I heard the muted sound of laughter. From a television set.

"Daremo imasen ka?" I called louder.

"Who is it?" came a raspy voice from down the darkened hallway.

"Okita Koda desu."

"Who?" the hoarse woman called back.

"Koda. I, um, deliver mushrooms."

"What?"

"I got your address from this girl . . . in a parking lot. She said you might have something for me."

You are the worst thief in the entire world! "Excuse me, ma'am, I'm interested in possibly stealing something from you—if you have the time, that is."

Shut up, brain.

"Who?"

"Her name was Moya. I have this piece of paper, if that helps."

Why would that help?

"Go away, young man. We don't need mushrooms here."

"No, I don't want to sell you mushrooms. My name is Koda Okita."

"I don't know who that is, young man."

"Right. I did just explain this, though. I'm Koda Okita. I received your address from a girl at Lawson's. I think you have, um, a memory for me?"

"I'm very busy," the voice said. "I don't have time for salesmen."

"I'm not—"

"Thank you, goodbye."

"Um."

"Please shut the door."

"Right. *Ojama shimashita.*"

I slid the front door closed. Well, that was a big fat fail. The dusty placard on the front read "Yamamoto." Which didn't help much. How many Yamamotos live in Kusaka? Fifty? A hundred? It might be the most common name in all of Japan. I still didn't know what I was supposed to be looking for. Or how it could possibly stop the crows that were killing people in this town.

Maybe this was a bad idea. When a girl who snubs cigarettes with her fingers hands you an address late at night, you don't visit that address. That's how people end up getting murdered. "Mountain Street." Moya was probably just some stresshead who actually knew nothing about me or Kusaka Town.

I shut the gate to the Yamamoto home and walked out into the street. Everyone in the world has stress, but in Japan we've turned it into a national art form. Think about all the stress heaped on us students: If you don't pass your exams in high school, you won't get into a good college. If you don't get into a good college, you'll never get hired by a decent company. If you don't get into a decent company, you'll become an outcast and probably die alone in an apartment the size of a broom closet while your ancestors look down and weep from shame.

Or you'll become a *shiitake* mushroom farmer. Which is pretty much the same thing.

Stress starts when you're a kid, and it doesn't let up until . . . I guess, until you die. There's social stress: Am I part of the in-crowd? Do people know my name? There's job stress: Am I the last one to leave? Does the boss know my name? There's romantic stress and parental stress and transportation stress and stress you get from walking down the street and wondering if that girl passing you will nod, or smile, or pretend you don't exist at all.

That's a lot of stress. Everybody has it. Old or young. Rich or poor. Nobody wants to be left on the outside. Nobody wants to be alone. And sometimes that stress builds up until something cracks inside.

I had met this guy the summer before on a train from Kōchi City. He smiled and sat down next to me, ignoring all the other empty seats in the car. I kept on looking out the window, but I could feel him watching the back of my head. I started to think he was one of those train perverts. You know, the kind who waits until the train lurches to the side, then reaches out to grope you. I scooted over a bit.

"I'm a very generous man," he told me.

I scooted over a lot.

"Do you know how generous I am?" he asked.

"Nope," I said, looking up at the ceiling.

"I would give you this book here."

He set down a tattered pile of loose papers on the seat between us. I looked over. They were pages ripped out of a 1996

Honda owner's manual. Looking back, I don't think he knew that.

"I like the part when the *rōnin* is caught between two warring families and he tricks them into killing each other," he said. "You should read that part."

Yep, I'm pretty sure he didn't know it was a car manual. Of course, I hadn't actually read that particular car manual. It could have been the most awesome *samurai*-themed Honda owner's manual ever.

"I've been more generous than this," the man continued. "I had a friend who'd been in a car accident and was paralyzed from the waist down. He came to me and said, 'I wish I could go to the school dance.' So I let him borrow my legs."

"Your . . . legs?"

The man frowned. "He gave them back, of course."

Stupid me.

"Just like he promised. Returned them the next day and the doctor sewed my legs back on. No problem."

Not a glint. Not a wink of the eye. Not a corner of a smile. Nothing. He was as serious as an old man with reattached legs could be. The brakes screeched as we pulled to a stop.

"Kusaka Station," the voice buzzed over the intercom. The doors slid open.

"This is where I get off," I said.

"Yes, me too."

"Oh. Good."

"I have to get to the doctor's office by noon. I'm lending out my brain today. I can't be late."

"Good luck, then . . . with your brain and everything."

He bowed.

I'm sure he won't miss it, said my own brain.

And that's what the daily grind can do to people here. It creates a nation of stress-heads. Moya was probably just one of them.

"*Oi!*" someone yelled.

I looked back at the house to see a man poking his head through the second-story window. He was pretty old—forty or something—and from what I could tell, he was wearing welding goggles, a cape, and a *sugegasa* straw hat. Speaking of broken.

"Koda-*kun?*" the man yelled. "Koda Okita?"

"Yes."

"What do you mean 'yes'? It's me!"

"I . . ."

He removed the hat and peeled the goggles off his face.

"Yori-*san?*" I said.

"Come on up, Koda. I'm really glad you came by."

"I didn't know you lived here, Yori. I would have asked your mother—"

"Sister."

"Yes . . . your sister. I would have asked your lovely sister if I could speak with you."

"She's not lovely. She's a hag, but don't let her scare you off. She won't move from the floor in the front room. Come in, come in."

So Yori the Bus Driver was my mysterious contact? Okay. I

walked back through the overgrown garden and slid open Yori's rickety front door. *"Gomen kudasai,"* I called in again.

"Upstairs, Koda."

"Sumimasen," I said, ducking inside. Yori's sister grunted and turned the volume up on the TV.

8

Yori's house was filled with junk. Newspapers. Picture frames. Broken-down appliances. Bicycle horns. Rusted tools. Stacks of old CDs and clear plastic bottles to keep away cats. Ceramic lawn ornaments. Piles of souvenirs collected from shrines. Folded paper decorations. Square pots for *bonsai* trees. His house hadn't been properly cleaned for generations. Not years. Generations.

In Japan it's not strange for several families to live under the same roof at the same time. Kids, mothers, fathers, grandparents, even great-grandparents, eating and sleeping and living together. Yori's house was like that—except without the people. It was filled with the clutter of three, four, five generations, stacked up against the walls, lining the stairs, touching the ceiling. But even though all these things had been collected over the years, only Yori and his sister remained. An ex–bus driver and an old woman who grunted at television sets.

I walked up the stairs, careful to avoid the piles of *anime* figurines and *manga* comic books. Through his bedroom door I could hear Yori talking. Shouting, actually.

"Donna shigoto demo, Sunabōzu kanarazu dekiru yo!"

A couple of days after Ichiro died, Yori had stopped driving the bus to school. He didn't say a word to any of us. He was sitting in the driver's seat one day, and the next he was gone. Haru was right about one thing—Yori *had* told the school board that a river troll tricked Aiko and Ichiro into killing themselves. Some of the students said he got fired for that. One of them said Yori's sister called in a few favors and got him an accounting job in the Kusaka town hall. That made sense. Numbers and spreadsheets and small marks in note books? That's the kind of work only someone like Yori could enjoy.

"Ojama shimasu," I said, pulling back the door to Yori's room. From the worn *tatami* mats on his floor to the splintered rafters of the ceiling, from the dusty shelves on his walls to the stained windowsills, on every centimeter of free space I could see piles of souvenirs and figurines. Some had bright costumes or plastic accessories. Some were large. Some were old. Some were worn, and some were still in the original packaging from years before. But all of them, every single one of them, were *kappa*. Yori's entire room was a collection shrine to the most famous river troll in Kusaka Town—Shibaten, part turtle, part freaky human child.

And in the midst of it all, like an emperor in his treasure house, stood the bus-driving accountant. Goggled. Caped. Holding out a military canteen with the word 水 painted across the front.

"Um, hi," I said.

"I'm sorry I didn't go to the door, Koda. You never know what creatures are lurking around out there. Come in. Sit down. Not there . . . or there. You know what? Let's just stand."

"Okay."

"Let me turn this off." Yori stepped carefully over to the desk and pushed a button on a small video camera.

"What were you recording?" I asked.

"Cosplay. I can't post it to the Net if I don't record it."

"Makes sense, I guess."

"My name is Kanta Mizuno," Yori started, folding his arms dramatically across his chest.

"Okay."

He stepped between the figurines and swept his cape toward the window. "I am Sunabōzu—the Desert Punk. I have joined forces with Kosuna to defeat Rain Spider in the wastelands of Tōkyō. *Donna shigoto demo, Sunabōzu kanarazu dekiru yo!* Whatever the feat, whatever the run, Desert Punk gets the job done!"

I just stood there. I mean, what are you supposed to say to that?

Yori turned back to me and held out the canteen. "Would you like a refreshment, weary traveler?"

"Um, is your camera still on or something?"

He lifted his hand to the sky. "There are no cameras in the deserts of Tōkyō, traveler! Drink this." He poured me a small cup of water from his canteen. "Nothing is more important in the desert than clean, clear water."

"Mmm," I said, sipping gingerly. "Just a little sour, though."

"That's the chlorine. River water is not safe to drink without chlorine."

I coughed water back into the cup.

Yori reached out and grabbed it from me. Before I could say anything, he poured the used water back into his canteen and screwed the lid on tight. Gross.

He walked over to his desk and pulled off the goggles and straw hat. "Fantastic, Koda, fantastic. Welcome to cosplay. Now to the business at hand. You are here because of Shibaten."

"I'm sorry, the river troll?"

"Yes. Shibaten is killing the students of Kusaka High."

Yori turned away from me, and for a moment I thought he might still be acting.

"Some people say Aiko and Ichiro committed suicide. But it isn't true. They were murdered."

He was not acting. He was serious. Well, as serious as a grown man in a cape can be.

"You're telling me Aiko and Ichiro were killed by a *kappa*?" I asked.

He turned back to me. "That's exactly what I'm telling you. He didn't murder them with his own hands, but he *tricked* them into killing themselves. Which in my books still counts as murder."

Maybe spending all day collecting and obsessing over one thing isn't good for a person.

"Why would you think that, Yori?"

"Because I saw him. Lurking around the school. Watching us. Watching the children. I tried to tell them, the teachers and the headmaster. I tried to warn them, but they wouldn't listen to me."

"You actually saw a *kappa* sneaking around the high school?"

"Well, not with my regular eyes, Koda. I could feel his presence around the school. And that's as good as seeing him."

Such a shame. I'd always liked Yori.

He frowned at me like he'd heard that. "You don't believe me, do you, Koda?"

"It's not that I don't believe you, Yori, it's just that . . . the words you're using are not, well, believable to me right now."

"Stories have been told about *kappa* for hundreds of years," he continued. "Countless people have been murdered by them for wandering too close to their rivers. Bodies have been found floating downstream all swollen and bloated, each one broken, with its life-energy sucked out. This isn't *anime*, Koda. This isn't *manga*. It's real life. The school sits dangerously close to Kusaka River. If not *kappa*, then what? If Shibaten didn't kill those kids, then who did? And why?"

"I . . . really couldn't say."

Yori untied the string at his neck and folded the cape over a used *ramen* box. "Shibaten is the only *kappa* in Kusaka. It had to be him." He walked quickly to the window. "Something has changed in this town, Koda. I can feel it everywhere. There is a monster out there with murder in his heart. He's obsessed with it. Driven to madness by it. I don't know why he killed those children, but I know this—he isn't finished yet." Yori turned back to me. "We have to watch the river, Koda. Never take your eyes off the river. Shibaten is watching us."

9

I clicked the tire lock on my bike, pulled on my tuba-sized helmet, and pedaled away from Yori's house. The *kappa* Shibaten is pretty famous here in Kusaka Town. *Kappa* trickster trolls were a scare tactic that mothers in ancient Japan used to keep their children away from rivers. Did I mention that a *kappa* is made from gluing turtle parts to a human child? Okay, then. You can see how that might have been an effective scare tactic. Anyway, kids who somehow ignored all that would still wander too close to the rivers and drown.

"Do you see the body that just washed up on shore?" the mothers would say. "That's what happens when a *kappa* gets its claws on you."

And the children would be totally freaked out. I mean, wouldn't you if your mother was shoving you at a bloated corpse? Then the children would ask, "Why do they look like that, Momma?"

Real answer: They drowned and their tissues are engorged with water and gases.

A mother's answer: "*Kappa* break your bones and drag you

into the river, child. They stuff you into their secret lairs and suck out your life-energy—through your anus!"

That's right. Your anus. Why it couldn't be your neck, or your fingertips, or pretty much anywhere else that isn't your butt, I don't know. I'm pretty sure that the kids of ancient Japan fell asleep each night crying and squeezing their little cheeks together.

Even today you can find irrigation canals with pictures of *kappa* posted as warnings not to swim there. So Yori's conclusion that *kappa* are real-life serial killers? Well, I got the feeling that the school deaths were a bit more complicated than that.

Yori knew nothing about the crows. He didn't have any memories of the suicides that would help Moya at all. He was just a middle-aged man whose brain was a little cracked. Being locked up in a tiny house or a tiny office all day makes some people go *kuru kuru pa*. Real life is so disappointing or painful that the only way they can survive is to pretend their problems away. Cosplay. Short for "costume play." Maybe they're dressing up in a cape to save humanity from sexy robots, or donning goggles and a straw hat to battle Rain Spider in the wastelands of Tōkyō. For some people, cosplay is the only way to cope with real life.

Looking out on my long future as a narcoleptic *shiitake* farmer, I kind of understood how someone's mind could pop. Some people dress up as *anime* characters, and others ride their bikes around town trying to save their school from a murder of crows. Maybe Yori and I weren't so different after all.

I steadied my bike with one arm and let the other stick out like an airplane wing. *Ladies and gentlemen,* I said to myself, *we've reached a cruising altitude of thirty thousand feet. The seat belt sign is now turned off, so please feel free to move around the cabin.*

Okay, yes, pretending my bike is a Boeing 777 Star Jet is a teensy bit like cosplay. But you can't compare airplanes and *anime.* Airplanes are real. They exist. Real people sit down in real Japanese airliners like MD-11 J-Birds or Flower Fleet 737s and fly all over the world. Does that make me an *otaku* nerd like Yori the Bus Driver? No. Well, Flower Fleets and Star Jets sound kind of cutesy, but no, still no. The Flower Fleet is awesome!

You're in for a treat, everyone, I could hear my copilot say. *The pilot tonight is Koda Okita, the boy from Kusaka who never sleeps.*

I have to correct him.

I'm sorry, the man *from Kusaka who never sleeps. Fly-Man, we call him. Everyone knows Koda flies very fast but also very safely. That's why he wears a helmet, even in the cockpit.*

No, no, no.

One more correction, folks, our pilot does not wear a helmet. He never wears a helmet anymore because helmets look stupid. It would be silly for a pilot to wear a bicycle helmet in a cockpit anyway. That was just a joke and I apologize to Fly-Man and all of his ancestors.

If my bike really had been a Star Jet, I would have flown around the corner of my street and immediately sensed something was very wrong. My tires screeched and shuddered to a halt in the middle of the road. Without even unbuckling my helmet I stepped off my bike and let it crash to the ground.

The eyes of a hundred crows stared back at me. From the housetops and the fence posts, from the fields and the trees and the cars and the road itself, a massive black flock silently stood and watched every move I made.

"What do you want?" I whispered.

They didn't answer. They just stood there, boring holes into my skull with their lifeless gray eyes.

"Get away from me."

They could have been statues. A hundred stone birds covered with real feathers and real beaks, staring, relentlessly staring. They pushed in on my brain like giant hands. The edges of my eyes felt cold. I smelled ice. My left pupil began to drift. I tore off my helmet, but the pressure wouldn't let up. The birds were all connected. Stitched together like bits of string, they were united in trying to crack my head like a melon using only their awful, beady eyes.

The flock suddenly lifted up into the air and dropped back down again. Fresh air rushed into my brain. The crows clicked their beaks and flapped their wings, darting their eyes from side to side. For some reason the strings were all tangled up now.

I flipped around when I finally heard the low growl.

"Whoa!"

A white fox crept past me toward the flock, hair raised and lips curled. The crows in the front hopped back. A few flew up into nearby trees. The fox gnashed its teeth and the flock lifted up into the air again. Some dropped back onto fence posts and car hoods, but the fox lunged and the flock finally exploded, cawing and darting off in every direction until the road was empty and quiet.

Huh. Maybe foxes aren't such bad luck after all.

The critter was calmly licking its front paws as I inched my way up behind it. I reached my hand out.

"Hey there, little friend, just gonna give you a scratch behind the ears for saving me—"

The fox flipped around and lunged at me, snarling and snapping its teeth.

"Foxes are not pets!" I squealed.

The wild animal ran off into a rice field, leaving me in the middle of the road trying to steady my breath. So now I'm thinking foxes aren't good luck *or* bad luck. They're just ornery varmints who lash out at anything. Anyone who tells you otherwise has obviously never tried to be friends with one before.

10

Kusaka Matsuri. Each October the people of Kusaka gather at Ōmura Shrine and celebrate the founding of our town. That doesn't sound so awesome, but believe me, it is.

On the night of Kusaka Matsuri there are food booths and games and festival performers. My parents even leave the *shiitake* farm—if you can imagine that. Haru and I race through the crowds, pushing our way past the booths and the hundreds of people. Maybe someone sells Haru a cup of *sake* and we take turns sipping at it until the lights turn fuzzy. That's never happened, but what if it did? Anything is possible at Kusaka Matsuri. Everybody gets into it. Everyone has a good time.

This year might have been different, though. Ichiro's funeral was held just a week before the festival. His body was cremated six days before. There was talk of canceling the *matsuri* altogether, but in the end the town went through with it. The decorations and the booths had already been built. The toys and food and fireworks already purchased. The performers had been rehearsing for months.

Some people said they wouldn't go. They couldn't dance and drink and toast Kusaka Town after two kids walked into our high school and killed themselves. "This isn't a time to celebrate," they said. "It would be a shame to the memory of the students."

"The unfortunate deaths of Aiko and Ichiro are a struggle for us all," the mayor of Kusaka said in response. "But that is precisely why we must continue with Kusaka Matsuri."

The mayor of Kusaka Town was a small man with a bald head. His suit always looked like it had swallowed him whole and was hungry for more. But if you heard the mayor speak without seeing him, you'd never know he looked like that. I guess that's why he'd been elected in the first place.

"There is something great about this town," he continued. "We have lived and thrived in this valley for more than two centuries. We have met disaster after disaster, and our people have overcome it all. Mudslides and earthquakes and floods have tested us, but we have always *isshō ni ganbarimashita*. We have never given up.

"The tragedies of Aiko and Ichiro tell me that something terrible has happened to us. We have become forgetful and lazy. We have ignored the signs that our children are hurting. The solution isn't to hide in our houses with the doors and windows locked. No, we have to show our children that life is good. That Kusaka is an amazing place to live and work and go to school. We have to celebrate who we are, not hide from it. Mothers and fathers, grandmothers and grandfathers, bring your children. Dress them in their *yukata* and *geta* sandals.

Take them to the booths and the lights and the games. Bring smiles to their faces. Show them why we have stayed in this valley for two hundred years."

Now, some might say that the mayor didn't want to lose the money he'd already put into the festival, but I don't think that was it. I think he believed the festival would save us. At least a little bit.

"What did you say?" My mother stood in the kitchen, spooning hot bowls of *shiitake* soup.

"Do you think dreams mean something?" I asked again, kneeling down to the table in the front room. "You know, in real life."

"One more time," she said louder.

"The boy asked if you believe in fortune-telling!" my father shouted across the table and into the kitchen.

My mother was frowning when she walked in.

"That's not what I said."

My father ignored me and blew his nose into a handkerchief. My mother rattled a bowl of soup down in front of me. My parents are so old! Not normal old either. Really, really old. My mother had me when she was fifty. "It's a miracle," the doctors had said.

"Yes . . . a miracle," my father had replied, rubbing his face and leaving the room.

So fifteen years later my sixty-five-year-old mother tried to steady her hands and not spill mushroom soup on our low dining table. She grinned and asked if I'd been seeing ghosts.

"What? Ghosts? No," I said. "Do you guys listen to anything I say?"

"It would be nice to see my sister again," she said to herself.

My father shoved his handkerchief back into his pocket. "Yes, Koda, give all the family our regards if you happen to see them wandering through the halls."

"Will Haru be attending the festival?" my mother asked, setting chopsticks next to my bowl.

"We go together every year. He should be there. As long as his uncle isn't trying to punish him."

"Perhaps it would help Haru to have more fun in his life. You could invite him to spend more time on our farm. I think he would like that."

"Um, no, he would not like that."

"Why not?" my father asked. "You like being a *shiitake* farmer."

"I do not. Not even a little bit!"

"Every boy wants to be a *shiitake* farmer," my father said.

"Why would anyone want to be a *shiitake* farmer?"

My mother pushed up from the table and shuffled toward the kitchen.

"You're in the dirt," my father continued. "With mushrooms. All boys like dirt. And mushrooms."

"What boys like mushrooms? Boys like TV games and

anime and, I don't know, ice cream. Nobody likes mushrooms. Mushrooms don't even like mushrooms."

"Well, you should eat them more often, then," my mother said, returning from the kitchen with a plate of steamed *shiitake* buns. "The more you eat something, the more delicious it becomes."

"I don't think that's true at all," I said.

"What do you want to be, then?" my father asked.

I stared into my stupid mushroom soup bowl. "You know what I want to be."

"Oh, a pilot. Mother, get JAL on the phone and ask them if they need someone to fall asleep and crash a plane into Mount Fuji."

"Stop it," my mother whispered.

"You're a *shiitake* farmer, Koda. You come from a long line of honorable *shiitake* farmers. The sooner you accept this, the easier your life will be."

"That's enough," my mother said.

"Honorable *shiitake* farmer," I said under my breath. "What would a *dishonorable shiitake* farmer be?"

"One who goes around with his head in the clouds," my father shot back. He turned to my mother. "That's the reason he has the problems he does."

"*Urusai!*" My mother almost never raises her voice. So when she does, we all know to keep our mouths shut. "This is supposed to be a happy night, both of you. Please, don't ruin this."

My father wiped his face and we finished our soup in silence.

11

I tied on my *yukata* and slipped into a pair of sandals. I'd have to hurry if I was going to meet Haru near the entrance to Ōmura Shrine. Before I could get through the door, my mother called from the kitchen.

"It's good luck to share an umbrella with a girl at Kusaka Matsuri."

Share an umbrella? Gods, my parents are *so* old. "Yeah, thanks," I called back.

"I'm just saying, in case you happen to meet a nice girl at the festival, take an umbrella."

"Well, I'm not going to do that."

I could tell from the silence she was frowning.

"I don't even want to meet a girl at the festival," I said. Because some girls want you to steal things. Some girls call you a little thief and send you on quests to steal memories that no one actually has. Some girls are best to avoid altogether.

"Da dee da dee dum da dee," my mother sang to herself, dancing in the kitchen. I guess she got over the umbrella thing.

"Stop spinning around in there," my father called. "You'll fall and break a hip."

"Don't listen to your father, Koda. Go to the festival. Have fun. It will be a magical night."

I was sincerely hoping it would not.

I left my bike and helmet in the parking lot of Ōmura Shrine and walked up between the two stone lions guarding the entrance. Haru wasn't there, so I sat down near the gates and waited.

As the students of Kusaka High School pulled into the lot with their friends and families, I noticed our school counselor standing near the entrance of the shrine, bowing and wishing everyone a happy evening. The parents would nod to Ino-sensei and say, "Konbanwa," before leading their kids inside. The headmaster walked by with his wife. He nodded at me without really looking. Shimizu-sensei didn't see me at all when he walked by. Probably too busy talking to ghosts or whatever. Even ex-sumō Ikeda-sensei lumbered through the gates without yelling about basketballs or algebra or any number of other things that usually make him angry. Festivals are nice.

After a while, though, I was the only one left. Haru never showed up. The lights and sounds of Kusaka Matsuri glowed behind me, but I was outside. Alone. And kind of cold.

"Hello, little thief."

Moya walked up and crossed her arms in front of her. She

was wearing a slim dress that seemed too adult for a fifteen-year-old. Her hair, pinned back with a silver barrette, shone bright black against the night. I'd never noticed how pretty she was before.

"It's Koda," I stammered back.

"I know your name. And you know your name, so I think we're ready now."

"Ready for what?"

"To go inside," she said, pointing.

"The festival?"

"Where else would two totally normal people go?"

"I don't know."

"Okay, then. Let's go be normal."

Moya looked up at the lights and took me by the hand. She tugged on my arm, pulling me through the entrance to the festival beyond.

"I didn't find anything at Yori's house," I said to the back of her head. "All he cares about is *manga* and river trolls. I don't think he even knows about the crows."

"You'll find the memory, Koda. I believe in you."

"If Yori doesn't know about the crows," I said, "how could he have a memory of them? Maybe we should be looking somewhere else—"

The fireworks over the *matsuri* started in an explosion of blue and red and green. Moya's face lit up.

"The festival is a safe place," she said. "It's a happy place. Let's just have fun tonight."

"I mean, you're the one who said this was urgent."

"Do me one favor, though," she said, letting go of my arm and facing me. "Don't steal my memories. I know it's in your nature, but just don't. Leave mine alone."

"I . . . How would I steal your memories?"

"Promise me."

"I mean . . . Okay, yes, that's an easy promise to keep. If you don't want me to know your memories, don't say them to me."

Moya stepped to the side and kissed me on the cheek. "You're cute. Dumb, but cute."

What was going on here?

"Follow me," she called, running into the festival.

I looked up at Ōmura Shrine and did the one thing I knew I'd probably regret. I ran after Moya.

I will be honest—I don't remember a lot of what went on the night of Kusaka Matsuri. My head felt . . . thirsty. That's the only way I can describe it. Thirsty to take in everything. To hold on to it and never let it go. It felt like I was watching a dream, but I wasn't cold and I knew I wasn't sleeping.

Moya and I slipped in between the crowds of people, making our way along the rows of rickety booths glowing under orange lanterns and strings of colored lights. There was food everywhere we looked: chicken shish kebabs, marinated eggs, boiled *daikon* and skewered *konyaku*, cabbage pancakes with brown sauce, *mochi dango* rice balls, squid-on-a-stick, frankfurters, pork dumplings, fish cakes and garlic pot stickers, fruit jellies, sweet bean paste, ice cream pastries. And fried *tōfu*. A lot of fried *tōfu*.

There were booths with toys and prizes hanging from every inch of free space. Bouncing-ball games, ring-toss games, guessing games, and fishing games. Moya pointed out a metal tub where players were trying to snag eels with a piece of string and a fishing hook. I'm guessing you got to keep the eel if you caught it, but I never saw anyone win. Leathery farmers lumbered by us, swimming in the fog of alcohol found on every corner. There were also bottles of Mitsuya Cider, melon soda, natchan! orange drink, bubbling Ramune, Pocari Sweat, white grape juice with floating bits of aloe, peach water, and cartons of strawberry milk.

There was an old man stumbling by on stilts, and in the corner a stage was set up where a play about Kusaka's founding was being performed. There were man-sized drums where *taiko* players pounded out a heartbeat to the night. There were priests and priestesses, businessmen and party girls, *kimono* and tiny sandals, papier-mâché floats and costumed parades.

Everything blurred together in a spinning haze of colors and wrappers and dripping skewer sticks, but by the end I never wanted to leave. I never wanted to be away from Moya for a moment. She was like a single point of light. A thread of clarity keeping my mind firmly in place. If she walked away, I knew the darkness would come toppling back down.

We walked to the last booth, and Moya ordered another

plate of fried *tōfu* along with a glass of rice liquor. The man behind the counter smiled and set down a plate of *agedōfu* and a glass of *sake*.

"*Arigatō*," she said, and the man bowed.

"How did you do that?" I asked.

"Do what?"

"How did you get him to give you *sake*? You're, like, fifteen!"

She adjusted her dress and touched her hair. "Do you think I look fifteen?" she asked.

"Well, yeah, I guess."

"Oh, good. Very good. *Tōfu* tastes like clouds, don't you think, Koda?"

"I . . . don't know."

"If you could fry clouds, I mean. I like clouds. And snow. And sunsets. What do you like?"

"Well," I said, walking along beside her. "I like airplanes. And hanging out with Haru."

"Boring. Let's talk about something else."

Moya shoved a huge piece of *tōfu* into her mouth and washed it down with *sake*.

"Wow," I said.

Then she belched.

"And that was the perfect end to a perfect night."

"I really like *tōfu*," Moya said, throwing her trash into a nearby bin.

"I can see that. And *sake*. How are you still standing? You should be in a gutter drooling on yourself by now."

"Koda," she said, "you are not as smart as you look." She sighed, leading me to the entrance of the shrine. The smell of rice liquor filled the air. "But you are one of the good ones. Even if you are a dirty little thief."

"Um, thank you?"

"I had my doubts about you, you know. People make such terrible thieves. But you, Koda, you really are one of the good ones."

"I'm sorry, *people* make bad thieves?" Maybe I was a little intoxicated, too, because that last sentence only seemed to bother me a bit.

"You have a good heart. You see things other people can't, and you care enough to try to help."

Moya's smile fell away and she stared off into the parking lot. "But some things can't be helped. Other people will be sad. Other people will be sick. Finding Shibaten is the only way to end all of this."

"Shibaten? The river troll?"

"Of course," Moya said. "Why else would I send you to that weird bus driver? No one is more obsessed with Shibaten than he is. He has to have a memory somewhere in that gross house of his."

"I thought we were looking for crows."

Moya reached out and touched one of the stone lions that guarded the entrance. "No. The crows are just the symptom, Koda. Shibaten holds the key to curing the disease."

"What does that even mean?"

Moya looked at me a little too long. "Find the memory,

Koda. Use your powers for good, and I will show you what that means."

"I guess it couldn't hurt to ask him," I said.

Moya slumped to the ground. "That's my little cutpurse—asking politely for things he's supposed to steal."

"Being polite opens doors."

"You know what else opens doors? Hammers. And rocks. And fire. Fire opens doors."

"Burning down an accountant's house is not a good use of powers," I said, sitting down next to her. "I think you're a little drunk."

"I'm a lot drunk, dummy." She looked over at me. "Do you know where the *kaki* tree is?"

"There are no *kaki* trees in this town, Moya," I told her.

"That's not true. There's one. It's the last *kaki* tree. I hid it. In a bamboo grove surrounded by camphor trees. Go to the westernmost part of town, and you'll see a road next to a small graveyard. Behind the last house on the road there's a footpath. Take the footpath and you'll find the bamboo forest. But don't tell anyone about this, Koda. Don't tell anyone or I will burn you alive."

"Okay, you probably don't realize how extreme that sounds right now."

"I will. I'll burn you alive." Moya looked up at me without a hint of a smile. "Do me a favor."

"This is an odd time to ask for a favor—after threatening my life and all."

"Don't look at me for a second. Promise me."

"I feel like this relationship is very one-sided, Moya."

Moya leaned forward until she was centimeters from my face. Her breath was sweet. Strange and sweet, with an alcohol sting. "Don't look at my eyes, Koda."

I looked down.

"Wow. Not at my boobs. What's wrong with you, kid?"

"Where am I supposed to look?" I said, jerking my chin back up.

"Just close your eyes, genius. Have you never done this before?"

"Done what?" I said.

Moya covered my eyes with her hand and kissed me. It's true, I'd never done that before. It was different than I'd ever imagined. It felt like the oxygen was being pulled out of my body and, with it, all of the fear and the sadness and the pain that had been collecting in my soul ever since Aiko died. When Moya pulled away, I felt the air rushing back in. My head swam in the alcohol on her breath.

"Good night, Koda. Be strong. There are harder times ahead."

Then she walked away. I wanted to follow her, but I slid down to the foot of the stone lions instead. The air blew crisp and raw against my skin. My eyes stung.

Moya was possibly insane and probably dangerous, but as she disappeared around that corner I felt the light inside me dim. It was like I'd invented fire and then someone took it away from me. Suddenly the night seemed so much bigger. So much darker. Suddenly I felt so much more alone.

———

The next morning, caretakers from Ōmura Shrine swept up the bottles and the lanterns and the plastic toys far away from Headmaster Sato and his small Mitsubishi. The headmaster pulled out his briefcase, locked his door, and walked through the high school parking lot. The day after the festival was usually a pleasant time for everyone. The teachers and staff would be in a good mood. A few would probably have hangovers, but nothing a little *kusuri* wouldn't fix. The headmaster smiled for the first time in weeks and rounded the corner. He saw a crowd of those same teachers gathered near the southwest wall of the building, near the school swimming pool that had been drained and abandoned for years. They were all looking up. Some of them were crying.

The headmaster shielded his eyes from the morning sun and stared up at the roof. A shadow balanced dangerously over the edge.

"Taiki!" one of the teachers cried.

The boy teetered on the roof for a moment, then stretched out his arms.

"No!" the headmaster screamed, and dropped his briefcase.

12

For days, the parking lot at Kusaka High School was blocked by police cars and flashing lights. The front doors were chained shut. The windows were bolted. Men in suits with briefcases flew in from Tōkyō and stepped over the barricades that had been set up.

When something terrible happens, people call it a tragedy. Aiko was definitely that—a tragedy. But when something terrible happens again, and again, there's another word for that: a pattern.

I sat on the floor of the front room with my parents, watching the glow of the television set. Watching as reporters descended from Fukuyama and Ōsaka and as far away as Sapporo. They held cameras and microphones and personal computers. They asked questions like "Why this town?" and "How did you miss the signs?" and "Who is responsible?" and "Who is to blame?"

What they really meant was *How do we feel safe again? What can you tell us that will explain away the nightmare?*

The teachers made no public statements. They bowed politely or tried to ignore the barrage of questions as they carried groceries from the Sunny Mart or mailed a letter or filled their cars with petrol. The tragic pattern in Kusaka was making national news, and the people of Japan wanted to know how this had happened and, more important, if it could spread.

Agents from the Public Safety Commission were set up in the school. They opened their briefcases and talked to every teacher and employee. The suicides were a disease. If they searched hard enough, they believed the cure for that disease could be found somewhere inside the interviews and notebooks and personal email accounts.

Some teachers, like Ikeda-*sensei*, got angry. His gym classes could never have led to the suicides, he said, or rather shouted in his huge *sumō* voice.

"But Aiko was found in the school gymnasium. And Ichiro died on the floor of your math room," the agents calmly answered.

"That had nothing to do with me!" Ikeda-*sensei* shot back.

"Perhaps it does. Perhaps it doesn't. We will see."

Other teachers, like Ino-*sensei*, withered under the questioning. "You are the school counselor?" the agents asked.

"Yes."

"Did you counsel your students not to take their own lives?"

"Is that supposed to be a joke?"

"We don't make jokes, Ino-*sensei*. If we did, though, they would go something like this: A counselor is supposed to help her students manage their stress, and that didn't happen in this school. See, that's not even a joke. It's just a statement."

"It's an accusation."

"It's an observation."

As it turned out, one individual couldn't endure the agents' questioning at all. Sato-*kōchōsensei*'s car was found in the parking lot of Ōmura Shrine. The headmaster had entered the grounds and sat down against the eastern wall next to the old *botan* tree. The newspapers said that when the priests came to rake the grounds in the morning, they found him doubled over. His heart had simply stopped beating.

An honorable man, the reporters wrote, Headmaster Sato felt the sting of each suicide deeply in his heart. While he may not have been the cause of the tragedies at Kusaka High School, he was certainly the watcher at the gate. Kids like Aiko and Ichiro and Taiki had slipped by unnoticed while he stood on the wall. There was only one thing an honorable man in Japan could do then. Headmaster Sato knelt down in a holy place and properly died of a proper broken heart.

This wasn't true, as I would find out later, but the newspapers didn't ask many questions. The headmaster was an admirable man, they wrote, a noble man. He was a true beacon of dignity in our troubled times. It was like they'd all forgotten that death was the reason they were here in the first place.

After Sato-*kōchōsensei* passed away, things in Kusaka changed. The investigation and the reporters moved quickly to close the case. Maybe the headmaster's death answered their questions. Maybe it softened their hearts. Maybe they thought Kusaka had faced all the tragedy a town could face for now. Who knows? But the agents gathered their papers, nodded to the reporters, and finally let the press conferences begin.

A new headmaster from Kōchi City leaned forward and bowed in front of a long table bristling with microphones that hummed against the floor of the school gymnasium. The men and women sitting around him lowered their heads as the cameras clicked and flashed. They were dressed in black. Teachers from school, mostly, but also the small mayor of Kusaka Town. Even the governor of Kōchi Prefecture sat nearby, and to each of their lapels a single *yamabuki* flower had been pinned.

Yamabuki means "mountain breath." Bright. Fresh. Unnervingly yellow. These flowers stood out like a snicker in a funeral. For some reason I didn't quite understand, *yamabuki* flowers came to symbolize the fallen students of Kusaka High School. Aiko, Ichiro, Taiki—they were called the Yamabuki Three. Whoever came up with the phrase thought that the spirits of the students would float along like the mountain's breath. Reverent and beautiful, right?

Or super creepy. Adults may have taken up the name Yamabuki Three, but we students never did. Adults can hang their wreaths of *yamabuki* flowers over the windows and the entrances to the school, but we're the ones who have to stay here and eat and walk through dark halls at the end of the day. No matter how beautiful or reverent the words, saying that the school might be haunted by dead classmates doesn't help anyone when they're trying to finish a math test.

In the gymnasium, the new headmaster bowed so low that his head almost touched the table. The other teachers did the same. They apologized for the shame that Kusaka now bore. They promised to make things right again.

Next to apologize was the mayor, and then the prefectural governor. Finally, the agents from the Public Safety Commission stood to address the reporters and answer the one question everyone was asking.

Their answer: *ijime*.

A single word to explain a tragedy that had claimed four lives in just a few weeks: bullying. According to the findings of the commission, the Yamabuki Three had killed themselves because they were victims of bullying.

Aiko Fujiwara's home life fell apart after her mother left the family, the agents said. She felt excluded and pushed to the outside. She was teased for talking to herself on the balcony during class breaks. She became an outcast in school and society as a whole.

It turns out Ichiro Kobayashi *had* lost his parents in a car accident. When he moved to Kusaka, he felt intense pressure to meet expectations on the baseball field. The conditions of his home life with his uncle were still under investigation.

Taiki Watanabe, the last of the suicides, was a *yowaiko*, a weak child, small, with a history of being picked on at home and at school.

Ijime.

Maybe there was some truth to the commission's findings, but I knew there was more to the Yamabuki Three. There had to be. The crows. The weird *haiku* poem about a traveler on the road. The bloody *kanji* on the floor and the cleaning fluid and how Taiki made it onto a locked roof in the first place.

The agents closed their briefcases and buttoned up their suits. They stepped back over the barricades and drove their vans away from Kusaka Town. Eventually the crowds of reporters thinned out until hardly anyone was left and hardly anyone outside our town cared.

Ino-*sensei* was required to undergo training in *ijime* counseling. Speeches were given and clubs formed. There was even a contest at school to see who could come up with the best antibullying poster. No one lost that contest, of course—all the entries were published in a calendar that we were told to hang in our bedrooms and look at each morning.

That was how Kusaka changed. That was how we honored the Yamabuki Three. That was how Japan forgot this small town. We patted ourselves on the back and said, "Now we understand. Now we see. Now the danger is finally over."

But you know what?

We were wrong.

13

By the time I reached Yori's house, the sun was just touching the high mountains of Kusaka Town and the cool smell of evening was drifting through the valley. I swung down the kickstand and left my bike on the street. I creaked open the gate, took a breath, and walked up to the front door. *"Gomen kudasai,"* I called, trying to slide it back.

It was locked.

"Hello?" I said louder. "Is anyone here?"

Nothing.

"Yori-*san*?"

The house was as dead and quiet as the weed path in front of it. I turned and sat down on the steps. Moya and her kiss were constantly on my mind. What kind of a name is Moya anyway? It means "mist" or "fog." What mother names her daughter Fog? Oh, nice to meet you, my name is Ms. Foggy von Misty Hair. See, totally normal.

I stood up and walked around the outside of Yori's house. Maybe there was something buried in all the junk inside that would help me find Shibaten. A few weeks ago I would have laughed at the idea of tracking a *kappa* with the help of a bus driver. But then crows started killing kids. And if you can accept crows who mind-control people into walking off school roofs, well, river trolls aren't such a difficult leap.

Shibaten and the crows were connected, though I couldn't imagine what that connection might be. People in Kusaka may not know too much about crows, but everyone knows at least a little about Shibaten. He's a *kappa*, obviously. He's older than the town itself. There's a forgotten statue of him in the southern part of town. The story goes that when Kusaka was founded two hundred years ago, the *rōnin* and the farmers made a deal with Shibaten. If he promised to stay in his river and not venture out into the valley, they promised not to hunt him down and make a floor mat out of him. Or something like that. I don't pay attention on school field trips.

I heard footsteps on the road in front of the house. I ran around the corner but didn't immediately recognize the man walking toward me. He was dressed in a brown business suit with a yellow tie and a tote bag for a briefcase. His clothes weren't old, but the man inside them looked tired and wasted away.

"Yori-*san*?" I said.

The man's face lit up. "Koda?"

I bowed a little at the waist. I was standing in his front yard, so it seemed like the proper thing to do.

"What are you doing here?" he asked.

"I need to find Shibaten," I said.

Yori stopped and looked around.

"Did he follow you here?" he asked.

"No." I looked behind me. "I mean, that would make my life easier, but no."

"That would not make your life easier, Koda. It would be terrible! Absolutely awful! Let's get inside."

Yori walked past me and up the steps. He yanked on the front door, but it caught on the lock and wouldn't budge.

"Ne-*chan!*" he called through the window. There was no reply. He turned on me suddenly. "Did you see anything strange when you came to the house?"

"Like what kind of strange?"

"*Kappa* are trickster demons." He rattled the caught door again. "This could all be some kind of . . ."

"Trick?"

"Exactly."

Yori set his tote bag down. "What did you do, Koda?"

"What did I do? I didn't do anything."

"You're not listening," he said. "*Kappa* are dangerous, Koda. Very dangerous. Shibaten will kill you."

"Kill me? Why? What did I do to him?"

"What did Aiko and Ichiro and Taiki do? Murder is just part of a *kappa's* nature." Yori looked past me to the corner of the house. "We need to get inside immediately. Follow me."

Yori led me around to the side of the house. He pushed hard on the window, and with a few creaks it gave way. Yori hopped up and squeezed himself inside. I did the same, landing on the dusty floor of his kitchen. Yori shut the window.

"Ne-*chan!*" he called, but his sister didn't answer.

We walked through the junk of Yori's home and into the front sitting room. The TV was dead. Yori opened his briefcase, pulled out his *keitai* phone, and dialed. Hello Kitty swung back and forth from a charm on the antenna stub.

"*Ne-san?*" he said into the phone. "*Ima doko? Sunny Mart? Itsu kaette kuru? Nandatte! Kagi ga shimatteru kara. Chigau, chigau. Baka ja nai, Shibaten no sei datte!*" He looked at me and lifted the phone from his ear. "She hung up on me. Guess she was the one who locked the door when she went to Sunny Mart. Said the back door is unlocked."

"It wasn't Shibaten, then?"

The fire that animated Yori died away. His shoulders slunk back into his drab brown suit. He pocketed his phone and asked if I wanted something to eat.

"No, I'm fine," I said.

Yori walked to the refrigerator and pulled out a *musubi* rice cake. He peeled off the plastic and bit lazily into the seaweed wrapping.

"You sure you don't want anything? I have another one," he said.

"I'm okay."

Yori took another halfhearted bite.

"I almost forgot." Yori reached under the counter and pulled out a pair of welding goggles. After snapping them to his face, he slumped back down and bit into the rice cake.

Sad.

"Yori, I need your help."

"Really."

"I have to find Shibaten."

"No, you don't." Yori crumpled the plastic from his rice cake and brushed it onto the floor. "That's the last thing anyone has to do."

"Something is wrong with this town, Yori. You can feel it. I know you can. If we find Shibaten, we can stop the suicides."

"I don't know who told you that," Yori said, "but they're stupid. Or trying to get you killed. A *kappa* is crazy strong. Shibaten will break every bone in your body with one hand. If you ever see a *kappa*, you should run as fast as you can in the opposite direction."

"Can't you help me find him?"

"How would I even do that, Koda? He doesn't usually stop by for a cup of tea. No one ever stops by to have tea with me."

I was losing him. "Think, Yori. Do you have a memory of Shibaten? Anything we could use to find him?"

"A memory?"

"You know: Do you remember something specific about where he hangs out, or whatever?"

"*Kappa* live on riverbanks, Koda. That's all I can tell you. I don't know where Shibaten goes when he's not killing kids. And it would be best if you didn't either." Yori laid his head down on the counter.

I'd completely lost him. I turned for the front door but stopped. "Who do you think will be next, Yori?"

"What?"

"Do you know what they call Aiko and Ichiro and Taiki?" I

said, stepping back to the counter. "The Yamabuki Three. Don't you see anything wrong with that?"

He lifted his head. "It's a little creepy, I guess."

"First of all, thank you. It *is* creepy. More important, it's the 'three' part. Everyone's already decided the tragedy has passed, and they fixed the number of victims at three. But you and I know Shibaten is still out there. So I'm asking, who do you think will be next?"

"I . . . I don't know."

"Maybe it's me, Yori. Maybe I'm Yamabuki number four. Or maybe it's another kid who has friends and family who care about him. I have to stop this and I can't do it without you. Help me."

Yori pushed the goggles up onto his forehead. "I don't know where he is, Koda. I swear to you."

"You have to know something—anything at all. Try to remember, Yori. Please."

My ex–school bus driver dropped his head into his hands and squeezed his skull. "Think, Yori, think!" he cried to himself. "You are the Desert Punk. You can do this. You are awesome. Where is Shibaten hiding?" He was quiet for a moment. "Ah!" he bellowed and then looked up at me. "Okay, I've got nothing."

"What? I thought you were remembering!"

"Sorry. Nothing at all . . . Wait." He closed his eyes again. "Nope, that . . . that was from a *manga*." Yori opened his eyes. "I've never actually seen Shibaten. I've only felt him from a distance, so there's no way I would have a memory of him. Like, at all."

I exhaled loudly. Moya was wrong. Yori was a dead end. Just because you obsess over something doesn't mean you really know that something.

"Taiki's father met Shibaten," Yori offered. "But then he was murdered by him. Everyone thought the guy fell into Kusaka River, but you don't break every bone in your body by falling into slow-moving water."

Tonight was just full of dead ends.

"It's getting dark," I said. "I should be getting home."

"I wish I could help you, Koda."

I stepped back toward the entrance. "Can I go out the front door, or do I have to climb through the window again?"

Yori walked past me and turned the lock. The door screeched when he pulled it back.

"Thanks, Yori," I said with a half smile. "I'll stop by some time for a cup of tea."

Yori smiled back. "Watch yourself out there, Koda. Stay away from the river. If Shibaten's hiding, it means he doesn't want to be found. I doubt even a *suri* could track him down."

I stopped. "A what?"

"A *suri*. You know, those nasty little pickpockets who feed on misery and suffering."

"When you say 'feed on misery and suffering' . . ."

"If your brain were a pocket, these awful sneak thieves break inside and pick the coins out of it."

"And 'coins' in this case are . . . ?"

"Memories of trauma. Obviously."

The air of Yori's house suddenly felt close and sickeningly raw.

"Stealing traumatic thoughts and memories is only the beginning, though," he continued. "Those are the first steps on the Tengu Road. Most *suri* become dark inside. They spend their days spying on people's misfortune until all their compassion drains away. At that point there's nothing human left inside them."

Yori's house started to sway. I felt light-headed.

"Their bodies eventually transform into mountain demons. They become lost. They become *tengu*. I'm pretty sure everyone knows this. Hey, are you okay?"

"I'm fine," I said. "I just need to get outside. I need some air."

I pushed through Yori's front door, stumbled to my bike, and threw on my giant helmet.

"Be careful, Koda," Yori shouted.

I slammed my foot on the pedal and didn't look back.

Kusaka High School was empty. There were no cars in the parking lot, but it wasn't that kind of empty. I parked my bike under the awning and walked up the front steps. The new motion-sensing lights came on, but after a few seconds they went out again. Lights and locks were the best people could do, but when faced with the strange emptiness that hung over the high school, their best wasn't good enough.

I walked through the side gate and over to the abandoned pool. It had been scrubbed clean just like the school gymnasium and the math room. I climbed inside and looked up at the roof. That was a huge jump. Even for a regular-sized person.

I got down on my hands and knees and inched forward, feeling the cement in the dark with my fingertips. I'd been hospitalized twice for narcolepsy since I was thirteen. I wear a helmet sometimes because I get too stressed and black out. I see weird things when that happens, but it's not like I'm spying on people. I'm just dreaming. Like a normal person. Like any other totally normal kid.

I hit a patch of cement that was definitely colder than the rest and jerked my hand back. My hopes of normalcy shattered and fell to pieces around me. The bottom of the pool was warm from the evening sun, but the area that had been scrubbed the most felt like ice. I ran my fingers back over the spot. The longer I kept my hand there, the dizzier I felt.

This is very stressful, I thought to myself. Of course I'd be feeling a little woozy, I'm climbing into an empty pool at night, a pool where someone died. Who wouldn't be stressed out by that? Time to ride my bike back home, eat a nice warm meal, and slip into a steaming bath. That sounded amazing, so I pushed myself up to my feet.

All that talk of hot food and hot water was just a mirage in my brain, though. The world around me was freezing cold. I'd fallen face-first onto the pool floor and hadn't even realized it.

Gravel crunched loudly above me. I didn't have to see him. I knew it was Taiki. He'd just pulled his bike into the awning. I could feel his pain.

Taiki Watanabe was too small. He was too small for his home, too small for Kusaka High, and perhaps too small to last long in this world. But he was just the right size to be the last of the Yamabuki Three.

Taiki's mother usually worked the night shift at a local gasoline stand, and before she would leave each night she would say, "You are a beautiful boy, Taiki. You are very special and someday you will do great things."

"Will I be tall?" Taiki would ask.

"Yes, of course, my son. You will be the tallest man in all of Japan."

But then she would take her coat from the hook near the front door and leave him. Alone. With his father.

"You are a stupid boy," *tō-san* would always say, pouring another glass of warm *sake*. "You aren't special. Gods, look at you. You aren't even normal."

Taiki would turn to leave the room, but his father would stop him.

"Say it," he said.

Taiki wouldn't turn around.

"Say it," his father repeated.

"*Iitakunai.*"

His father would slam the *sake* bottle on the table. "Say it!"

Without turning, Taiki would whisper, "Will I be tall, Father?"

Then his father would laugh and laugh until spit trailed from the corners of his mouth and Taiki would run from the room. When the house had become still, Taiki would sneak out to sit in an abandoned truck on the banks of Kusaka River. He pictured himself as a giant. Not the kind the villagers would fear, no, just a normal giant who grew tea in steppes on the mountainside.

Do you see that, child? the villagers would say. *That is a real giant.*

Will he eat me, Mother?

No, child, no. You shouldn't fear that giant. He only wants to grow tea and to be left alone.

Taiki's father died one night after falling into the river. His mother cried for days.

"What was he doing out there?" she sobbed. "He never left the house that late. He was too inebriated."

"You may have answered your own question," the policemen said softly.

Taiki sat in his room imagining what the accident might have looked like. The policemen were puzzled by his father's body. The official cause of death: drowning. But that wasn't the whole story. So many bones were shattered.

"Falling in is one thing," Taiki heard them say. "But it looks like he was dragged along the bottom of a raging torrent. And then went over a waterfall."

"How many raging torrents and waterfalls do we have in Kusaka?" asked one of the policemen.

"Not a single one," the first one said.

Taiki knew something that the policemen didn't, though. Not everything small in Kusaka is weak and scared. Some small things are powerful. Some small things are strong enough to grind a man's bones to dust. Taiki couldn't help picturing the look on his father's face when the river reached out and dragged him under.

Taiki stood outside Kusaka High School and searched the windows on the second floor. There it was. The one that led to Toriyama-*sensei*'s art room. After Aiko and Ichiro died, the school windows were shut and latched each night. All of them except for the tiny window above the art room. Without ventilation the paint fumes will fill the school, Toriyama-*sensei* thought to herself. Surely that's more dangerous. Besides, no one can get through that window. It's just too small.

Giant, the art room window said.

"Me?" Taiki replied through the dark, frigid air.

Of course, you. You are a giant, aren't you?

"Yes. I am a giant."

Giants aren't afraid of walls or balconies, are they?

"Giants aren't afraid of anything."

That's right. Giants go wherever they want to go.

"Wherever."

They climb the tallest mountains, don't they?

"The tallest."

Climb this mountain, Taiki. Stand above the world below. Look down on everyone like the giant you are.

"They won't fear me?"

No, Taiki. They will love you for it.

Taiki walked around the school and stood beneath the balcony.

"I can't jump that high."

You are not small, Taiki. You are the tallest man in Japan. The balcony is easy to reach. It is easy for you.

The window was right. Taiki leaped with all his might and grasped the frozen concrete ledge. After struggling for a few moments, he managed to pull himself up and over the railing.

You are so close now.

Taiki ran along the balcony and slid easily through the art room window.

"How do I reach the top of the mountain?" he asked.

From the maintenance hatch. In the kitchen. The key is in your pocket.

"The key that the crow gave me?"

Yes, that is the one.

Taiki climbed to the roof of Kusaka High School.

You did it, Giant, the voice said.

"I did it," Taiki repeated.

He walked through the flock of crows nesting on the roof and looked out over the town of Kusaka. He was taller than everyone else. Morning broke out over the mountains behind him. The birds hopped around his legs. Taiki stood and looked and smiled. For the first time in his life, he was totally and completely happy.

Nothing is impossible for you, the voice said after a while.

"Nothing is impossible."

You could even fly if you wanted to.

"I could fly."

To higher mountains than this. Do it, Giant. Spread your arms and soar through the air.

"With the crows?"

Fly with them, child.

"Crows fly," Taiki said.

"A traveler on the road
Is lost."

Taiki Watanabe spread his arms as wide as he could. He didn't notice the crowd below at all. The crows lifted up, storming away into the sky. The last of the Yamabuki Three followed them. Over the roof. Over the sidewalk. Above the fence that ringed the freezing pool. Until the moment he landed behind me, Taiki soared with the birds.

14

It was long after dark when I finally walked into the house that night. Father had gone to bed, but Mother was waiting up for me. Well, sleeping up for me. She was snoring on the floor in the sitting room with a paperback novel in her hand. She'd probably been like that since five o'clock. Did I mention my parents are super old?

"*Okaeri,*" I whispered to her. "It's time to go up to bed, *Okā-san.*"

She looked up and smiled at me.

"You took the long way home from school," she said, totally unaware of what time it actually was.

"Yes, Mother, I did."

I helped her to her feet.

"Good night, Koda. There's *shiitake* in the refrigerator if you're hungry."

Nope. Never hungry enough to pop open a bag of snacking mushrooms.

"*Oyasumi nasai,*" I said.

"*Oyasumi,*" she said back.

I was exhausted and slept through the whole night without dreaming at all.

My parents were both gone when I came downstairs the next morning. That wasn't so unusual for a Saturday. Since the cycle ends in October, they would both be harvesting the remaining *shiitake* from oak logs stacked outside the house.

I ate a bowl of rice and *miso* soup, and sat outside on the front steps. I breathed in the mountain air and tried to push yesterday out of my mind. The *haiku* wouldn't budge, though. During class breaks Aiko used to stand on the balcony and talk to a three-legged crow that wasn't there. I figured the poem was just something she'd made up. But then Ichiro said it in the math class, and Taiki said it on the roof. I wasn't so sure it *was* a *haiku* anymore. It sounded more like a warning. Or a cry for help.

> *"Crows fly.*
> *A traveler on the road*
> *Is lost."*

If people are getting lost on roads in this town, maybe it would be best if I found a new place to walk. I should listen to Yori. Whatever I am, nothing good will come from following this road to its end.

"Koda," my mother called out to me.

I looked up and saw her pushing a baby carriage from the direction of Route 33. I stood up and unlatched the front gate.

"I brought you your favorite treat, Koda."

My mother handed me two shopping bags and then parked

the carriage in the carport. Parked it. We *do* have a truck, but since my mother's vehicle of choice is a baby carriage she purchased ten years ago, the truck was moved to the side of the house to make room.

"Your treat is in that one," she said, pointing to one of the bags.

"Oh, Milky . . . yep, that's my favorite all right."

No, it's not. I mean, it was. When I was six. Old people always seem to be stuck in the past. They tell the same stories about you over and over and over again, and they're always from when you were six.

It's true that Milky is a very popular candy in Japan. It may be the *most* popular candy along with Pocky sticks and Kit Kat bars. But once I turned seven, something about the bag seemed really weird. There's this cute girl on the front—Peko-*chan*. She's got pigtails and big eyes. She's licking her lips with this huge smile on her face and staring off to the side. But just above that, there's the slogan for Milky candies.

ミルキーはママの味
Milky: The Flavor of Mom

Wait. The Flavor of Mom? What exactly is Peko-*chan* licking her lips at? Suddenly I felt like I'd outgrown milky mom candies.

"Will you be seeing Haru today?" my mother asked as we walked inside.

"I think so."

"I hope the boy's all right and nothing was too damaged in the fire."

I set the groceries on the counter next to the sink.

"What fire?"

"At his uncle's house. The night of the festival."

"Haru's house burned down?"

"Not down. Just burned. They never did find the cause of it. Smoke can still damage your things, though."

"I haven't seen Haru since we were supposed to meet up outside the *matsuri*," I said. "I'll ask him, though."

Wait, Moya wouldn't set a house on fire just to get me alone, right? No. I mean, what kind of a person would do that?

A person who is not a person, my brain said.

After my mother finished with the groceries, I picked up my helmet and walked to the front door. I stopped with my hand on the glass and then ran back to my mother. I gave her a hug.

"That's nice," she said.

My mother is old, but she's happy. There's no trauma or cold-dreaming at all when I hug her. I'm going to go ahead and say it—that's how hugs should always be.

I turned back to the front door.

"Don't forget your Milky," she said, holding out the bag of candy. "It's the flavor of mom. That's me!"

Oh wait, there's the trauma.

Wing flaps up. Increasing throttle to 2,000 rpm. Increasing back pressure. Here we go. Gaining speed. Going full throttle now. Lifting the nose. Carefully. Carefully. Climbing. Hold on to the stick. A little crosswind, but that's no problem for Fly-Boy of Kusaka Town. Seventy-five knots. Got it now. Cruising. We are cruising.

Fly-Boy, everything look all right up there?

"Smooth sailing, Ground Control, smooth sailing over Kusaka Town."

You going to be up there for a while, Fly-Boy? Over.

"That's a negative, Ground Control. Don't have time for sightseeing today. Got a shipment to make."

Shiitake mushrooms again?

"That's another negative, Ground Control. Boys on bicycles deliver mushrooms. My shipment is top secret. Comes straight from the emperor."

So you're flying to the Imperial Palace, then?

"First off, Ground Control, don't ever assume you know where I'm flying."

That's kind of our job, Fly-Boy. Over.

"Second of all, no. This shipment needs to arrive at Lawson's."

Your top secret delivery from the emperor is to a convenience store?

"Umm."

We need a confirmation on that, Fly-Boy. Over.

"Yes. To the most important convenience store in—"

That's a roger, Fly-Boy. Make sure to pick up a top secret box of strawberry Pocky for the emperor. Over.

"Real funny, Ground Control. Guess that's why I'm flying

this plane and you're stuck down there cracking jokes like some . . . uh . . ."

Like some narcoleptic loser?

"I'm not really narcoleptic."

Insult received. Over.

"Fly-Boy out."

Did I just lose a fight with my own imagination?

Checking my air-speed indicator and carburetor heat. Green lights on both. Lawson's coming into view now. Ease the stick. There we go. Circle a few times, and then go in for a smooth landing. Wave to Haru.

"Koda."

Slowing down to seventy knots. Flaps down thirty degrees.

"You are so weird, man."

Making the final turn. Keeping it straight, keeping it straight. Turn the rudder just a bit.

"You're making me dizzy. Stop."

Ignoring Haru. Floating. Lift the nose. Floating some more. Elevator to the back and . . . touchdown.

"Where have you been lately?" Haru asked.

I took my foot off the pedal and kicked my bike stand down.

"Permission to exit the plane, Ground Control."

"Permission to be an idiot, granted," Haru said, blowing out a mouthful of smoke.

"What are you doing out here?" I asked.

"I'm on break. What are *you* doing out here?"

"I always ride out here."

"I haven't seen you for almost two weeks. I thought maybe you'd crashed your imaginary plane into a very real semi truck."

"I've had a lot to deal with," I said, sitting down next to him.

"Yeah." Haru snuffed his cigarette on the sidewalk.

"You didn't fall asleep with one of those and burn your house down, did you?" I asked.

"Nope. For your information it was electrical. Probably. Nobody knows."

"Huh." I picked up a pebble and tossed it into the parking lot. "Are you okay from the whole fire thing?"

"I'm fine. Even my uncle's fine, unfortunately. The bastard. I don't want to talk about it."

"So, Sports Day is Monday," I said, changing the subject.

"Right." Haru flicked his cigarette butt at a trash can and missed. "Your parents aren't going?"

"They never go. Like, anywhere."

"You want me to show up and cheer your team on?" he asked.

"Only if you dress up like one of those game show contestants."

"In a Speedo, covered with vegetable oil, and swinging around a plastic lobster?"

"That was specific," I said. "And very accurate. Yes, that's exactly what I want."

"I'll pass," Haru laughed. "What team are you on, Red or White?"

"I don't know."

"Where's your school pride, Koda?"

"We're a little low on that right now," I said. "Besides, I don't think it will matter. I have a feeling no one's going to lose Sports Day this year."

Haru smiled. "Everyone's a winner."

"That's what the posters say."

A truck roared by on Route 33. I fiddled with the air valve on my front tire. Things were a little awkward between Haru and me. He was probably upset that I'd been ignoring him for so long.

"Guess I should get back to work," Haru said.

"Um, yeah, I've got *shiitake* to deliver, so . . ."

Haru pushed up from the curb and turned to the convenience store. "Hey," he said, "you didn't go off to that kitten graveyard, did you?"

"The what?"

"The address. The one that girl gave you. You didn't actually go, did you?"

"Oh, kind of. But it just led to an old pool."

"A pool graveyard?"

"You could say that."

"I knew it," Haru said, walking to the front doors. "Nothing good comes from following strange girls who lie about who they are."

Very good point, Haru. Very good point.

15

Kusaka High School had lost its unity. That's what they told us, anyway. And what better way to bring the school together than the Annual Kusaka Sports Day Celebration of Smiling Times and Positive Thinking?

Huh. I don't remember the title being that long last year.

Danketsu. Unity. The word literally means "bind one to the group." So if we were all bound together, I guess that would prevent one of us from sneaking off to commit suicide. And hey, what better way to bind a group together than to dress them up in white shirts and blue shorts, split them into rival teams, and make them race each other for a plastic trophy?

Ikeda-*sensei* blew his whistle and we formed military lines on the dirt track. I looked around for Haru. Sure enough, he'd come. Minus the Speedo, vegetable oil, and plastic lobster.

"Attention!" Ikeda-*sensei* shouted. We slapped our arms to our sides. "Students of Kusaka High," our *sumō* gym teacher bellowed, "welcome to the Annual Sports Day Times . . . of . . . Positive Smiling . . . and something else, gods, I can't remember because I'm a normal adult."

A few of the students giggled.

"The eyes of the town are now on you. Bring honor to yourself and your school by displaying the true qualities of a student of Kusaka High. Do your best! Never give up! And be polite to everyone, or I will *sumō*-punch you through a wall."

He didn't say that last part, but honestly I'd stopped listening.

"Hey, little thief."

"Whoa!" I twisted my head around. "Moya, what are you doing here?" I whispered.

"Standing uncomfortably in a line. Just like you."

"No, I mean, why are you here at my school?"

"I go to this school," Moya whispered back. "I told you, I moved in down the street."

"I don't believe you."

Moya shrugged.

"Where are your parents, then?" I asked.

"Where are yours?"

"At home because they're old."

"Well, mine are, too."

"They're at home or they're old?"

"They're whatever you want them to be, little thief. Turn around."

The metal speakers of the school popped and slowly whined to full volume. The sad notes of "Kimi Ga Yo" drifted over the school grounds.

"The first event is the forty-meter sprint!" Ikeda-*sensei*

shouted when the national anthem ended. "Red Team to the right! White Team to the left!"

I glanced back to see where Moya was going. The Red Team with me? Well, that's good. Not that I care what team she's on.

"Runners, take your marks," Ikeda-*sensei* called.

We all clumped together at the starting line.

"I-I think I need my helmet," I whispered out loud.

"Are you serious?" said Kenji from homeroom, whom I still hated.

"I don't think I can do this. I really hate running. I'm going to fall."

"If you do go down," Kenji whispered, "cover your head with your arms. That's how people survive getting trampled by mobs."

"Oh gods, I need my helmet. Stop the race!"

"Don't pick on Koda," came a girl's voice behind me. "If anyone's going to have his butt dragged across the finish line, it'll be you, fat-ass."

"Hey," Kenji said.

"Breathe," Moya whispered in my ear. "You don't need the helmet. When the whistle blows, run. Don't overthink it."

The piercing shot of Ikeda-*sensei*'s whistle sent both teams stampeding down the track. Dust billowed up and swallowed me like a whale. I focused on the red tape at the end and kept my feet moving. Moya was right. This wasn't so bad. Now if I could be flying a plane it would be even better. I would lift up off the track and soar through the sky clear as glass. I'd pull back on the stick and climb higher than any mountain in Kusaka before diving again to buzz the crowd.

Who's flying that plane? my classmates would shout.

That's Koda.

Koda? Isn't it dangerous for a narcoleptic kid to be flying an airplane?

Nope. Turns out those weren't sleep attacks after all. He's actually a mind thief who steals traumatic memories.

"Wait, what?"

And that's when I ran face-first into the back of some girl's head.

"*Nani shiteru no!*" she cried, rubbing the knot on her head.

Was that the same girl I hit with a basketball in gym class?

"The race is over, Koda! Gods, what is wrong with you?"

Yep.

"I'm sorry," I said. "I was thinking of something else."

"Get away from me." She pulled deeper into the crowd of the celebrating White Team. My nose started to bleed. Who runs a race and ends up with a bloody nose? I wandered off to the side, tilting my head back to stop the flow.

The next event was the three-legged race, and as luck would have it, the Red Team had an odd number of runners. Guess who ended up without a partner? Surprise, surprise— the only kid who managed to wound himself in the forty-meter sprint.

"Does everyone have a partner?" Ikeda-*sensei* shouted.

I didn't raise my hand.

"Does anyone not have a partner?"

I tried to pull back into the crowd. Maybe they wouldn't notice.

"Anyone who can't find a partner, please step up to the front where we can all see. Everyone take a look around. If you see someone who doesn't have a partner, please point at them now. Nice and big. Point right at them."

"Koda's alone," Kenji shouted gleefully.

"Who? Koda? Koda Okita? Come up to the front, Koda. Hurry, we all need to look at you."

"Gods and goddesses," I breathed, and squeezed my way to the front of the line. Ikeda-*sensei* looked back to the teachers in the tent.

"Look, Koda, you can just run by yourself," Ikeda-*sensei* said.

"But it's a three-legged race."

"Well, you can just run with the Velcro on your leg. That'll be fine for you."

"Wait a minute," came a female voice. "Hold on just a minute, Ikeda-*sensei*."

Oh, good. Moya's come to save me from this mortifying experience.

"Koda, your nose is bleeding."

But it wasn't Moya.

"I think you should be wearing this." The school counselor, Ino-*sensei*, jogged over and stuck my helmet on my head. She yanked on the chin straps and fastened it with a click that echoed across the track. Oh. My. Gods above.

"Hey, I'll be his partner."

I turned around to see Moya finally pushing her way through the Red Team.

"Whatever," Ikeda-*sensei* said. "I really don't care. Runners, make your way to the starting line."

Moya knelt down beside me and fastened the Velcro around her leg and mine.

"Gods, Moya, you couldn't have stepped forward five seconds earlier?"

"You can still run by yourself," she said, avoiding my eyes. "I mean, if that's what you want, I'm not going to stop you from going out there and looking like an idiot again."

"No, no, I'll run with you."

"That's right." She stood up and hooked her arm around my waist. "Just do me one favor for saving you up there."

"Anything."

"Stay out of my head."

"I . . . okay."

"I'm trusting you, Koda. Just because we're touching doesn't mean you can take whatever you want."

"I don't even know how to do that."

"Put your hand over here on my hip. Whoa, not on my butt."

"I didn't, I swear!"

"Relax. I was joking, kid. Let's get to the front of the line."

"Moya," I said, "I can't tell if you're a nice person or a really mean one."

"Yeah, well, keep that hand above my panty line, Koda, or you'll find out fast."

Ikeda-*sensei* blew his whistle for a second time, and the Red and White teams lurched off down the track. We were supposed to make it around twice, but to tell you the truth, I was more focused on making sure my hand didn't violate Moya's panty rule. Not an easy thing to do when you're hopping along on one leg, trying to keep a helmet out of your eyes.

But we crossed the finish line in one piece. Not first place or anything, but at least there weren't any more injuries or inappropriate gropings. So I counted that as a success.

Sports Day carried on into the late afternoon with the racing and the dust and the sweat. But for the rest of the time Moya stayed nearby and, you know, the day didn't seem that bad. I knew she was just using me to find a memory, or whatever, but when I crossed a finish line or passed off a baton, she was always there. That was something I'd never really had before.

"Get ready," Moya said to me as we lined up for the Ramune race. "I've seen this race before. It's brutal. Do your best to wait until after you cross the finish line to throw up all over the place."

Which is a pretty good way to sum up a Ramune race. Take my three favorite things in the whole world: running, spinning, and chugging soda pop. Then do all of them at the same time until liquid comes squirting out of every hole in your face. That is a Ramune race.

"Go!" Ikeda-*sensei* shouted. The Red Team launched forward, sprinting to the table on the side of the track. We each spun around in a circle ten times and then popped open a fresh bottle of Ramune soda.

"Drink! Drink! Drink!" the teachers shouted from the tent. "Run! Run! Run!" the parents in the bleachers cried. Seriously, who sits in their dark little lair and comes up with ways of torturing high school kids like this? Don't they have better things to do?

The fizz of the soda pop scorched my throat. I could feel it bubbling up through my teeth and behind my eyes. "Run!" Moya shouted. I dropped the bottle and threw myself forward onto the track. *I'm in first place!* I screamed in my brain. *Wait, nope, I'm in last place. Very last place. Kso.*

I put my head down and ran with every bit of energy I had. The Ramune sloshed around in my gut like a volcano ready to explode. I could feel the hot sting of bile rising up the back of my throat. I looked ahead of me and saw Moya's legs. She'd waited for me, I knew it. She could have been at the front of the line, but she chose to hang back. I pushed harder. The cheer of the crowd rose in my ears.

Sometimes in extraordinary circumstances people are capable of extraordinary feats. Maybe they lift a car off someone or kick their way through a steel door. Well, this race was my car. That track, my steel door. I'd keep the soda down and blaze across that finish line even if it killed me. My knees started to buckle beneath me, but I ignored them and pushed on. My helmet fell over my eyes. I didn't care. I could smell the soda coming up through my nose. I swallowed hard. The finish line was right ahead of me. I belched but cupped my hands over my mouth just in time. Yes!

"*Dekita!* I did it!" I yelled. Well, mostly yelled. Stopping suddenly made all that soda come rushing back up. And it splashed right across someone's shins.

"What the hell, Koda?" shouted the random girl I keep assaulting. "Are you kidding me? That is so gross! Why me?"

I lifted my helmet and tried to say sorry, but soda throw-up dribbled out of my mouth. She started to cry.

Ino-*sensei* took the girl by the shoulders and led her away to the girls' bathroom.

"Don't worry about her," Moya said. "Her shins looked dirty anyway."

The final event of the day was the *masuto nobori*. The mast climb. Two stories of bamboo trunk set up at the end of the track with little red or white flags on top. The object is to run as fast as you can and at some point leap into the air and grab on to the bamboo. Then you scurry up the mast, grab a flag from the top, and shimmy back to the earth below.

Whoever invented this must have been like, "What would happen if we chased little kids up a tree? Then, and here's the really genius part, we *told* everyone it was a Sports Day event?"

"Why, it would be the greatest Sports Day event ever devised," answered the evil villain who thought up the Ramune race.

"Go!"

"What?" I turned to face Kenji towering over me.

"Go! It's your turn!"

"My turn?"

Then, keeping in line with his very helpful nature, he

shoved me down the track. My helmet and I rolled a few times, but I picked myself up, trying to slap away the dust all over my shorts.

"Run!" my team shouted.

"All right, all right, *wakatta*," I shouted back. The runner from the White Team tore past me and leaped for the mast. He jumped out of his shoes and over the gymnastic pads, slamming into the pole hard enough to shake a few flags loose.

I think I'll do this a different way, I decided to myself. Instead of running fast, I'll run carefully. Instead of leaping for the mast, I'll slip off my shoes and do a little bunny hop onto the bamboo. Instead of scurrying to the top, I'll safely plant each foot and palm so my grip won't slide. I won't be of any use to my team if I'm dead, now, will I?

"What are you doing?" my teammates shouted. But they weren't halfway up a giant trunk of bamboo, so I ignored them. Carefully, carefully. Just like that. Almost there. Keep your eyes on the prize. Slow and steady. So close now. One little red flag coming up.

It was about that time that I made the mistake of looking down. Normally I'm not afraid of heights, but when the only thing keeping you in the air is bamboo and sweat, you develop the fear pretty quickly.

I hooked my shoulder onto the mast so fiercely that the bamboo shuddered and began to sway. The ground seemed to be rotating, spinning slowly to the left. I buckled my knees onto the pole and stared up into the sky. That didn't help. The clouds started spinning, too. I squeezed my eyes shut. I could

feel my heartbeat pounding my body as if it were actually trying to knock my grip loose. Stupid heartbeat.

"*Kso*," I hissed through my teeth. "I'm going to die, I'm
going to die."

"Koda!" I heard Moya's voice from somewhere far away.

The swaying stopped.

"Let your body slide down," Moya called up to me.

I opened my eyes, but instead of seeing the ground below, I
saw something much worse. Actually, a whole flock of some-
things.

"Moya!" I yelled. "Crows!"

There was a pause and then I heard her say, "Oh, shit."

They came in a storm of spiny feathers and tiny sharp toes.
Their quivering bodies slammed into me as their cries filled
up my ears and spilled into my brain.

"Slide down!" Moya yelled.

But there was so much screaming. All around my head.
Pecking at my fingers and snapping at my knees. My head felt
dizzy. I locked my arms and legs around the bamboo that was
swaying from side to side. Behind the flurry of feathers and
beaks I could barely hear Moya's voice. Her words were like a
single ray of light cutting through a tornado of screeching.

"Move your feet and slide down! You can do it, Koda.
Focus!"

I closed my eyes and let my knees go. I loosened my grip.
The bamboo slid between my arms faster and faster. I tried to
brace, but it didn't make much difference when the ground
raced up and sucker-punched me unconscious.

16

Moya was the first to reach me when I hit the ground like a stack of wet fishing nets. She grabbed my hand and called my name. Her voice sounded dull and distant. My brain was all scrambled inside my skull. I looked up at her face. Into her eyes. That was a mistake. Instantly the world turned to ice.

Before the war in the Pacific there was a boy named Seimei who lived in Kusaka Town. He was about my age and didn't have any brothers or sisters. Other than that, I don't really know too much about him. I don't even know his family name. I only knew his first name because his mother was shouting it in a park as I watched her die.

"Run, Seimei! Run!" she screamed.

Seimei's father was lying on the frozen ground nearby with a jade-handled *samurai* sword sticking out of his back. He was groaning in the darkness surrounded by a hundred crows.

"Leave him alone!" Seimei's mother shouted, throwing herself on her husband's body. A huge mountain demon stepped forward and yanked the sword from the dying man's spine. It turned and threw the mother aside.

There wasn't much that the woman could do, really. The *tengu* stood almost as tall as the rusted swing set she slammed into. Seimei's mother untangled her leg from the poles and stumbled to her feet.

The demon towered over Seimei's father, barking with laughter. Through his elaborate robes the *tengu*'s skin was thick and patchy like boar's hide, and as red as the blood that seeped from his victim's back. The monster stroked his white beard and touched the sockets where his eyes used to be.

"Oh, how I wish I could see you suffer with my own eyes," he said to the father, leaning in so close that his absurdly long nose almost scraped the ground. "And I know what suffering is. I have waited more than a century to repay the debt I owe you and your kind."

The *tengu* reeled back and lifted the sword above his head. "But with a hundred eyes watching for me, I will remember this as a glorious day."

Seimei's mother rushed forward. The crows lifted up in unison and the demon spun around, slicing her across the stomach. She crumpled to the side.

"That is what happens when you interrupt people!" the demon yelled. "Gods above, I was trying to do something nice for this suffering man, and you went and ruined it."

"Seimei," the woman spat onto the concrete. "Climb, my son, climb to the top of the tree."

The *tengu* grabbed Seimei's mother by the back of her *ki-*

mono and flung her across the park. She slid along the icy ground and buckled around a streetlamp.

"Seimei," the father groaned, reaching out to his son, who was hiding in a nearby tree.

The mountain demon stomped past Seimei's father, beheading him with a flick of his sword hand.

"Man-child," the monster said up into the branches. "Man-child, come down from there."

Through the frigid air I could see Seimei snapping twigs and pulling himself through the gnarled branches of the thick oak. His brown school uniform caught for a moment, but he tore the sleeve free and climbed faster.

The crows hopped along the ground, fixing their collective gaze on the scrambling boy above them.

"I see you, man-child. I'm an old blind *tengu*, but through the eyes of my crows, I see you. You can never hide from me. You cannot climb high enough. You cannot run far enough. Your blood is mine and I will have it."

Seimei kept climbing.

"If you come down right now, man-child, I will wait until after you're dead to eat your eyes. I promise. You really won't get a better deal than that."

"Inari," Seimei's mother whispered. "Goddess of life and protection, the *tengu* has erred. He has cut me. I am dying, Goddess. Oh, please save my son." She tore a pendant from a chain around her neck, a small silver fox from the Shrine of Inari where her grandparents used to pray. When the policemen found her body later, they had to pry that pendant from her fist with a metal bar.

"I'm not climbing up the tree after you," the *tengu* yelled to Seimei, but the boy didn't look back.

"I have to use birds for eyes, and now you're making me climb all the way up a tree in order to murder you? Well, I'm just going to say it—you are an inconsiderate child."

The monster sheathed his jade sword and wrapped his arms around the oak tree. He rested his long nose and white beard against the bark. The branches shook and the trunk whined and cracked as the great red arms of the *tengu* crushed and popped the wood. The tree rocked from side to side. Seimei locked his arms and legs into the branches, but it didn't make any difference—the monster wasn't trying to shake him loose. With a sound like that of a cannon, the trunk finally gave way.

The *tengu* turned and roared as the tree crashed down into the abandoned park. "See," the monster growled. "That was inconvenient for everyone. Now I'm going to pluck your eyeballs out and make you watch me eat them, which you won't be able to do without eyes, but we'll give it a try anyway."

Then something very strange happened. Well, stranger than a blind *tengu* pulling down a tree to eat a kid's eyes. There was a whispering, carried on the freezing air itself, floating through the park, winding its way into the frozen branches of the tree.

"What is this?" the *tengu* snarled.

The whisper became visible, like a ghostly trail of petrol

fumes. It swirled over Seimei and spread out from the broken trunk.

"Inari?" the *tengu* cried.

The whisper slithered across the ground and brushed against the demon's red feet. He stepped back.

"Inari! This isn't your concern. Keep your minions away from here. I only want the boy. It's my right!"

"You have taken more than that already," the minion whisper sighed.

The *tengu* looked over at Seimei's mother, who was cold and still as stone. "That wasn't my fault!" he growled, baring his teeth. "It was technically my fault, yes, but she interrupted me!"

The whisper ignited. Fire surged through the air, swallowing the tree and the abandoned park. The shock of the sudden heat threw the *tengu* off his feet.

"Seimei," the whisper said. "Seimei, open your eyes."

The boy obeyed and all around him the world burned.

"You are safe."

When Seimei looked up he saw a girl in a silver *kimono* covering him, shielding him from the flames. She smiled, just centimeters from his face.

"Who are you?" he asked.

"Who do I look like to you?" she replied.

"A girl. In a gray *kimono*."

"Then that is who I will be."

———

The next thing I knew, every teacher at the middle school was huddled around me. Ino-*sensei* pressed her hand against my forehead. Moya was nowhere to be seen.

"Koda, are you all right?" she asked.

I looked up at the bamboo mast above the teachers' heads. I tried to nod, but my chin straps wouldn't allow it.

"That was a bit of a fall, Koda. I bet you're glad you have this helmet now. You're like a superhero," she said, forcing a smile. "Able to fall off bamboo masts with barely a scratch."

"That would be a particularly useless superpower," I answered, clenching my stomach.

Ino-*sensei* set her hand on my back and helped me into a sitting position.

"Is everyone looking at me?" I asked.

"Um, yes. Want to do a little wave?"

"I'd rather not."

"He's fine, everyone," the new headmaster announced to the parents in the bleachers. "He's fine, isn't he?" the headmaster whispered, kneeling next to Ino-*sensei*.

"Thanks to his helmet," Ino-*sensei* said, "and to Ikeda-*sensei* for setting up these gymnastic mats."

"I knew this was a bad idea," the headmaster said. "Kids shouldn't be climbing those things. They're so tall that birds run into them. Who invented such a horrible Sports Day event?"

Thank you. That's what I thought.

Ikeda-*sensei* towered above me, pointing his huge hand at my legs. "He didn't break anything. He doesn't have a concussion. Just a little dazed. He'll walk it off."

"Do you have medical training?" the headmaster asked.

"I've seen plenty of concussions and shattered bones in the *sumō* stables. The helmet broke his fall. He'll be fine."

I wanted to point out that Ikeda-*sensei*'s go-to solution for probable concussions was walking it off, you know, like a man, but thought better of it and kept my mouth shut.

"Where are his parents?" the headmaster asked.

"They're not here," Ino-*sensei* whispered. "They almost never come to the school."

"Let's carry him out to my car and I'll drive him home," the headmaster replied. "I should stay with the family and explain what happened. The mayor will probably call when he hears of this."

No, he won't. Nobody cares about a narcoleptic kid who can't make it through a Sports Day without hurting himself and the people around him. Ino-*sensei* knew that drawing attention to me was the last thing we should be doing. She waved to Haru, who was finally allowed to jog onto the track.

"Who is this?" the headmaster asked.

"Haru Maeda," Ino-*sensei* told him. "He used to be a student here. He and Koda are neighbors. Haru will make sure Koda gets home safely. Is that all right with you, Koda?"

"Gods, yes."

"Good thinking, Ino-*sensei*," the headmaster said. "I should stay here in my office . . ."

"In case the mayor calls," Ino-*sensei* finished.

"Exactly. Ikeda-*sensei*, jump to the award ceremony. And

take down those masts before another child is assaulted by migrating birds."

Haru pushed my bike and I walked alongside him.

"Do you want to talk about it?" he asked, once we were clear of the school.

"Nope."

"Okay."

And that's why Haru and I are such good friends. We know when to shut up and just let the other person think.

17

"You're sure you feel all right?" Haru asked when we got to my house.

"I just need something to eat. I'll be fine."

Haru locked up my bike for me, nodded, and walked in the direction of his uncle's home. When he was out of sight, I unlocked my bike, clicked my helmet on, and rode off to find the last *kaki* tree in Kusaka Town.

The logs of the footbridge thumped beneath my bicycle tires, jostling my helmet over my eyes. I stopped and pushed it up again. A wall of camphor trees stood before me like the front lines of a *samurai* army. I couldn't see any way around.

"Koda, over here," a voice called from behind the lines.

"What about my bike?"

"Leave it."

"What if someone steals it?"

"Lock it, then leave it."

"I don't know. It might look abandoned way out here."

"A flock of crows just tried to break your neck and you're worried about someone stealing your bike?"

"Well, it's a good bike."

"It's a pink bike."

"It's a red bike," I clarified. "It's been . . . used a lot. The color's faded."

"Listen, Hello Kitty–*chan*, lock up your pink bike and get your ass in here."

"Then we can talk about keeping my neck unbroken?" I swung my leg over the seat. "I feel like we skipped over that part when you were saying rude things to me. Also, do you think I should keep my helmet on?"

"Does your helmet have any Hello Kitty stickers on it?"

"Of course not," I said.

"What about Pokémon?"

"Not on the outside."

"Dear gods and goddesses," Moya said. "Of all the kids in Kusaka, you had to be the pickpocket. Get in here now."

I left my awesome not-pink bike by the footbridge and squeezed through the line of camphor trees. On the other side stood a thin bamboo forest, and in the middle of that— a single *kaki* tree. Moya walked through the bamboo and sat down beneath the withered branches of the tree.

"How did you find this place?" I asked.

"It's a safe haven. I brought her here when the *kaki* trees began dying out. She's the last one left."

"She?"

"Persimmon trees are unlike any other trees, Koda. They have gender. This one is female."

"Does your girl-tree have a name?" I asked with a smirk.

"Does your ugly pink bike have a name? No? I didn't think so. Stop hovering out there and come inside."

"The tree?"

"Yes. Sit down."

I ducked under the branches and knelt down next to the gnarled trunk. Moya watched me but didn't say a word.

"So," I asked, "how do you know this tree is a she?"

"You don't see it?" Moya said.

"Am I supposed to be seeing something? I don't even know where to look. That part over there looks weird. Is that it?"

"What? No! Gods, I mean the *soul* of the tree, you pervert. Can't you see the soul of this tree?"

"Um, no. Can you?"

"*Kaki* trees are special, Koda. Do you know why?"

"Because they're trees that have souls?"

"They are resilient. They represent the goodness in this world and the will to survive."

"This one looks like it's already given up," I said.

"No, you're wrong. It is very difficult to kill a *kaki* tree. Floods and insects and birds and disease—those are all things that kill regular trees like those mighty camphors out there. But not the thin, sickly-looking *kaki* tree. Even death cannot kill a *kaki* tree."

"What?" I said.

"Before the *kaki* tree sends out its fruit in late fall, it dies. Or at least, it mostly dies. The branches shrivel, the leaves fall away, the trunk takes on this twisted, gnarly shape. And then in the midst of its own death, when it looks like it should fall over and be forgotten, it suddenly sends out this explosion of persimmons. Dozens of bright orange fruits pop out. The tree is reborn! For the next several months, the *kaki* tree pieces itself together and goes on living stronger than before. It's almost impossible to kill a persimmon tree."

"Then why is there only one left?" I asked.

Moya's face dropped. "They're *almost* impossible to kill." She picked up a brittle leaf from the grass. "There is an infection in this town, Koda. A cancer much older than Kusaka itself. It isn't a person or a god or a spirit you can fight against. It's darkness, hopelessness, emptiness, despair. It exists everywhere in the universe where the light doesn't shine. Eventually everyone and everything everywhere will succumb to it."

"Now see, you go talking all normal for a while—well, normal for you—and then you say totally freaky things like that."

"That kind of darkness is a long time off, though. Maybe a thousand billion years from now. But when the nothing of the universe encounters a particularly bright light, it's drawn to it. The darkness surrounds the light, tries to twist and fold and consume it. That is the Tengu Road."

"The Tengu Road?"

"It is the nothingness that's all around us," Moya said. "The Road breaks down the universe piece by piece until everything you see will be black and empty and cold. Normally people don't even notice the Road, but Kusaka is different. The Road is seeping in here faster than anywhere else. And whatever it touches, it eventually destroys."

"So do you, like, ever get invited to sleepovers? No? Here's a hint: it's because you say things like that."

"I don't know what a sleepover is, Koda, but the Tengu Road probably hates that, too."

"Right."

"Listen to me, the Road infects things differently. The *kaki* trees were points of light and hope in this town. As the Road flooded in, though, it suffocated them one by one."

"Gods, Moya, this is not the conversation I pictured us having."

"And humans don't fare any better. Those who become infected by the Road go mad. They wander down empty paths of hopelessness. Some survive this encounter, but most do not."

"The Yamabuki Three were on the Road."

"Despair overtook them. When the crows started watching, the cancer flooded their minds."

"Watching them? Gods above, Moya, they're watching me! I see the crows!"

"Calm down, calm down, Koda. You're freaking out. Just listen to me."

"Okay, fine, what?"

She waited until my breathing returned to normal.

"You are going to die."

"I'm going to what? Are you serious? Have you ever given bad news to anyone before? You are absolutely terrible at it!"

"No, no, that's a good thing."

"How is that a good thing?" I shouted.

"Because the Road won't take you like it took the others. You're different. If you're very lucky you'll die in about eighty years like a *normal* human being."

"I hate how you said 'normal' there."

"You're a dirty little memory thief, Koda. That's not really normal."

I dropped my head into my hands. "Moya."

"Yes?"

"Why am I on the Tengu Road? I'm a nobody. I'm a sick, weak kid who is constantly hurting myself. I'm the kind of person you forget five minutes after meeting me. I'm a *shiitake* farmer with no future. I'm not important to anyone, anywhere."

"You're a *kaki* tree, Koda."

"I'm pretty sure that's not true," I said, looking up.

"Not literally a tree, no, but you have great strength inside you. You may be scrawny and goofy-looking and incapable of running forty meters without injuring yourself—"

"Bedside manner, Moya."

"But you have potential in that gnarled trunk of yours."

"What am I?" I asked her.

"You're someone who sees things that other people don't," she said.

"I see misery that other people don't."

"Yes. But unlike the *suri* who enter the Tengu Road and lose themselves, you want to help people. You want to reverse the pain and suffering you see, not poke it and spread it around. That makes you more *kaki* tree and less—"

"Tengu?"

"Well, technically, yes."

"But that's where most *suri* end up?"

"Certain *suri* do . . . make a home of the Tengu Road."

"I don't want to make a home on any road. Especially not one that leads to freaking mountain demons."

"That's why I sent you to Yori's house, Koda, to steal a memory about Shibaten. That river troll holds the key to breaking the Tengu Road in Kusaka."

I leaned back against the trunk of the *kaki* tree. "I was at Yori's house, Moya. He doesn't know where Shibaten is hiding. There's nothing in his house but cosplay videotapes and *anime* figurines."

"He has to have the memory," Moya said quietly.

"I'm sorry. He doesn't."

"But the bus driver said he saw Shibaten."

"He *felt* his presence around the school. He didn't actually see anything."

Moya stood up and walked to the edge of the *kaki* tree. "No one else has seen Shibaten in two hundred years. Yori was our only link. If we can't find someone who has a memory of the *kappa*, then Kusaka is lost."

"I wish there was something . . ." I started, but trailed off. I suddenly jumped to my feet and ran to Moya. "I have to go."

"What? Why?"

"I'm a *suri*. Those traumatic memories aren't going to steal themselves!" I tried to give Moya a peck on the cheek, but I was really excited and smacked her in the chin instead.

"Ow, Koda, gods!"

Whatever, I had a town to save. No time to worry about awkward kisses. I ran out from under the *kaki* tree and darted through the bamboo forest.

"All right, then," Moya called after me. "Ride like the wind on your little pink bike, my brave thief."

"It's red!" I shouted back.

18

"Yori!" I called. *"Imasen ka? Are* you there?"

"Koda?" came a voice from the second floor. Yori walked to the window dressed in his *sugegasa* straw hat, his cape, and goggles. "What are you doing here?" he asked.

"Yori, I need to talk to you. Can I come up?"

"Is it about the *kappa* Shibaten?"

"Yes, it absolutely is."

Yori's face lit up. "Do you need the Desert Punk?" he asked.

"That is, yep, exactly why I'm here."

Yori pumped his fist in the air. "Come up, Koda. The door's unlocked!"

"Sumimasen," I said, after I walked up the stairs and into his room.

"Here, have a seat, Koda. First question: Did you ride all the way here?"

"Yes."

"Next question: You're out of breath."

"That's not a question. I was riding hard."

"Drink this," he said, handing me a canteen. "You've lost a lot of water. I can see it in your face. You need to rehydrate. Our bodies are ninety-eight percent water."

"I'm pretty sure that's not true."

"Drink it anyway."

I took a swig. "Done. And really gross."

"All right, your turn."

"I think my girlfriend is a *yōkai*," I blurted out.

Yori stopped dead in his tracks. He slowly turned around. "You have a girlfriend?"

"Yori, that wasn't the important part—"

"What's it like to have a girlfriend? Someday I'm going to have one. She can be Rain Spider in my cosplay videos. I definitely need a girlfriend."

"So that really wasn't the point. And I shouldn't have said 'girlfriend.' We've never actually, you know, defined our relationship."

"A girlfriend who doesn't know she's your girlfriend?" Yori said. "Oh, okay, I've had those before."

"I mean, we kissed once. But the point is, I think she's a *yōkai*."

Yori walked to the window and removed his straw hat thoughtfully. "I don't know, Koda. Having a supernatural creature for a girlfriend could complicate things . . . in the romance department, if you know what I mean." He turned back to me. "Do you know what I mean? Because I do not know what I mean. Women are a complete mystery to me."

"If my girlfriend is supernatural, is she dangerous?" I asked.

"It's possible. It depends on what kind of *yōkai* she is. She could be good or malicious or something in between. She could be a *yūrei* ghost. She could be a shape-shifting *obake*. Does she seem more like a snake or a badger or a spider? Oh! She could be *tsukumogami*—an inanimate object that comes to life every hundred years! I once dated a porcelain teapot for three months thinking it had a woman's soul inside."

"But it didn't really?"

"We broke up," Yori shot back.

"When you say 'broke up,' do you mean you 'broke it'?"

"I don't want to talk about it. It was a very delicate teapot!"

Yori untied the strap on his cape and laid it over a nearby *ramen* box. "The first thing you need to do, Koda, is find out what kind of *yōkai* she is. This is very important. If you're compatible enough, you might be able to marry. If not, she could suck your soul dry and leave your body a withered husk. Just like a *kappa*," Yori said, spinning on me. "You aren't dating a *kappa*, are you? Koda, are you dating Shibaten?"

"What? No. Gods, Yori, no. But if I can find out what kind of *yōkai* she is, I'll let you know."

"All right. And if she *is* an inanimate object with a soul, I will not judge you. Heaven knows those relationships are hard enough."

"I'm really here because I need a favor." I lowered my voice. "One that isn't strictly legal."

"Illegal?" Yori asked. "Like criminally illegal?"

"That . . . Okay, what other kind of illegal is there? No, I just need you to borrow something for me."

"What kind of something?" he said, removing his goggles.

"You work at the town office, right? You work with records and stuff?"

Yori took off his straw hat. "I work with tax records."

"What about different kinds of records?"

"How different?"

"Police different."

"What would you want with police records?" Yori asked.

"Not police records." I handed him a piece of paper.

Yori opened and read it.

"You remember how Taiki's father was murdered by Shibaten two years ago?" I said.

"Sure. They found him in the river."

"Well, I need any evidence they still have at the town office. This is a top secret mission, Yori. Only the Desert Punk can do it."

Yori looked up at me. "What are you talking about, Koda?"

"The case was ruled accidental, and any evidence was probably filed away somewhere. I need you to get it for me. I need whatever he was carrying at the time. A watch, maybe. A wallet. A key. There might be clues that will lead us to Shibaten."

"This is incredibly dangerous, Koda. What do you think you'll do if you find the *kappa* anyway?"

"Something larger than Shibaten is happening to this

town," I told him. "It's bigger than me and you and the Yama-buki Three. Bring me any evidence the police have, and I will show you a conspiracy that makes Shibaten look like a sneezing kitten."

"Why a sneezing kitten?"

"I tried to think of the opposite of scary. That's what popped into my head."

"Cats give me the hives."

"I'll remember that. Will you do it for me, Yori?"

He looked down at the paper. "I don't know, Koda. I could get in trouble. I don't even know if I can get into those archives."

"I need help," I said. "I need *your* help. And when people need help, who do they call?"

"The police?"

"No. They call a hero. They call the Desert Punk."

"Sure."

"Yori," I started, "you are a simple town employee. You were fired from being a bus driver because you saw things and refused to back down. And what did you get for it? Thanks? No. A medal? Hell, no! You got stuck behind a dusty desk in the basement of the town hall. You sit around all day under the glare of fluorescent lights making sure that numbers in Column A match numbers in Column B."

"It's not that bad," he said.

"No one sees you," I continued. "No one pays you any mind. If you suddenly stopped existing, they would just replace you with some other mindless drone who is willing to waste his life away over a mountain of papers."

"Hey."

"That's no way for a person to live," I said. "That's not a real life, is it? But I will tell you what it is, Yori. It is a perfect cover. The perfect secret identity. Who would ever suspect that Yori Yamamoto, failed bus driver and town hall accountant, is really the Desert Punk? Out there solving murders! Changing lives!

"You come home each night and dress up in front of your camera. You put on that cape and the hat and goggles, and you pretend you're making a difference. But I'm offering you something here, Yori. I'm offering you a chance. A chance to be someone. For real."

"Koda," Yori said.

"Help me, Desert Punk."

"It's just, if someone saw—"

"Help me, Yori. I need the Desert Punk."

"I don't—"

"Please, Sunabōzu. Please."

Yori folded up the paper and pushed it into his pants pocket. "All right, Koda. I'll bring you the evidence. But promise me you won't keep it for long. I have to return it. I could get fired for this. Or worse."

"You have my word. On the honor of the Desert Punk, you have my word."

Yori walked me to his front door. "Give me a couple of days, Koda. I need to reconnoiter the premises."

"Sure thing. Whatever you just said."

I walked out into the growing darkness of Kusaka Town.

"By the way," I said, turning back to Yori, "there's this strange *haiku* that keeps popping up. I wonder if you know anything about it."

"I like *haiku*."

> *"Crows fly.*
> *A traveler on the road*
> *Is lost."*

"Nope. I can look into it, though, if you want."

"Don't do that. I'm just glad you've never heard it before. Have a good night, Yori."

"*Oyasumi,*" Yori said.

I walked out to my bike and kicked up the stand. Looks like I am an awesome thief after all. Step one: Tell your victim he has access to something you want. Step two: Ask him to get that something and bring it to you. Step three: The victim says he'll do it.

Being a master thief is way easier than I thought.

19

Moya wasn't at school the next day, which was fine with me—I had a very important errand to run. After the final bell, I rode my bike along the backstreets to the town library. And when I say library, I mean a small reading room tucked in between town hall and the Sunny Mart grocery store. It may not be very big and it may not have a wide selection of, you know, books, but if something happened in Kusaka (and it usually doesn't), this library would be the best place to learn about it.

"I'm, um, doing a report for school," I told the old lady behind the desk. "And I was wondering if a family was ever murdered in a park with a *samurai* sword."

The librarian squinted at me over her wire-frame glasses. "Well, that is morbid. And oddly specific. This is for a school report, you say?"

"Yes. So do you know where I can find some information on that, and also did it really happen?"

"That was a very long time ago, young man," she said.

"But it did happen?"

"Oh yes. It was very strange and very tragic." She set down the book she was reading.

Hey, they do have books here.

"Come with me," she said.

The librarian led me through the run-down room toward a table in the back corner. One, two, three, four . . . nine. They have nine books here.

The librarian pulled down a fat three-ring binder with the date Shōwa 6 written on the spine.

"This is a collection of all the *Kusaka Town Newsletters* from the year 1931 to the present. Let's see," she said, thumbing through the pages. "Here it is. May." She laid the binder out in front of me. "A young man lost both his parents that night. He was about your age."

"Seimei? Was his name Seimei?"

She looked over the edge of her glasses and ran her finger down the page. "That's right. Seimei Nakagawa. What was the topic of your school report?" she asked, but I'd stopped listening to her. I was staring at the front page of the next month's newsletter.

At first it was difficult to tell what I was seeing. The charred remains were apparently part of a shrine. It could have been any building, really, from what was left, but in the corner of the picture, you could see the trunk of the old *botan* tree. Anyone who attended the fall *matsuri* would instantly recognize it.

"Is that Ōmura Shrine?" I asked.

"It is. Two tragedies in two months," the librarian said. "All centered on this boy Seimei."

The doors in the picture were seared and shattered. Around the handles, though, you could make out a blackened chain. Someone had locked it. Fastened it tight.

"What ever happened to Seimei?" I asked.

"He died in the fire that burned Ōmura Shrine to the ground."

"He died?"

"Seimei and his family were the last Nakagawas in this town. Their ancestors went all the way back to the founding of Kusaka Village in 1805. When Seimei died, his family line went extinct. I suppose that makes three tragedies in two months."

"Gods," I whispered.

"Do you need a photocopy for your report?" the librarian asked.

"Sure," I said, blankly.

As we walked across the room to an ancient-looking machine, I asked the librarian if the man who set the fire had ever been caught.

"Oh no, no one set that fire," she said. "It was an act of the gods."

"Why do you say that?"

"Because the shrine was struck by lightning. And not normal lightning, young man."

"What kind of lightning?" I asked.

"The kind that explodes a shrine from the inside out."

"Oh," I said. "That kind."

I folded up the grainy photocopy and shoved it in my pocket. After clicking my helmet on, I turned my bike toward Lawson's.

Moya didn't know it, but I'd already stolen two memories from her. One while we were at the funeral, and the other after my fall during Sports Day. Both memories were about Seimei Nakagawa.

In one of those memories, Moya was screaming at Seimei to run. In the other, she looked like she was protecting him from a blind *tengu* by torching an entire park. But then Seimei died a month later when Ōmura Shrine was locked and detonated like a firebomb. Did Moya do that?

On the night of the town festival she did get drunk and threaten to burn me alive if I told anyone about the *kaki* tree. *Gods above, Yori was right. My magical girlfriend who lives in the woods might actually be dangerous!*

I slid my bike into the Lawson's parking lot. I left my helmet on the handlebars and ran into the convenience store.

"Haru," I said.

He looked up from the counter.

"You know that weird girl, Moya? I think she's an arsonist. Or the ghost of an arsonist. I'm not sure which one yet."

"Koda, quiet," Haru whispered.

"What?"

He smiled at the back of the store and jogged around the cashier's counter. He grabbed me by the shoulders. "You have to play it cool, kid. There's a new employee here."

I looked down the aisle at a woman in her twenties stamping price tags on noodle sandwiches.

"Who is that?" I asked.

"That's Emi," he said.

I looked again. "Her name tag says Natsuki."

"Okay, fine, you caught me. I don't remember her name. But it should be Emi. That's a really pretty name, don't you think?"

"Hey," Natsuki called from the back. "My hands are cold because of the refrigerator, so I'm going to take a smoke break."

"I'll just be here watching the store," Haru called. "Take all the time you need."

She stopped to look at me and Haru, rolled her eyes, and then pushed her way outside the store.

"She does not care for this job," I said.

"She hates it!" Haru said with glee. "We're perfect for each other."

"Right. Anyway, I have to talk to you about Moya."

"Who?" Haru said, rounding the front counter.

"The girl from a couple of weeks ago. The one who snuffed your cigarette."

"Oh, yeah, the kitten-graveyard girl. Whatever happened to her?"

I was about to tell him that Moya might, *might* be murdering boys my age, when Natsuki stormed back into the store.

"*Kore hidoi,*" she said. "This sucks!"

"What is it, Emi?" Haru immediately asked.

"My name is Natsuki!"

I shook my head.

"You stare at me too much," she continued, pointing at Haru. "And the store is too cold, and I can't even smoke outside because of all the birds."

Birds?

Natsuki marched into the backroom to grab a coat. I ran over to the front window. Crows lined the curbs of the parking lot. They must have flown over the roof, because they kept dropping onto the asphalt in front of me. They kicked to their feet and hopped onto the sidewalk and the garbage cans and the recycling bins. They clicked their beaks and stared straight at me.

"Are you seeing this?" I said to Haru.

"Never mind that," he said. "I need you to take off."

"What?"

"Emi is in a delicate place right now, and she needs me to be there for her."

"Listen to me, my friend, I really think you're misreading the situation."

"Take an ice cream bar on the house and come back later, Koda."

"You might want to— A free ice cream bar, you say? Like, any ice cream bar?"

Natsuki walked back into the room and started fidgeting with the cash register.

"*Hayaku,*" Haru mouthed to me.

I stepped up to the freezer unit near the door and quickly slipped a vanilla ice cream bar into my pocket. Haru laughed and then stopped when Natsuki turned to look at me.

"What the hell?" she said.

Kso! She saw me! I turned to Haru, but neither he nor Natsuki were actually looking at me.

"Run, Koda!" Haru screamed.

Because of the ice cream bar? You said it was on the house! Do something, Haru! But he wasn't yelling about the ice cream. He was looking past me, through the huge window. I turned around.

Have you ever noticed how time plays out differently in your memories? A van spun off Route 33, barreled through the parking lot, and skipped the curb. It flew through the window and smashed the ice cream freezer in front of me. The force of that blow knocked me down and jarred my senses so badly that everything was fuzzy until I woke up later in a Kōchi hospital.

But that's not how you remember traumatic events. I looked back, and in my memory the world ground to a halt. I remembered the van in the air, wheels slowly turning, bearing down on me. Behind that van, across the parking lot, sat a ghostly white fox. Black, shining eyes staring through the flying gravel and the broken crows.

A fireball blossomed under the van, and the front fender burst gently through the window. Witnesses standing nearby thought the petrol tank had exploded. I remember seeing glass and wood and plaster flying through the air like slow-motion confetti. I remember the look on the driver's face. Clearly. It must have only been a fraction of a fraction of a second, but I remember it like a photograph.

Terror. That's what you thought I'd say. How else would someone look as they bounced their vehicle through the front of a convenience store? But that wasn't it. The driver didn't look terrified. Or even concerned in the slightest. He looked bored. As if losing control of his vehicle was an inconvenient thing to happen on his way home from work. Even when his arms buckled at the elbows and shattered from the force of the steering wheel, his face looked blank and totally separated from what was happening.

The force of the blast knocked me to the ground. The van flipped onto its side, demolishing half of the Lawson's back wall. I remember hearing screams. The world rocked in and out. Stripes of black raced across my vision. I heard Natsuki screaming behind the counter.

"Shinde iru wa! Shinde iru!" She was crying.

I rolled over. Why is she screaming like that? I'm not dead. The store jerked back and forth. Then I saw Haru's feet beneath the counter. I tried to focus. He wasn't moving.

20

As I was lying in a hospital bed, waiting for my parents to take the train to Kōchi City, I expected Haru to walk into my room at any minute.

You're a mess, kid, he'd say. *Guess that's what you get for stealing ice cream bars. How's that for karma? Do something bad and somebody runs you over with a car. Immediately. Through a window.*

"I wasn't stealing," I'd say.

I told you to take it without paying. Which is pretty much the definition of stealing. That's how karma works, kid.

"I think there's a little more to it than that," I'd say.

Haru would shrug and pull out a cigarette.

"Koda?" my mother said, shuffling through the door. "Oh, my poor baby boy."

"The van missed me. I'm okay," I said, trying to sit up. The nurse in my room reached out and pushed me back down.

"Relax, dear," my mother said.

"I can't," I said, kicking my legs. "She's hurting me."

"I'm barely touching him," the nurse said.

"Our boy is not strong in the conventional sense," my father repeated.

"He has a wonderful spirit," my mother shot back.

"I didn't steal the ice cream bar," I blurted out. "Where's Haru? He'll tell you. This has nothing to do with karma."

My mother drew close to my ear. "Haru's fine, Koda. They told us he's just fine."

I stopped kicking my legs. "Are you sure?"

"Yes, dear."

"But I saw his feet."

"Haru is going to be fine. He has a broken leg and some bruises, but they're fixing him up now."

"Is he here? Is he in the hospital?" I asked.

"Yes. He'll be here for a few days. You can see him when he's ready."

"When will that be?"

"We're not sure, dear."

"Okā-san?"

"Yes, my boy?"

"Am I naked?"

"You have a hospital gown on. Well, you did before you started kicking around like that."

"Mom?"

"Yes?"

"Is the nurse looking at me?"

"Umm."

"I think I can go now," the nurse said. "If you need anything, press the button near his head." She straightened her skirt, bowed, and left the room.

Mother covered me up with a hospital blanket.

"All of this was for an ice cream bar?" my father asked.

"Haru said I could have one. I got distracted because I was trying to choose between vanilla and strawberry. I like the strawberry, but you could win another vanilla bar by finding a Hello Kitty under the wrapper."

"Hello Kitty?" My father buried his face in his hands and whispered, "Gods above."

"Hello Kitty Dancing Ice Cream Party happens to be a delicious vanilla dessert bar!" I shouted. "I won't apologize for that."

"Quiet, both of you," my mother snapped. "Ice cream has nothing to do with this."

She was right. The *Kusaka Town Newsletter* wrote about the accident and published it the next week. The driver, a forty-three-year-old businessman, survived the crash. He said he didn't know what happened. He was driving down the road and then came to, upside-down in the van. Several witnesses reported seeing a massive fireball erupt beneath the vehicle, but the petrol tank was untouched and whole.

"There was no reason for it," one policeman said. "The

traffic on Route 33 was light at the time. He probably got drowsy and drifted off the road."

"But how would that explain the driver's injuries?" a reporter asked. "Both his arms were shattered. The steering wheel was bent around the driving column. That doesn't sound like a man who was drowsy. That sounds like a man who was bracing for impact."

"I don't know how to explain that," the policeman said.

Well, I do.

During the crash I saw a white fox staring at us from the parking lot. With no rational explanation, old librarians might describe the crash as an act of the gods. You know, the kind that sends vans flipping through windows in fiery explosions for no reason. Or, and I'm just throwing this out there, it might be the act of a supernatural girlfriend. One who, coincidentally, has also blown up a shrine.

The night after the hospital released me, I snuck out of my house. The words "snuck" and "night" are a little misleading. I walked out of the front door at 5:30 p.m., thirty minutes after my parents had fallen asleep.

I didn't mean for Haru to get messed up in all of this. He had been in and out of surgery, and "visiting" meant peering through a small window in his hospital room door and watching him sleep. By the time I got home, I knew I had to figure out what I was really dealing with here. I strapped my helmet on and rode my bike to Yori's house.

"Tell me everything you know about *kitsune*," I shouted up to Yori's window.

The Desert Punk slid back the glass. "I thought you got hit by a car?" he said.

"I did. Well, a van, actually."

"You don't look like you were hit by a van," he said. "Did Shibaten trick everyone into thinking that? That sounds like something Shibaten would do."

"Nope. It wasn't a *kappa*. And the van missed me, so I'm fine. Can I come up?"

Yori waved me inside.

"Tell me about foxes," I said, marching into his room. "And not just any fox. A fox spirit. A real-life *kitsune*."

Yori turned his cosplay camera off. "Your girlfriend is a *kitsune*?"

"Did I say she was my girlfriend? Oh, right, I did."

"Well," Yori said, "how many tails does your girlfriend have?"

"So, first of all, I'm not sure she's my girlfriend anymore. We might break up. Because she tried to kill me. And, second, as far as I know she doesn't have a tail."

Yori looked at me like I was an idiot. "I'm talking about her animal form, Koda. How many tails does the *kitsune* have?"

"Of course. I'm going to say just one tail."

"So it's a young *kitsune*, then."

"I guess. She's like fifteen."

Yori laughed. "That doesn't mean anything. You can't tell how old a *kitsune* is by looking at its human form. She could be nine hundred years old. But probably not if she only has one tail. She's definitely less than nine hundred years old."

"Well, great, I was worried there'd be an age gap."

"Do you know what type of *kitsune* she is?"

"Like big or small? She's definitely a white fox. Kind of medium size."

"No. Is she *zenko* or *yako*?"

"I don't know what that is."

"*Zenko* are benevolent fox spirits associated with the goddess Inari. *Yako* are the opposite. They're evil field foxes. Mischievous. Cruel."

"Definitely the last one. Maybe."

"*Kitsune* are shape-shifters. They usually take the form of girls. So yeah, it's reasonable that she could be your fifteen-year-old girlfriend."

"Oh good. I was afraid this wasn't a totally reasonable conversation."

"Now, if she's one of Inari's foxes, having her around is a good omen, Koda."

"And if she's the dangerous kind?" I asked.

"Then she will shoot fire at you."

"Okay, let's talk about that one for a minute."

Yori sat down on a *ramen* box. "It's called *kitsune-bi*. Fox fire. It comes out of their eyes. Or their mouths. Or their tails. They can shoot fire, that's really the point."

"Okay."

"I'm pretty sure she's not *yako*," Yori said. "If she'd wanted to burn you alive, she would have done it by now. Unlike their mischievous cousins, benevolent *kitsune* are fiercely loyal. That's probably what you're dealing with. If she has chosen you, it will be difficult to separate yourself from her."

"And why would a *kitsune* choose someone?" I asked.

"Who knows? Maybe you saved her life. Maybe it's a blood oath from the goddess Inari. Maybe you have something she wants."

"Yep," I said under my breath.

Yori jumped up and snapped his welding goggles over his eyes. "So are you going to ask me?"

"Ask you what?"

"No matter the feat, no matter the run . . ." he sang.

"Huh?" I said.

"C'mon. No matter the feat, no matter the run . . ." He gestured for me to finish.

"Oh, right. No matter the feat, no matter the run, uh, Desert Punk gets the job done! Did you get the evidence, Yori?"

"I didn't get it."

"What? Then why did you—"

"The Desert Punk did!" Yori pulled a thick manila envelope out of his tattered tote bag and set it in my hand.

"You got it!"

"Please," Yori scoffed. "Did the Desert Punk thrash Rain Spider all over the wastelands of Tōkyō?"

"I'm going to say yes because I don't really understand what you just said."

"Of course I got it! It was amazing!"

"Did you have to, like, sneak into a high-security room and trick the cameras and knock out a few guards?"

"Yes! Well, no. I mean, they were in a cardboard box in the basement. No guards and no cameras, but there was tape on the box. A lot of tape. It took me like ten minutes to get it off. And someone could have seen me, Koda! What would I have said if some guy was like, 'Hey, Yori, what are you doing down here?'"

"You could have said, 'I'm looking for tax records.'"

"Then he would have said, 'Why?'"

"And you could have said, 'Because I'm an accountant.'"

"Okay. Yes, I see where you're going with that. But the point is—I didn't have to!"

"No one saw you go into the basement?"

"Like four or five people saw me go into the basement, but they didn't see me take the evidence! I was in and out like a ghost. No—a shadow. A desert shadow!"

"And no one said a word to you?"

"Kazuo from accounting said, 'Hey, Yori, what were you doing in the basement?'"

"What did you say?"

"Nothing! I ran right past him! He's so stupid!"

"So that's it? That's the evidence?"

"Yep, and that's not all. I grabbed these, too."

Yori opened the envelope and pointed at a stack of folded files.

"What are those?" I asked, peering in.

"These are the case files on *all* of the Shibaten murders." He looked around. "They were on a shelf that was mislabeled—CROWS / TRAVELER / ROAD. Just like the *haiku*."

I stepped closer to Yori. "You stole police files on the suicides? Are you insane? The police are going to know they're missing."

Yori's face fell for a moment. "But Aiko, Ichiro, Taiki, the headmaster. They're all here, probably."

"These are open cases, Yori. Someone's going to notice!"

"Read through them, and then I can take them back."

"You can take them back right now," I said, pulling them out of the envelope. "I never told you to steal active police files—" I stopped. From the cover of a girl's diary, a three-legged crow stared up at me.

"What is this?" I said. I set the manila envelope on the ground, ignoring whatever Yori said in return.

藤原愛子
Fujiwara, Aiko

The drawing of the crow on the front stayed still as lead, but I could almost feel something stirring beneath the cover.

"I said I'll take them back first thing in the morning," Yori repeated. He reached out to take the diary, but I yanked it away.

"No, you're right, Yori. It's . . . it's all connected." I picked up the envelope and dropped Aiko's diary inside. "I'll bring these back in a few days. I promise."

"Two days."

"In two days."

"Good."

"Thank you, Yori."

"Hey," he said, sticking a stubby finger in my face. "Don't thank me."

"Okay," I said, opening the door to his bedroom.

"Thank someone else."

"Oh, right. Thank you, Desert Punk."

"Whatever the feat, whatever the run . . ."

"Desert Punk gets the job done," I finished, walking out into the hall.

"Yes! Wait, can we do that again?" he called after me. "I want to record it and post it on my website."

"No. Absolutely not. That is a terrible idea."

"Right. No, I get it. Next time, then."

I ran through the rusted gate, buckled my giant helmet, and rode down Yori's street, overflowing with confidential police files and murder evidence. I looked back. Yori was standing in front of that small metal gate in the dimming sunlight with his hands on his hips, grinning from ear to ear. You could almost see his cape billowing in the wind.

21

I passed my house and kept riding to the secret bamboo grove.

"What are you?" I demanded, ducking under the *kaki* tree.

Moya looked up at me. "A girl."

"What kind of girl?"

"I don't think I like your tone, Koda."

"Well, I don't like vans driving over my face!"

"First," Moya said, "it didn't drive over you. Your head would have popped like a grape if it had. Second, how did you not see a van trying to hit you through a convenience store window? A van. It didn't exactly sneak up on you."

"To be fair, I wasn't watching for runaway vans. I was inside a building!"

"A building with windows. That's what windows were invented for."

Moya reached out and patted the grass. "Sit down, Koda. You're hyperventilating."

"I was riding my bike very intensely. Are you trying to kill me, Moya?"

She looked up at me. And then laughed.

"I'm serious, Moya. If my girlfriend is trying to murder me, I think I have a right to know."

"Ah, you think I'm your girlfriend."

"That was totally not the point! And no, I don't think you're my girlfriend. I don't know why I said that. I was probably thinking of someone else."

"We need to talk," she said.

"Well, you don't have to break up with me." I dropped onto the grass obediently.

"No, I just want to talk. See, there *is* someone trying to kill you. But don't worry, it's not me."

"Okay, this is worse than a breakup."

"Did you see the crows, Koda? Out in the parking lot before the van veered off the road?"

I nodded. They forced Natsuki to cut her smoking break short.

"Think back to every interaction you've had with the Yamabuki Three. Did you see the crows then?"

The flock that flew after Aiko. The cries in the math room. The birds taking off with Taiki.

"Crows and *tengu* have a long history together. The very first *tengu* were *karasu-tengu*—small humanoids with beaks and claws and crow wings. Then came the mountain *tengu*—fallen humans that the Road had corrupted until their skin had turned red and their noses had grown ridiculously long. Kusaka Town is sick, Koda. But the crows are just a symptom, not the disease."

"Who is behind the crows?" I asked.

"Not so much a 'who' anymore," she said. "More of a 'what.'" Moya picked a blade of grass and held it up to the last rays of the setting sun. "The Seven Noble Families first entered Kusaka Valley two hundred years ago, but they weren't the only ones here. A powerful *tengu* called Kōtenbō led a clan of demons in the mountains above them. They had a war and all the *tengu* disappeared. Almost all of them, anyway."

"Why didn't you tell me any of this before?" I said.

"What would you have done," she asked, "if I'd walked up to you in a parking lot and asked you to mind-loot the location of a river troll so we could fight a mountain demon together?"

"I'd have called the police."

"Because . . ."

"I'd have thought you were clearly a danger to yourself and those around you."

"I thought it best to take baby steps. At least until I knew for sure that you were one of the good ones."

"Why would Kōtenbō stay in Kusaka?" I asked with resignation.

"Hate. Revenge. Spite. He is the source of the Tengu Road in this town. He is the magnet that's drawing it here. As long as he's hiding in this valley, the sickness will remain."

"If this *tengu* is behind the crows, why would he go after Aiko, or Ichiro, or Taiki? What did they ever do to him?"

"Aiko Fujiwara. Ichiro Kobayashi. Taiki Watanabe. C'mon, Koda, don't you know anything about your town's history?"

I shrugged.

"Inari, goddess of light, do you ever pay attention in class?"

"If I like the subject, I pay very close attention."

"But since there aren't many high school Pokémon classes . . ."

"I do not often pay attention."

"Fujiwara, Kobayashi, and Watanabe are three of the noble families."

"Wait a minute."

"Here we go."

"Stuff we learn in school . . ."

"Almost there."

". . . has real-world applications!"

"*Yatta!* You did it, dum-dum." Moya leaned back against the trunk of the *kaki* tree. "Kōtenbō is hiding out somewhere, so he uses the crows to break into his victims' minds. And the lingering Tengu Road is the side effect. Think of it like muddy footprints left behind when a thief leaves a house. Only these prints seep into your brain floor and infect everything they touch. The Road spreads through your mind, replacing happiness with fear and despair and loneliness. Kōtenbō needs the crows to control people, but he knows that in order to destroy his victims, all he has to do is nudge them onto the Road."

"How do we stop that nudge?" I asked.

"I don't know if that's possible," Moya said. "But we can cut off the source. The *kappa* Shibaten is the first step. If we find Shibaten, I think we can find Kōtenbō."

"But no one's seen Shibaten for two hundred years."

"Yori's obsession with Shibaten would have piqued the *kappa*'s interest. I thought it would have been enough to draw the troll out of his hiding spot."

I looked out at my bicycle in the dimming light and the murder evidence tossed so nonchalantly in its basket.

"You're sure you weren't trying to kill me with a van?" I said.

She smiled. "About as opposite as you can get, Koda. With the help of the crows, that driver temporarily took leave of his senses and tried to park his vehicle on your skull. I bumped him off course a bit."

"With a fireball?"

She shrugged. "We all bump in our own way."

Moya leaned forward and took my hand. She laid her head on my shoulder, and together we watched the sunlight disappear from the bamboo grove around us. It felt nice to be with Moya like this. It could have just been the sweet glow that comes from realizing your girlfriend isn't trying to murder you, but it felt good. Maybe Moya was my *zenko* fox spirit after all.

The sky grew dark and a little cold. It reminded me that there was one nagging question that I simply had to ask. "Who is Seimei?"

Moya's hand stiffened. "You promised you would never steal from me," she whispered.

"I didn't mean to," I answered. "I don't know how this whole *suri* thing works."

Moya pulled away from me. She hugged her knees and

looked down at the ground. "How much have you seen?" she asked.

"I saw the park," I started. "I know what Kōtenbō did to Seimei's parents. I know you saved him."

Moya dropped her head lower. "I watched them die," she said in a small voice. "His father was being hunted by Kōtenbō, but his mother's death was a mistake."

"The Nakagawas were one of the noble families," I ventured. "But Seimei's mother wasn't from that line?"

Moya shook her head. "With her last breath she called on the goddess Inari to save the life of her son. Inari granted her request. She let me come down to protect him."

"I saw all of that, Moya. But what happened next?" I asked.

She looked over at me with swollen eyes. "I failed, Koda. That's what happened next."

Tears rolled down Moya's cheeks. But instead of, you know, normal human tears, they dissolved into smoke, leaving black streaks down her face. I wanted to press her about the explosion at Ōmura Shrine, but if you're wondering when it's a good time to give a girl space—it's probably when she starts crying smoke.

"I think you should go," she said.

I slowly pushed up to my feet. Moya dropped her head onto her knees.

"I'll see myself out," I said, ducking under the branches of the *kaki* tree.

22

NOTEBOOK/FUJIWARA, <u>AIKO</u>
DATE: 2006年9月19日

my hair hurts. my eyes hurt. everywhere i look i see
them. watching me. perched outside my window perched
on the fence perching perching watching watching. i watch
him watching them watching me. it makes my eyes hurt. it
makes my skin push and pull. fly away black bird. fly away.
i didnt hurt you. i didnt know you then you came and
perched and watched and perched and hurted. someone
is angry. thats why he sent you. the angry one. you have
no teeth. you have no arms. but he does. Hhhhhhhhhhh
heeeeeeeeeeeee dddddddddddddoooooooooeeeeeeeesssss
sssssssssss. i am hurting. you are hurting. he is hurting us.
black feathers no shine. strong feet cracked broken. deep
eyes cloudy blind. so beautiful. so lovely. where is the crow
with three legs? why wont he save us? fly away, black birds.
fly to places he can never find. i will follow. fly away from
here.

                                                                    fly.
                                                         fly.
                                                   fly.
                                             fly.
                                       fly.
                                 fly.
                           fly.
                     fly.

ffffffffffffffffffffffffffffffffffffffffffffffffffffffffffffffffffffffffffffffffffffffffff
ffffffffffffffffffffffffffffffffffffffffffffffffffffffffffffffffffffffffffffffffffffffffff
fffffffffffffffffffffffffffffffffffffffffffffffffffffffffffffffffffffffffffffffffffffllllllll
lllllllllllllllllllllllllllllllllllllllllllllllllllllllllllllllllllllllllllllllllllllllllllllllllllllll
llllllllllllllllllllllllllllllllllllllllllllllllllllllllllllllllllllllllllllllllllllllllllllllllllllllll
lllllllllllllyyyyyyyyyyyyyyyyyyyyyyyyyyyyyyyyyyyyyyyyyyyyyy
yyyyyyyyyyyyyyyyyyyyyyyyyyyyyyyyyyyyyyyyyyyyyyyyyyyyyyy
yyyyyyyyyyyyyyyyyyyyyyyyyyyyyyyyyyyyyyyyyyyyyyyyyyyyyyy
yyyyyyyyyyyyyyyyyyyyyyyyyyyyyyyyyyyyyyyyyyyyyyyyyyyyyy
yyyyyyyyyyyyyyyyyyyyyyyyyyyyyyyyyyyyyyyyyyyyyyyyyyyyyyy
yyyyyyyy crows flyyyyyyyyyyyyyyyyyyyyyyyyyyyyyyyyyyyyyyyyy
yyyyyyyyyyyyyyyyyyyyyyyyyyyyyyyyyyyyyyyyyyyyyyyyyyyyyyy
yyyyyyyyyyyyyyyyyyyyyyyyyyyyyyyyyyyyyyyyyyyyy a traveler
on the road is lost

Yori hadn't lifted a lot of files from the town hall basement.
There was a report about the headmaster's suicide at Ōmura
Shrine. There was an interview between a social worker and

Seimei just after his parents died in the 1930s. And there was Aiko's journal. The official files on the Yamabuki Three had already been moved to some central police station in Kōchi City.

More than anything else, the journal reached out to me. It was like the book was sewn together from the chills that run up your spine on a cold night. Aiko had obviously spent a lot of time decorating the front cover. The three-legged crow was carefully drawn and painted like some kind of tribute. She must have done that while she was still thinking clearly. As the journal went on, her writing became more and more muddled. At the end, she was just furiously scribbling crows with dark lines shooting out of their eyes.

I slid the journal under my *futon* and turned over the last item in the manila envelope. A single wristwatch fell out. We all have secrets. Moya didn't want to tell me about the shrine fire? Well, I didn't want to tell her about the memory I might have found. Not yet, anyway. Not until I knew for sure. I poked the watch with my finger. It wasn't particularly cold. Other than the face being cracked, there was nothing strange about it. Maybe the trauma trapped inside had faded.

"Okay, so how do I do this?" I said to myself. "How do I start the cold dream?"

I picked the watch up and turned it over. Nothing happened.

"Maybe if I had a phrase or something? Maybe 'Genkaku Power Go!'"

Did I just shout that in my bedroom at eleven at night?

Yep, my brain said.

"That did not work at all."

It would have worked, said my brain, *if you were in an anime and you were a crime-fighting princess.*

"Hey, I like Sailor Moon," I blurted out.

Can we just do this now? My own brain was getting impatient with me.

I lifted the watch into the air and closed my eyes as tight as I could.

Is it working? my brain asked.

"I don't know. Should I, like, rub it or something?"

It's not a genie!

"Well, usually things feel cold right before I faint."

Does it feel cold to you?

"Not really." I dropped my hand onto my *futon.* "Stealing memories—especially about death—does seem like a terrible thing to do."

But there's no other way to find the kappa.

"Yeah."

Just take that part of you that feels weird about spying on someone's misery and strangle it.

"Strangle it? That's a harsh choice of words."

If you want, I can do it for you. I am your brain.

"Good point, I guess. If you think you can, go ahead— Oh, see, now I feel the cold—"

I flopped forward on my *futon* as the world turned to ice.

From the reeds along Kusaka River, an ancient hand reached out. It could have belonged to a very unfortunate child. Small. Thick. Wrapped in turtle skin. Not the kind of hand you want to see poking around as you drunkenly stroll the edge of a river late at night.

Taiki's father tossed his empty *sake* bottle into the black water. The boy had run at least this far, he reasoned. Normally Taiki hid out in an abandoned truck near the river, but he wasn't there now. It didn't make sense for the boy to throw a rock through the window and then run to his usual hiding spot. If he'd been thinking straight, Taiki's father would have just waited until the boy returned home and then whipped the stupid out of him with a broom handle.

But Taiki's father wasn't thinking straight at all. How many times had he yelled at the boy for throwing pinecones at the side of the house? Soon he'd be throwing rocks, and then this would happen. Taiki ran fast, though, and by the time his father reached Kusaka River, the boy had already vanished.

Unfortunately for Taiki's father, his son was nowhere near the river. But the real vandal was.

Shibaten had been hiding on the banks of Kusaka River for two centuries, feeding off the life-energy of bugs and rodents in the mud. In all that time, he'd never ventured far enough to watch a human. But then the small one came along. He sang a flattering nursery rhyme and threw cucumbers into the water. The small one was lonely. He was a throwaway, like the metal carriage he hid in at night. The small one looked over his shoulder and was constantly afraid. Like Shibaten with the crows.

But if the small one could find Shibaten, maybe the *tengu* could, too. Shibaten thought he might have to kill the small one and eat him. That would be the safest thing to do. The small one was sad and alone, so perhaps it would be better if he stopped existing anyway. Shibaten would decide what to do with Taiki in the future, but the fate of the man he lured out to the river tonight had already been decided.

Shibaten watched Taiki's father as he kicked through the reeds, yelling into the darkness, screaming for the small one. The large human would draw out the crows in the area if he wasn't silenced soon. Shibaten could break the man's neck now. It would be so easy. Like a dry stick. The *kappa* pushed through the river grass.

"Who is it?" Taiki's father screamed. "Who's there?"

The reeds drifted in the breeze. The shadows along the bank shifted without a sound. Taiki's father stared so hard into the darkness that he lost his balance and stumbled to the edge of the water. Taiki's father rocked back and forth, drunken to a stupor on warm rice wine.

"Taiki!" he screamed again.

The boy he called for didn't emerge. Something else that was small and hated did. Taiki's father looked up and screamed for the last time.

Grabbing his wrist and shattering the watch, Shibaten yanked Taiki's father off his feet and folded him backward until his spine popped. Shibaten was sorry that he might need to kill the young boy, so he gave him a gift—an agonizing death for the one person who tormented him most in the world. Taiki's father groaned softly, moving his chin from side to side. The man's spirit seemed old and sour like his breath, so Shibaten nudged his body into the water and let Kusaka River carry the folded man away.

Shibaten turned and leaped back across the freezing water. I stood on the other side, watching him through the icy air and the terror that still hung there. Shibaten crept up to an old barberry bush. He reached his hand out, and the thorny branches sank into a hole in the ground. The half-turtle, half-troll dropped to his stomach and slid into the cold darkness of the earth. The barberry rose up again, covering the entrance to Shibaten's den.

I opened my eyes and stared at my *futon* with its warm electrical blanket. The broken wristwatch was tightly wedged in my fist. I forced my fingers free and brushed the murder evidence onto the *tatami* mats. I felt overwhelmingly tired. Maybe misery visions take their toll on you. Or maybe the week was finally catching up to me. Either way, I flopped forward and couldn't keep my eyes from falling closed again.

23

My parents thought it would be a good idea for me to attend my high school field trip the next morning. I wasn't so sure. Who knows how people would react? Fainting from the top of a bamboo mast is understandable—it's almost expected of a kid who wears a helmet during Sports Day, but getting hit by a car through a convenience-store window kind of gets people talking.

"*Ah, Koda-kun, ohayō gozaimasu.*"

"And good morning to you," I said to a second-year girl I'd never met.

"*Ogenki desu ka?*" her cute friend asked.

"I'm feeling fine, I guess."

"*Yokatta ne.*"

"Yep. Good."

I took off my street shoes and set them in the cubby with my name on it. I stepped out of the school *genkan* and into my slippers.

"*Oi, Koda.*"

I looked up to see Kenji walking straight at me. I braced for impact.

"*Soba ni sawaranai ka?*"

"What?" I said, opening my eyes. "Like, right now?"

"No, stu— I mean, no, Koda. On the bus. Do you want to sit next to me on the bus?"

I caught our school counselor watching us from the other end of the hall.

"Oh, right. The field trip. I guess so," I said with a strained grin.

He grunted and lumbered up the stairs.

"*Ohayō,*" a group of third-year guys said as they passed me on their way to homeroom.

"*Genki de ne,*" said a gaggle of girls.

Huh. Who'd have thought that the secret to popularity is getting hit by a van? In high school, people will either like you based on your merits or pity you. Hey, you get to the same place either way, right?

"How are you feeling, Koda?" Ino-*sensei* asked. "Everyone was very worried about you."

"I'll bet."

"It's true," the school counselor said. "Many of the students asked about you."

"And you had nothing to do with that?"

"I had very little to do with that," she said, walking me up the stairs. "There are many people here who care about you. That is a wonderful thing."

"Well, thanks," I said awkwardly.

After we got to my homeroom, Ino-*sensei* crossed her arms in front of her and bowed. "Well, you better get inside. Have fun today, Koda."

I bowed back and then walked inside. The students were sitting around the classroom talking and laughing.

"Don't forget your *bentō* lunches," Shimizu-*sensei* said from the front of the class. "There will be vending machines, but you will only be allowed to buy drinks. Cookies and Hi-Chew taffy do not constitute a meal. I'm looking at you, Kenji-*kun*. Stay with a partner, and when you're ready walk quietly down to the buses."

As the students filed out, Kenji walked up and got very close to my face. "You have to be my partner."

"Actually, I already have a partner. Her name is Moya and we're in love. No, we're not in love. She's nice. I like her. It's complicated. The point is . . . I have a partner already, so . . ."

Kenji looked at me for a second and then turned and walked away.

"Koda," Shimizu-*sensei* said, "could you stay behind for a few minutes?"

"Okay."

After everyone left the room, Shimizu-*sensei* told me to sit on a chair next to his desk.

"Am I in trouble? I just got here."

"No, it's nothing like that, Koda. It's about your accident. I'd like to ask you . . . what it was like."

"To get hit by a van?"

"No, not that." He glanced behind him at an empty corner. "I wanted to know what it was like to leave Kusaka Town."

"To leave?"

"You had to go to the hospital, didn't you? In Kōchi City? What did it feel like to finally leave this place?"

"I've been outside Kusaka before. You know that, right?"

"Wonderful. Just wonderful. Tell me all about it."

"I mean, you've been outside of Kusaka, too."

"No, I haven't."

"I'm pretty sure you have."

"No," he said. "In my entire life, I've never left this town."

Except I knew that wasn't true. Shimizu-*sensei*'s mother was from the northern island of Hokkaido. Her family tended sheep on a farm, and Shimizu-*sensei* used to tell stories about spending summers there running through the pastures and the birch wood forests. A faded picture of that farm even hung in an old frame on the wall behind him.

"Tell me what it was like, Koda," he said. "Please."

Shimizu-*sensei* had different-colored eyes. One was brown. The other was light green. How had I never noticed that before?

"Well," I started, "leaving Kusaka wasn't so hard. First, I had to find a van that was speeding out of control. Then I had to stand in front of it. For the last part, and this was probably the most important step, I had to stay very still while it attempted to park on my face. The rest was easy. I woke up in a hospital in Kōchi City."

"Fascinating," Shimizu-*sensei* said with exaggerated hand movements. "Just like that, you woke up outside Kusaka Town."

"Well, yeah, but from the way you're looking at me, I feel like I have to mention this: There are easier ways to leave Kusaka. A car. Or a train maybe. You don't even have to get hit by any of those. Just get inside and ride them out."

"I love it. I really do. Ride them out. Brilliant."

I thought he was mocking me. But he wasn't.

"Have you ever tried to leave Kusaka?" I asked him.

"I see where you're going with this. The short answer is yes. I would like to leave Kusaka."

"That wasn't my question."

"The long answer is no. I've never been outside."

How is that the long answer?

I looked up at the picture behind him. Those rolling grassy valleys weren't from anywhere on *this* island. "Why have you never left this town, Shimizu-*sensei*?"

My teacher leaned back in his chair. "No, no, no. That is something I can't discuss with you, Koda."

"Well . . . okay."

"I cannot talk about it."

"All right."

"Even discussing it could put you in great danger."

"Then let's definitely not discuss it."

"The doctors say it's a condition."

"I thought we weren't discussing it."

"Have you heard of agoraphobia, Koda?"

"Um . . . no."

"Agoraphobia is a fear of open spaces or crowded public places, but it's also a fear of leaving safe places. That's what the doctors say I have. Agoraphobia. Kusaka is my safe place. Whenever I try to leave it, I feel like my body is melting and coming apart. My brain shuts down. My fingers lock up. My feet stiffen into cement blocks."

"How would knowing that endanger my life?" I asked.

"Because they're wrong," he said, leaning forward. "Kusaka is not my safe place. I hate this place. I hate this town. And I hate this school."

As a teacher, that's probably a secret you should keep to yourself, I thought.

"I've tried to leave, I really have. I've gone to the train station. I've sat in a car. I'd crawl out on my hands and knees, but every time I try, they stop me. They are doing this to me. They won't let me leave."

"Who are 'they'?" Which was the worst question I could have possibly asked.

And his answer was probably the worst he could give: "Do you know what happens when you die?"

"Well, I've never died before, so . . . no?"

"I don't know either. Maybe you're reborn. Maybe you float up into the sky to meet the sun goddess Amaterasu. Maybe you attain enlightenment and contemplate the cosmos from your castle in the middle of space."

"I'm pretty sure you made that last one up."

"But what you don't do, Koda, what you absolutely should

not do under any circumstances, is stay around in the exact same house and torment all of your living relatives that come after. That doesn't makes sense, does it? Who would want to do something like that? They just showed up one day. Who would want to spend the rest of eternity haunting your own family? It's crazy! Simply crazy!"

"That *is* the word that came to mind," I said.

"What if I needed to go to the hospital? Did they ever stop to think about that? What if someone put me into an ambulance and just drove me out of town? Would my body tear apart? Would my brain melt into a puddle? Would my ancestors actually let me die?"

"I don't know how to answer that. But if you're thinking of getting hit by a car so you can leave town, my recommendation would be not to do that."

"Shut up! Just shut up!"

"Okay."

"No. Not you, Koda. Them." He glanced back over his shoulder. "I'm with a student. You know that. You can see him." His greenish eye drifted off a bit.

I looked behind him. No one was in that corner. "If you have company, I can go," I said, backing away ever so slowly.

"He doesn't know how we can leave. I already asked him. He said ride a train. Of course I know that's a stupid idea. I know we would have tried it before. What do you want me to do? Punish him? Give him more homework? He isn't the key to anything. You were wrong! I hate you! I hate all of you!"

"I would like to go on my field trip now," I said.

Shimizu-*sensei*'s one creepy eye drifted back over to me again. "Yes. The field trip. Ikeda-*sensei* will be waiting. Go now. Please shut the door on your way out."

I bowed and quickly left the room.

"The door, Koda. Please. You'll let the crows in."

I ran back and slid the door closed.

24

I was looking out of the bus window when Kenji tried to squeeze in next to me.

"Koda, I need the window seat."

"I'm doing something right now."

"What are you doing?"

"Thinking about something. It's very important. I shouldn't be disturbed."

"I need to sit there," he said.

"No, you don't."

"I'm serious. I get motion sickness."

"Ugh. Aren't you supposed to sit with your partner?" I said, scooting over to the aisle.

"You *are* my partner."

"No, I'm not."

I slid my backpack onto my lap and sucked in. Kenji tried to push himself over to the window, but the seat wasn't cooperating.

"Just—like, turn your head."

Yep. I'd rather not have your butt shoved into my face.

"A little more. One last squeeze. Almost there . . . *yatta*." The springs of the seat shuddered in defeat.

"I get sick if I'm not by the window," Kenji said again, adjusting and reaching into his backpack.

Yeah, well, I get sick when sweaty butts are shoved in my face. We all just have to deal with stuff in life, I thought.

"*Uso*," squealed a girl from my class. A whole mess of them were sitting at the front of the bus giggling and talking about Hello Kitty, probably. Or makeup. Or Hello Kitty makeup. I bet they have that.

In the middle sat the jocks. Well, as close to jocks as Kusaka High School gets—so in the middle of the bus sat the guys who could run a race without getting a bloody nose.

In the back of the bus sat the delinquents. These were the kids who talked back to the teachers, hardly ever did their homework, and probably did macho things like fighting with knives, wrestling boars, and riding bikes without safety helmets.

Then there was me. And Kenji. He was sitting hunched over a portable video game. He was easily the biggest and loudest kid in class, but no one wanted to actually hang out with him. If he hadn't spent so much time being a jerk to me, I might have felt sorry for the guy.

The bus suddenly rocked from one side to the next. Students grabbed their seats. The talking and the giggling instantly died. Ikeda-*sensei* pushed his huge frame onto the small bus with the small hired driver.

"That's more like it," he said. "You think Hayashida-*san*

likes driving a bus with you chatterboxes working your jaws nonstop? Would you like it if someone came to your house and crammed cicadas in your ears? You wouldn't like that, would you? All day. High-pitched *semi*. Squealing. In your ears. That's what you sound like every single day."

Ikeda-*sensei* adjusted his thick glasses and turned to the bus driver. "*Gomen, ne*. Children are rude little monsters. No getting around that."

The driver smiled and nodded in his blue blazer, cap, and white driving gloves.

Ikeda-*sensei* turned back to us. "Tell Hayashida-*san* thank you for being willing to drive your noisy, yapping mouths around all afternoon."

"*Arigatō gozaimasu,*" we said.

"Louder!" Ikeda-*sensei* barked, slapping the back of the nearest seat.

"*Arigatō gozaimasu!*" we yelled in unison.

The bus driver lifted his gloved hand and gave us a little wave.

"We can go now," Ikeda-*sensei* said.

The bus engine started up, and the first-year class from Kusaka High School pulled away from the parking lot. I closed my eyes, trying to shut out the noise of Kenji's video game. I pictured myself in the cockpit of a Boeing 777 Star Jet, feeling the vibrations through my seat as the plane roared down the runway. The nose finally tipped up and the acceleration of the plane pushed heavy on my chest.

From the window, I watched my town fade into the distance

below. At this height, Kusaka sat awkwardly between two mountain ranges. I'd never really thought about it before, but imagining the town from above, I wondered why anyone would have settled here. Sure, Kusaka River would be nice for crops and fishing, but there wasn't much else around. Kusaka was just the middle of nowhere.

From way up here I could see Kōchi City in the far distance. There were other towns dotting the horizon, too: Sakawa. Nōzu. But Kusaka was isolated. Lonely. Hidden deep in a valley overflowing with bamboo forests, leafy green ferns, and dried persimmon stumps.

Maybe that was the point. Maybe this was all on purpose. Maybe the families who came here two hundred years ago chose this valley precisely because this was the one place no one would come looking for them.

"Koda."

I jumped a bit. Moya was leaning over the aisle with a cellophane bag in her hand.

"Moya, what are you doing here? I didn't see you get on the bus."

"Well, I did." She untied the gold ribbon at the top of the bag.

"Shimizu-*sensei* is on the Road," I whispered frantically.

"Right. And that ogre sitting in the front is, too."

"What ogre?" I said.

"Koda!" Ikeda-*sensei* barked. "Keep it down."

"That ogre," Moya whispered.

"Ikeda-*sensei*?"

"Here, take one," she said, offering me the bag of cookies.

"What is it?" I asked.

"Just some *kappa* eggs I found."

"*Kappa* lay eggs?"

"I like to steal them out of their nests at night," Moya said. "Then I boil the babies inside and dip them in chocolate."

"That sounds kind of gross. But I like chocolate, so—"

"What is wrong with you, Koda? I was joking."

"I've never had *kappa* before," I said.

"*Kappa* babies!"

"Dipped in chocolate," I reminded her.

"You're sick. They're just cookies."

"Are they good?"

"Well, they're not made from babies, if that's what you're asking. You monster."

I picked out a cookie and put it in my mouth. "Mmm. Does not taste like a dog biscuit."

"That's a rude thing to say!"

"I said 'not.' Your cookies do *not* taste like dog biscuits."

"*Baka*. See if I ever bring you dog biscuits again."

"These *are* dog biscuits! I knew it!"

She shrugged. "They're cookies to me."

I spit the not-cookie into my hand and dropped it on the floor. Kenji looked over at me. I tried to smile, but I still had biscuits in my teeth. He shook his head and went back to his game.

I leaned forward and glanced across the aisle. Moya was pretty. Not your average J-pop-singer-whose-poster-hangs-in-the-train-station pretty, though. She had a foreign look to her. Her eyes weren't very dark; they were almost gray in the sunlight. Her nose was thin, not short. Her cheekbones sharp instead of round. She didn't have *maru-gao* like a lot of the girls in my class. A round face isn't a bad thing, of course. It's soft and cute. Kind of the ideal Japanese girl. But Moya didn't have *maru-gao*; she had *kitsune-gao*, a sharp, angular face—a fox face. It was pretty, but it made her look cunning. Devilish in a way. In hindsight, it should have been obvious what kind of *yōkai* she was.

"I know what you're thinking," she said, crunching on another biscuit.

"I bet you don't."

"You were wondering—why Kusaka?"

"Nope."

"Why did the seven noble families come here and not to some other mountain village in Japan?"

"Not what I was thinking."

"Look at this place, Koda. It's secluded. Completely cut off. Its only tether is that freeway that runs through the town. It's obvious, isn't it? This valley is where people—and others—come to hide."

"What are they all hiding from?"

"Koda!"

I flipped around to the front of the bus. "Yes, Ikeda-*sensei*?"

"I understand you were hit by a van, I do. Congratulations

for that. But unless that vehicle knocked the ears clean off your head, I know you can tell when you're talking too loud. I can tell. Hayashida-*san* can tell . . ."

The bus driver blankly waved.

"Everyone can tell. Now you're going to keep your chatty mouth shut, or I will come back there and shut it with my hand. *Wakatta?*"

I nodded. "*Wakarimashita.*"

Ikeda-*sensei* turned back to the front of the bus. Kenji giggled but didn't take his eyes off the little flashing screen in his lap. I leaned back in my seat and looked over at Moya. She slid down and crossed her arms over her chest, glaring at the back of Ikeda-*sensei*'s head. It was going to be a quiet bus ride after all.

Thankfully we arrived at the Kōchi Cultural Center without Ikeda-*sensei* having to physically shut anyone's mouth. Moya stood up and quickly left the bus. Her face didn't have that follow-me-around look, so I decided not to chase after her.

I walked between the seats and stepped off into the parking lot. The teachers were wrangling the students, lining us up according to height.

"*Yoku kiite kure,*" Ikeda-*sensei* started. "While you are here at the Cultural Center you will be representatives of Kusaka High School. There will be art projects from schools all over Kōchi Prefecture. You must be respectful. You must not separate from the group. You must not, under any circumstance, touch anything. Not the watercolors. Not the pottery. Not the mobiles. Nothing. Do you understand?"

"*Hai*," we said.

"I don't think you understand," Ikeda-*sensei* said, pushing his glasses farther onto his face. "If you break any one of these rules, you will be bringing a great dishonor upon your own head, as well as upon your school, your teachers, and your family name. You don't want that, do you? That would make me very unhappy. I don't like to be dishonored. I don't like to be shamed. If you separate from the group or touch anything at all that doesn't personally belong to you, I will knock your head through a wall of my choosing! Do you understand now?"

"*Hai*," we said.

"*Wakatta?*" he yelled.

"*Hai! Wakarimashita!*" we yelled back.

"Let's go."

Now, you might be thinking that a field trip to a cultural center sounds like about as much fun as a trip to a library or a prefectural government office, and you wouldn't be that far off. *Look at all the fun things to do,* you might say. *Look at that bench. You could, like, sit on it and stuff.*

Good point, good point. Who wouldn't love that?

Exactly. And look over here! Paintings! By elementary school students! Isn't this awesome?

Well, I got bored of elementary school paintings in about eight seconds. Ikeda-*sensei* tried to act interested as he walked us by wall after endless wall of watercolor paintings, but it was a losing battle. Farms. Zoos. Families. Pets. More farms.

More pets. Smiling faces. I'm so bored. Look. Another room of watercolors. Farms. Zoos. Families. Pets. Gods, get me out of here, please. What did I ever do to deserve this?

"Stay with the group," Ikeda-*sensei* barked at a delinquent kid. He thundered past me to snatch the wandering punk by his collar.

Now's your chance, my brain said.

"Chance for what?"

Your chance to get out of here. There has to be cooler stuff than this. Kids suck at painting.

"To be fair, you suck at everything when you're six years old."

Let's go!

"Shut up, brain."

Seriously, who's going to notice if you sneak off?

"Um, that giant ex-*sumō* who likes knocking kids through walls."

He'll never see you. He's too fat and slow.

"Ooh, if he heard you say that, he'd slap you right out of my head."

Now! He isn't looking!

"You go. I'll stay here."

Just say you were looking for the bathroom, my brain said. *Do you really want to stay here? Look up ahead. There are nine more rooms of these watercolors.*

"That can't be right. Oh, wait, yes it is."

Now look over there. Tell me what you see.

"Shodō?"

That's right. Calligraphy.

"We'll get there eventually," I said.

Will we? After the watercolors, then comes the pottery, then the mobiles, then the who-knows-what. By the time we get to the shodō *exhibit, it'll be too late. We'll have to go home. We'll miss it.*

"I guess I could say I was looking for the bathroom."

*Besides, you'd hear Ikeda-*sensei *coming from across the building. He's so fat. And ugly. And stupid. Go! Right now! Hurry!*

I stepped out of the line. Yes, I'd lost an argument. With myself. It wasn't the smartest thing to do if I was trying not to get punched through walls, but it was *shodō.* Old-style Japanese calligraphy *does* look pretty cool. Stupid brain with its observations and reasoning.

A couple of the kids around me started whispering. I ignored them and scurried off around the corner. They might tell Ikeda-*sensei*, but I doubted it. What prison inmate rats out an escape plan to the guard everyone hates? Besides, it'd be more fun to see Ikeda-*sensei* punch me through something, so they'd probably let me skip out for as long as I could and then laugh while I was broken and bleeding. School friends are really the best kind of friends.

I quickly and quietly jogged over to the *shodō* display. The walls were lined from top to bottom with bright white papers and deep black ink.

I took my time walking through the calligraphy exhibit. Most of the *kanji* were painted by students from high schools in the prefecture. Some showed real craftsmanship and skill. Others were rushing to get their assignment done.

I stopped. From across the room I saw it. The one *kanji* I love more than any other. Okay, "love" is a strong word to use for a symbol painted on a piece of paper. But, no, I think I might actually be in love with this *kanji*. I want to marry it.

飛

Tobu.

To fly.

It looked like an airplane to me. Two wings with rudders. A seat. A steering column. It was all there. Ready to take off from the paper at any moment. So complex. So beautiful. I reached out to feel it. Someday, I'd climb into one of those things. I'd point the nose right at the sky and I'd just fly up and away from everything. I'd keep going and going until I broke through to the other side. I'd fly past the gods and goddesses and on to the place where lost souls go. I'd look down and watch for people I know. People like Aiko and Ichiro and little Taiki. I'd look for—

"*Omae, nani shiten da yo?*"

I flipped around.

"I said, what the hell do you think you are doing?" Ikeda-*sensei* yelled.

I hate my brain right now.

"Nothing," I said. "I was just . . . looking for the bathroom."

"Did you find one? On that piece of paper?"

"No . . . I just saw it and thought—"

"You thought you'd stroll over and deface a work of art!"

"I wouldn't really call this one art. I mean, it was a good effort . . ."

A few of the visitors in the exhibit looked at me and then quietly slipped around the corner.

"Koda, get out," Ikeda-*sensei* whispered. "Now."

"Okay."

I put my head down and hurried toward the exhibit door. *If he hits me, brain, he's going to get you first,* I thought.

But Ikeda-*sensei* didn't knock my head into a wall as I walked past. Instead I heard a thousand talons scuffling in the ceiling above me. I stopped and looked up.

"*Sensei?*" I said.

"Caw," the ceiling answered.

My gym teacher's giant hand locked on to my shoulder. Without a word, he lifted me off my feet and threw me into the brass handlebar of a side exit. I couldn't keep myself from yelping like a puppy before crumpling to the ground.

"*Sensei?*" my teacher repeated. "*Sensei?*" he mocked again. "Oh help me, *sensei*. The scary birds are coming to get me, *sensei*." He dragged me through the door and tossed me against a wall. "Disgusting man-child."

Ikeda-*sensei* turned back to the exit and slammed the door behind us.

25

"Let me in!" Ikeda-*sensei* roared, shoving my head against the outside wall of the cultural center.

"*Yamete kudasai!* Please!" I screamed.

Ikeda-*sensei*'s fingers dug into my face, squeezing my eyeballs shut.

"You're breaking my head," I cried, beating at his arms and face.

"Nothing will break this head! Where is it? Where is the part that keeps me out? I'm going to find it. I'm going to dig around in your brains until I can pull it out with these fingers."

I kicked and jumped but couldn't break his iron grip. "Please, Ikeda-*sensei*, please," I cried. "I'll give you whatever you want."

"I want this mind!" Ikeda-*sensei* screamed.

My thoughts raced around like mice trying to escape a fire. *This is it,* I thought. *I'm going to die. Just like Aiko and Ichiro and Taiki. I'll be the fourth. A possessed* sumō *is going to smash my brain and I'll become one of the Yamabuki mountain-breath-kids.*

I clawed at Ikeda-*sensei*'s arm and shook my head until I was able to open one eye.

"Let me in!" Ikeda-*sensei* bellowed.

But my gym teacher's voice suddenly sounded distant. His bloodshot eyes transformed the world around us. Heaven didn't look the way I'd always imagined. I don't know what I'd thought, really. More light. Less freezing air. A few floating Shintō temples in the background. A sun goddess or two. Heaven looked more like walking into the kitchen of a cold apartment building.

The front door slid open, but the wintry temperature remained the same. I jumped back as Ikeda-*sensei* stumbled into the room. He was dressed in a pair of boxer shorts and a robe.

"Father, please," he said.

I looked around but didn't see anyone else in the room.

"I swear to you, Father, I haven't been bad. I make tribute to your shrine every night. Just like you asked. Fish and seaweed. Every night. I promise."

As soon as he said it, the stench of Ikeda-*sensei*'s apartment cut through the freeze and overpowered me. I stumbled back to cover my face. In the corner there was a small mountain of rotting fish. Dripping with ooze. Sliding off the bone and plopping onto the stained floor below. Above it all stood a single crow, cawing at the ex-*sumō*.

"Please, Father, no," Ikeda-*sensei* begged.

Eat, came a dark voice from somewhere in the frigid shadows.

"No, I don't want to eat tonight. Please, I ate last night."

Go to the shrine. Kneel down before my face and eat.

"Father."

Do this and you shall sleep another night.

"Please."

Do it not, my son, and I will come for you. I will come tonight and I will tear out your soul.

Ikeda-*sensei* fell forward and dropped to his knees in the sludge and the slime.

"No," I whispered.

But Ikeda-*sensei* couldn't hear me. He reached out his huge hands and plunged them deep into the mountain of rot. As he lifted a fistful of slime to his face, the voice called out again.

You are a disgrace, Nobu. You are a filthy man. And so you will eat filth before my face for all of your days.

Ikeda-*sensei* chewed through the thorny bones until his mouth bled.

Abandoning your mother to become sumō. *You are no hero! You are a rotting sack of meat! You have dishonored me. And so you will kneel before my shrine and eat nothing except rotting flesh.*

Black slime oozed out of Ikeda-*sensei*'s mouth and dripped down his chin.

You should have stayed by our side, Nobu. You never should have left her to die alone. Money and fame and whores were all you sought. So now you will kneel and feast on the only thing you gave her in return.

"Father," Ikeda-*sensei* blubbered.

Open your mouth and eat death, my son.

"Caw," cried the crow above him.

Ikeda-*sensei* collapsed next to the mound of runny meat and moaned like a child.

"Koda!"

The smell of rotten fish disappeared.

"Koda!"

I opened my eyes.

"Koda, get up! We have to go!"

"Moya? Where am I?"

"Stand up!"

My head was groggy, but I could hear Ikeda-*sensei* moaning on the ground near the wall. His arm above the wrist was burned, like it had been yanked over a bonfire.

"You have to get out of here," Moya said, lifting me to my feet.

"Where are we?"

"Can you walk? You need to run. Get away from here."

"But his arm. What did you do to Ikeda-*sensei*?"

"Go!"

"Where?"

"Down the hall. Into the restroom."

"The restroom?"

Moya opened the door and pushed me inside. "Go! They're coming."

Outside the door, Ikeda-*sensei* continued to moan. "Father," I heard him say. "Oh, Father, what have you done?" Above me, the ceiling filled with tapping and scraping. I ran back to the door and peered through the open crack.

Moya the girl was gone. Hundreds of crows poured from

the outside vents and swarmed a snarling, writhing white fox. It twisted on the ground, snapping its teeth and tearing at the flock. All the while a silent mist of fumes snaked across the ground. Then, in a single flash, the crows burst into roaring flames. In the midst of it stood the white fox, untouched, enveloped in fire, licking its stained fur.

"*Kitsune,*" I whispered.

The fox looked up and growled at me. I slammed the door and ran down the hall.

"What. Was. That?" I yelled when Moya slipped into the men's restroom.

"I'm sorry, kid. I had to let Kōtenbō make his move. What did you see?"

"What did I see? I saw Ikeda-*sensei* trying to tear my head off my body!"

"Skin and bones can be fixed, Koda. Did he have a memory that would help us?"

"Did you kill him, Moya? Did you kill my gym teacher?"

"No! I don't kill innocent people. Even huge jerk-faced innocent people. His arm's just a little singed."

"That was a third-degree burn!"

"Second-degree at most. His mind was so scrambled he won't remember how he got it, anyway. Did you find a memory?"

"And why are we meeting in the men's room? You're not a man. Or a human. Someone could just walk in here!"

Moya marched to the door and slapped her palm on the frame, melting the metal and welding it shut.

"There," she said.

"The lock, Moya! Use the lock on the door!"

"What did you see in there?" she asked again.

"Gods," I breathed out. I walked over to the mirror and held on to the sink. "Ikeda-*sensei* believes his father's ghost is punishing him," I started. "And Shimizu-*sensei* thinks he's being followed by dead ancestors. But it's not true, is it? They're both on the Tengu Road."

"You need to focus, Koda."

"Are they going to die?" I asked through the mirror.

"Probably."

"Can we stop him? Can we stop Kōtenbō?"

"We might have a chance if you find me the memory I keep asking for."

"I don't get it. Why use crows? He's a *tengu*. Why doesn't he just stroll down from the mountain and murder us all?"

Moya walked up behind me and leaned against the wall. "He could have done that at one time, sure, but not anymore. He's hiding."

"Right. But why doesn't he stop hiding? He's a *tengu*!"

"He's a blind *tengu*. And from what I can tell he's mostly blown up."

"What?" I said, looking into the mirror.

"I blew him up the last time we met," she said nonchalantly. "It didn't work."

"Didn't work? You mean the explosion at Ōmura Shrine? How does an explosion not stop a *tengu?*"

"Well, you jerk, this one is not so easy to kill."

I turned around. "Why me, Moya? I'm not a threat to anyone! Maybe to bicycle helmets and my own face, but not to a mountain demon."

"You're a *suri,*" Moya said. "And from what I can tell you have an unusual talent for it. Most *suri* only ever lift feelings from their victims. Maybe they see colors or hear weird tones. Sometimes, with enough practice, they can learn to capture an image or two. But you, Koda, you lift entire memories from people's minds. You break inside their heads and clip whole conversations. You steal interactions, spy on what you should not be able to spy on. You're a potential danger to anyone you come in contact with—especially people who don't want to be found."

"Then why doesn't Kōtenbō just possess me and walk me into Route 33? I wouldn't be that hard to kill!"

Moya smiled. "You're like a *kaki* tree, Koda. You might look weak on the outside, but believe me, there is great strength inside you. You are a very dangerous little mind-thief."

"Not against Kōtenbō."

"Kōtenbō is just a *more* dangerous mind-thief."

I looked up at Moya. "Kōtenbō is a *suri?*"

She nodded. "Was, anyway, at one time. It's the only thing that explains his ability to possess humans."

"Wait, can I possess people?"

"Afraid not, kid. That is some dark magic. Kōtenbō embraced the Tengu Road a long time ago. It's hard to say for sure, but he was likely a priest. Or maybe a pilgrim who wandered mountain paths to separate himself from the traumatic memories of man. At some point, though, Kōtenbō changed. He began to thirst for strength and power."

"Or he could have just been lonely. You know, isolating himself to protect the people around him and then marching all over the countryside with no one to talk to. I can see how that could break a person's mind."

"Okay, do not sympathize with the bad guy, please," Moya said. "If you're having trouble with that, try counting the number of urns he's created since Kōtenbō entered the Tengu Road. His humanity withered away until all that had once been good was replaced by hate and despair. Whatever man Kōtenbō was doesn't exist anymore, and hasn't for hundreds of years. He is a *suri* on the Road. And when *suri* enter the Road, they become something else. Their minds turn viciously on the human race, which had once been their own. They start not only to steal memories but to manufacture ones in their place. And worst of all, when Kōtenbō cracks open a human mind, the Tengu Road comes rushing in. The Road invades places that were never meant to be invaded. It infects them. Breaks them down from the inside. The Road fractures their hold on reality, and in the end it almost always destroys them."

"But my mind is different."

"*Suri* cannot invade the minds of other *suri*. That is why

Kōtenbō doesn't walk you into Route 33. He thought he was powerful enough to break into your mind. He's now realizing how wrong he was."

I slid down along the wall to the floor.

"The *tengu* is changing tactics," Moya said. "He's desperate. He's trying to use his puppets to reach you."

"Why doesn't he just use *you* to kill me, then? I can steal memories from people who are not so human, so why doesn't Kōtenbō just use his crows to force you into barbecuing me?"

"I feel like you said 'not so human' in a way that means 'less than human.'"

I looked up at her. "That's obviously not what I meant, since you can start bonfires out of thin air. That's 'more than human' to me."

Moya paused for a moment. "The Tengu Road doesn't affect us like it affects you. I think it's because we accept the inevitability of an end. Humans—they cling to life with both hands. They dig their nails in like they're terrified of what comes next. A large part of the madness of the Road involves loosening that iron grip.

"And without that grip the Road has much less influence. Kōtenbō can still lift memories, like any *suri*, but his ability to influence . . . people like me is severely muted. That's not to say *tengu* aren't a danger, though."

"Well, they are huge," I said.

"Which doesn't matter at all. It's the swords they carry. *Tengu* taught swordplay to humans in the first place. They are very skilled at it."

"Even when they're mostly blown up?"

Moya nodded.

"If we can stop this sword-swinging puppeteer, though . . . You know, like"—I dropped my voice to a whisper—"if we can kill . . ."

"You mean tear Kōtenbō's head off and shove it down his neck hole? Yes, go on."

"Gods, Moya."

"A *tengu* just possessed your elephant of a gym teacher and tried to physically remove your head with his bare hands, and now you're getting squeamish?"

"Look, if the *tengu* isn't around anymore, will that cut the strings? Will the Road disappear and will everyone go back to normal?"

Moya shrugged. "I don't know. It's a nice thought, though."

"Then I have a confession to make."

Moya cocked her head to the side.

I took a breath and said, "I wanted to wait until we were under the *kaki* tree, but I know where Shibaten is hiding."

"You found the memory?"

I looked around, which was stupid since we were the only two people who could have been in the restroom. "Yori was right. Shibaten *did* murder Taiki's father. I convinced Yori to steal the evidence from the town hall, and last night I lifted the trauma from the watch Taiki's father was wearing."

"Gods," she said. "I'm impressed. You *are* a dangerous mind-thief."

"Can we cut the puppeteer's strings, Moya?"

"Well, we're a whole lot closer to finding out."

"All right, then, let's do this," I said, walking briskly past her. "Let's go find ourselves a river troll and stop the Tengu Road."

"And *try* to stop the Road," she corrected me.

I yanked on the door, which didn't budge because Moya had welded the stupid thing shut. I did lose my balance and took a face-plant into the door frame, though.

"Gods, Moya!"

"Maybe we should take the window?" she said.

"You think?"

"Wow. You are cranky when you're acting heroic and stuff," she said with a smile. "I don't hate it."

I gave her a heroic look as I walked over to the window and shoved it open.

26

POST—INCIDENT POLICE REPORT

Case No. 121719-03   **Date:** 2006年 10月 14日

Prepared by: 森

Actions Taken:

Arrived at Ōmura Shrine at 3:14 a. m. A male subject at the scene (identified afterward as fifty-two-year-old Headmaster Manabu Sato) was unresponsive. All of the bushes and trees, including the *botan* tree, were filled with crows.

Called out to the subject. He had his back to me and did not answer. Shined my flashlight and asked for identification. He didn't answer. Informed him he was trespassing. No response from the subject. Walked closer and saw he was holding a knife. Radioed in my location and pulled out my baton.

Instructed the subject to drop the knife. He refused to comply or turn around. Repeated this instruction numerous times. About the time backup arrived, the subject turned. He had no eyes. His face was mutilated. The wounds appeared to have been self-inflicted.

The subject's head seemed to follow the flashlight. He said something about a traveler who was lost on a road. The subject then turned and ran. On the wall, the vandalism was clearly visible. It was scraped into the wood with the knife. It read: CROWS FLY.

Pursued the subject to the southern wall overlooking the drop-off. He climbed the wall. Called out to the subject to get down and lie on the ground. A flock of crows from the *botan* tree flew off. The subject jumped. Or was startled.

By the time I reached him, the subject was barely breathing. Bones were visibly broken, and there were lacerations on the face and neck. Little could have been done to save him.

REPORT UPDATE: THE SUBJECT (MANABU SATO) PASSED AWAY AT KŌCHI PREFECTURAL HOSPITAL ON THE MORNING OF OCTOBER 15, 2006.

TRAUMA COUNSELING/UNKNOWN
昭和6 (1931年) 5月28日

SUBJECT: <u>SEIMEI NAKAGAWA, AGE 14</u>

He sits in the concrete room, alone,
a thin blanket covering his shoulders. He won't eat or drink.
He stares at the wall. He says he is waiting for "her"
to return and take him away from here. He must be speaking
of his mother. But she is dead. The boy is unresponsive.

Last night a man, who has eluded capture, murdered
the boy's parents while he watched from a fallen tree.
The police arrived and the killer ran. The police officers found the boy
talking to himself, hiding in the branches. They asked
his name, but the boy was unresponsive.

They brought him here, to a place of punishment
and shame. He had nowhere else to go, they said. He has no family.
All that existed in life ended in that park two nights ago.
They offered him tea and rice, but the boy was unresponsive.

The mother saved his life, the reports say.
She threw herself between him and the sword.
I asked him if he was waiting for her. He wouldn't look up.
What have we created? A world of suffering. A world of war.
Men kill each other in the streets. Their sons and daughters
left in rooms cold with cement and thinly covered by wool.

This is what we made. A boy mumbling to himself in the
dim light. He is difficult to understand. He speaks low.
Crows fly, the boy whispers,
A traveler on the road is lost.
That's what we've become. The boy is unresponsive.

Ikeda-*sensei* wasn't at school on Monday. None of the students
had seen him since the field trip. Toriyama-*sensei* drove out to
ride home with us on the bus but wouldn't say anything. It
was probably better that way. No one suspected a thing.

After school I raced home to grab the murder evidence and
the files. I wanted to return everything to Yori and distance
myself from him. Things were getting too dangerous. Even
for the Desert Punk.

"Koda," my mother called to me from the front door.

"Just returning something to a friend," I said without looking back. I fastened my helmet and kicked up my bike stand.

"Haru stopped by the house a little while ago. He's home
from the hospital now. He said he was going to Lawson's."

"Um, all right. I'll swing by there on my way home."

"He's on crutches. You can probably catch him before
he makes it too far."

I really did want to see Haru, but I *had* to return the police
files to Yori.

"I'll hurry, *kā-san. Oyasumi*," I said, even though it was
four o'clock in the afternoon.

"Good night." She waved. "I'll leave some *shiitake* rice in the steamer."

"You don't have to do that," I called back.

"Wear your helmet. And stay far away from Route 33. Promise me, Koda!"

"I promise!" I said, and stomped down on my bike pedal.

When I finally got there I dropped my helmet in the basket and called up to Yori's window. "I brought the police files back."

Yori's head shot up over the sill. "Are you insane? Why would you shout that? They'll hear you!"

"Who'll hear me?"

"They!"

"Oh, right. Rain Spider. Gotcha. I'm winking here. You can't see it, but I'm winking."

"What? No. The police, Koda. The police will hear you!"

"You know, screaming at me to keep my voice down kind of defeats the purpose."

"Get inside!"

"Is the door unlocked?"

"No."

"So will you come down and unlock it?"

"No. My sister will see me. Crawl in through the window, Koda."

"Yeah, that's not going to happen."

"Then go home."

"I have to give you back the files."

"No, you don't! Go away, Koda. Leave me alone." Yori slammed his bedroom window shut.

Huh. That went differently than I'd expected. I looked at the overgrown corner of his house. *Guess I don't have much of a choice,* I thought. *The window it is.*

I stepped over the weeds and old soda pop cans and pushed on the glass of the kitchen window. It slid back with a spurt of dust. *His sister is going to hear me fall inside their house and then she really will call the police. Not the brightest idea you've had, Desert Punk.*

My first foot landed in a sink of old dishes. Gross. Gross. I pulled my body through the window, but my backpack caught on the sill.

"C'mon. Let go," I said.

Yori's sister grunted from somewhere down the hall. "Yori? Is that you in there?"

I slid past a table stacked with old newspapers and ran upstairs to Yori's room.

"Don't give them to me," Yori said when I walked in.

"But you can just put them back. Put the lid on the box. Retape it if you have to. No one will ever know."

"They already know, Koda."

"How could they? No one saw you. You're the Desert Punk! On the outside you're a town office employee with a bad suit—"

"I like my suit."

"I know you do, but it doesn't matter because no one else notices it. You fade into a crowd. Which is perfect for a secret identity. By day you're a boring accountant, yes, but by night you're this fearless desert survivor who breaks down the—"

"Stop it!"

"What?"

"Just stop it!"

"Yori!" his sister bellowed. "What's going on up there?"

"Nothing's going on up here, *ne-chan*. You should just mind your own stupid business!"

"What did you say?" she shouted.

"That you should mind your own business! Also your face is ugly! And I hate your TV! And you smell like rotten meat!"

Yori's sister didn't say anything back. I just stood there while Yori breathed loudly.

"I'm not an idiot, Koda. I know there's no Desert Punk, no secret hero. I'm just Yori Yamamoto and I work at the Kusaka Town Hall and that's all I do. All that I'll ever do. I knew you wanted the evidence, and I knew you were using me to get it."

"Yori—"

"But I didn't care. Do you know why? Because I have nothing, Koda. I'm alone. I live with my horrible sister, who watches game shows every day, and when I get home at night I drag myself upstairs and dress up for a tiny video camera. That's all I have: my sister and a small box of glass and electronics. I would have done almost anything if you'd promised to be my friend."

"We are friends, Yori."

"No. No, we're not. Because a real friend wouldn't do this to someone he cares about just for some game he made up.

They're really watching me. Do you understand that, Koda? I stole something from them. Maybe they missed the files, maybe they saw me walk out with the evidence—somehow they know what I did and they are angry and they are watching everything I do."

"Who is watching you, Yori?"

"I can feel them. Like eyes in the darkness staring down into my soul. Have you ever walked up a dark flight of stairs and you could swear someone was right behind you? That's what it's like for me every minute of every day. I can't get away from them. I can't get away from their beady eyes! They're inside me!"

"Listen to me, Yori," I said, stepping cautiously toward him. "I think I know what's happening. There's someone who can help you. Her name is Moya and she'll know what to do. We can ask her. She'll tell us what to do."

"It's too late. They'll follow me until they've seen enough and then it will be over in a flash. They'll fly down and steal my soul. My fat, smelly sister will cry, and she should. Her brother couldn't even grow up to be a boring accountant. I've failed at everything I've ever done, Koda. Everything! Even at being me."

"I can stop this, Yori. I promise. Let me help you."

"Get out, Koda. I can hear them outside the window. I can hear their awful wings. I can feel them staring and watching. They hate me. I'm a traveler on a road that I've never seen before and I am lost."

"Yori."

"They are coming," he whispered. "The crows are coming."

27

I was panicking when I left Yori's house and there was only one thing that made sense: ride to the library as fast as I could. Yori sounded like he was on the Tengu Road, but if the Yamamoto clan *wasn't* one of the founding families, Kōtenbō might not be targeting him after all. Yori might just be cracking after years of stress and make-believe. I had to make sure, but the problem was—I couldn't remember the names of all of the Seven Noble Families.

"I hate you, history!" I yelled into the wind, but history ignored me.

I dropped my bike in the dirt parking lot and ran inside the library to find a copy of *Kusaka Monogatari*—the tale of Kusaka Town. "Do you have this book?" I wheezed at the old librarian.

"*Kusaka Monogatari*," she said, looking over her wire-rimmed glasses and clearly disapproving of my heavy breathing. "That's a very old book, young man. Written in the year Bunsei 13 by Hotaru Kobayashi. Let's see, that would be 1830."

"I'm not really interested in a history lesson right now. Well, yes, I am. Just not from you. Can you tell me where the book is?"

"I don't care for your tone," she said, looking down at me again.

"Do you have to like my tone in order to do your job?"

"I suppose not."

"Then, please, stop wasting my time and help me find that book!"

The librarian snapped her notebook closed. "You are an exceptionally rude boy."

I tried to control my breathing. She pushed her glasses higher up her nose and led me to a shelf of older-looking books. She pulled down a worn copy of *Kusaka Monogatari*.

"I'd like to check this out, please," I said.

"Oh, would you? Well, I'm afraid that would be impossible. This is a very rare book. You can read it, but you must stay here. At that table. In the corner. You mustn't take it out of this room." She glared at me over her glasses. "And you mustn't touch the pages, either. If you want to turn one over, I'll do it for you."

"Fine, I don't care. Gods," I whispered, dropping into a seat at the corner table.

The librarian laid the book open to the title page.

"*Itadakimasu,*" I said, with more than a little bitterness in my voice.

"What?" she said.

"It's like you're a waitress and you're serving me a book."

"Do not eat the book."

"I was joking."

"Not even a corner. When you need the page turned say: *Tsugi onegaishimasu.* I will turn it for you."

"*Arigatō.* Let's see, the book was written in 1830, a few decades after the village was first founded."

"To whom are you speaking?"

"No one. Just reading out loud."

"Don't talk on the book."

"What does that even mean?"

"If you're going to talk, do it to the side, like this. Or cover your mouth."

"All right! To the side."

"Do not shout on the book."

"*Kusaka Monogatari,*" I whispered. "Written by Hotaru Kobayashi. An epic tale of the founding of Kusaka Town. C'mon, c'mon. *Tsugi onegaishimasu. Tsugi onegaishimasu. Tsugi onegaishimasu. Tsugi onegaishimasu.* And . . . *tsugi onegaishimasu.*

"Just say the page number you want!" the librarian shouted.

"I didn't know that was an option. Or that shouting is now allowed."

"Just say the page you want to see!" she whispered loudly.

"*Thirty-two.*"

The Tengu Wars.

There wasn't much there. The Seven Noble Families arrived in Kusaka in the year Bunka 2. There was a map. They weren't alone—clan of *tengu* in the mountains. There were a bunch of wars with the humans. And . . .

"*Tsugi onegaishimasu.*"

And then there was a truce. The humans got the valley, and the *tengu* agreed to stay in the mountains. Things went well for a while, let's see, until the Ikeda clan made a deal with the *kappa* Shibaten. Ikeda? Like Ikeda-*sensei*?

Shibaten agreed to play a trick on the *tengu* leader. He snuck into his camp and stole his eyes. What? Gross. Oh, the blind *tengu*. Right. In return, the humans agreed to give Kusaka River to Shibaten, but instead they shot him full of arrows and dumped his body into the river. Humans cannot be trusted. I felt like this was the moral of the story.

"*Tsugi onegaishimasu.*"

And that's it. "Well, who are the Seven Noble Families?" I said out loud.

"They are the founders of Kusaka Town," the librarian replied.

"I know that, but the names aren't written here."

The librarian lifted the book and thumbed to the first chapter. She ran her finger down the page, then flipped to the back.

"Fujiwara. Kobayashi. Watanabe. Then . . . Sato, Ikeda, Shimizu, and Nakagawa."

Aiko, Ichiro, Taiki: the Yamabuki Three. Headmaster Sato, Ikeda-*sensei*, Shimizu-*sensei*, and that kid Moya was protecting: Seimei. Yamamoto was definitely *not* one of the founders.

Yori's ancestors had nothing to do with the Tengu Massacre. Yori was safe after all!

"Can I see that map again?"

The librarian grumbled but set the book back down.

"Where is that?" I asked, pointing to the *kanji* that read 天狗大虐殺.

She adjusted her glasses and ran her finger over the map. "The Tengu Massacre. Here it is. Just south of Kusaka River. Where the high school is now."

"I have to go."

"No. Don't. Stay here and bother my books some more."

I slipped my arms through the straps of my backpack. "I know you don't mean that, but it's okay. Coming here was the right choice after all. I thought someone's life was in danger, but it turns out I was wrong. See, libraries *are* still good for something!" I made a little jump in the air like *anime* characters do at the end of their shows.

"Wait, whose life did you think was in danger?" the old woman asked.

I ignored her and ran out of the front doors.

"What were you doing in there?"

"Aahh!" I yelled, nearly somersaulting over my bicycle. "Gods, Moya! Were you following me?"

"Of course," Moya said. "What were you doing in there?"

"I was reading a book."

"Reading a book?"

"It *is* a library." I picked my bike up off the ground. "I was worried there for a bit, but it was all a misunderstanding. I get what's going on here."

"Do you?" she said, crossing her arms.

"Yep. It has to do with the Seven Noble Families."

"Right. I told you that."

"But while other people are running around looking for crows and starting fires, I'm doing something productive. I'm reading. And figuring things out. With my brain."

"And just what did you and your brain figure out?"

"That Yori isn't from one of the founding families. He was all paranoid about birds following him around, but he probably just read that in the police reports. Or maybe it's part of the Desert Punk. I don't know and it doesn't matter. Kōtenbō doesn't care about Yori. Nobody cares about Yori! He's going to be perfectly safe." I struck another triumphant *anime* pose.

Moya turned and sprinted down the street without a word.

"Hey, where are you going?"

She didn't look back or call to me. She just kept running down the street as fast as she could.

"Wait up!" I called, swinging my leg over my bicycle seat. "And . . . you're already gone."

I pedaled down the road after Moya. Each time I rounded a corner I would catch sight of her, but then she would disappear again. After a few more turns I lost her completely. I knew this road, though. I knew where she was running.

I may have made a mistake.

28

Yori's house was dark. I called up to him. I banged on both the front and back doors.

"He's not here," Moya said, running through the side garden.

"Can't you, like, smell him out?" I cried.

"Smell him out? What does that even mean?"

"With your nose! With your fox nose. Gods, Moya, don't you care?"

"Of course I care!"

"Then find him!"

But all my yelling didn't do any good. Yori was not at his house. He was nowhere near his house. The Tengu Road had carried him far away into the wastelands of Tōkyō. Once there, Rain Spider rushed forward to battle Desert Punk for the honor of all of Japan. Those wastes, however, were actually a set of train tracks north of Kusaka. And Rain Spider was a thirty-ton railcar.

KUSAKA TOWN NEWSLETTER
2006年10月31日

Yori Yamamoto, age 41, expired last night in an accident on the JR line to Kusaka. Witnesses reported seeing Yamamoto running back and forth on the tracks, yelling and swinging at several cars before the fatal accident occurred. At approximately 5:30 p.m., Yamamoto charged the *kakueki teisha* from Kōchi, attempting to, as the conductor stated, "punch the front of the train." Yamamoto expired at the scene. An investigation into the mysterious cause of the accident is ongoing. Intentional death has not been ruled out. His sister claimed no knowledge of Yamamoto's whereabouts prior to the accident, stating that she thought he was still in the house. Yori Yamamoto worked as a driver for the Kusaka Motoring Company for ten years until he took work at the Kusaka Town Hall. He is survived by his sister and mourned by the town of Kusaka.

The police cars were pulling away by the time Moya and I got there. The body and whatever parts could be found were hurried away so the trains could run again. I reached down and picked up Yori's welding goggles. The left lens was cracked. I slipped them quickly into my pocket because I really didn't want to see those last traumatic moments. A flock of crows hopped along the ground, bowing here and there to peck at the gore on the tracks.

"You should leave," Moya said. "Go to the *kaki* tree. Wait for me there."

"Leave me alone," I shouted, turning and pushing through the weeds and bushes. Moya didn't reach out to stop me.

"You have to see how desperate he's becoming," she called behind me. "Kōtenbō knows he can't break into your mind, so now he's just trying to break it."

"He didn't do anything wrong!" I yelled, wiping furiously at my face. "Yori was a nobody."

"Innocence doesn't mean anything to Kōtenbō. We're on the right path here, Koda. Kōtenbō knows it. He's moving his final pieces into play."

I spun on Moya. "Is this a game to you?" I asked.

"What?"

"Is that what people are to you . . . you creatures? Pieces in some sick game you play to pass the time?"

"Koda—"

"Is that why Aiko died? And Ichiro and Taiki and Yori? To amuse your disgusting boredom?"

"No."

"It's not like you're in any real danger. You won't die! We're the ones getting poisoned and broken and cut open! Not you! Not Kōtenbō! Why can't you all just go back to where you came from and leave us alone?"

Moya looked down at the ground. I turned back to those horrible tracks, my breath coming on in sharp, painful bursts.

After a few moments Moya said, "Why do you think I won't die?"

"Because you're not human!" I yelled back. "None of you are human."

"Death doesn't only belong to humans, Koda. Death is change and transformation and loss. Everything dies. Humans, plants, animals, stars. Even . . . us creatures."

My vision rocked from side to side. My knees caved inward.

"If we can find where Kōtenbō is hiding," she said quietly, "I'll make sure he never does this again."

The crows hopped from one side of the tracks to the next, flapping up here and there to fight over a wet spot. Their beaks were cracked, their feathers missing in big patches. Their eyes were dead and watching. Always dead and watching. I stumbled away from the tracks, pushing the crows out of my mind.

"Burn them," I said.

"What?"

"Go to the tracks and burn them. Burn Kōtenbō's eyes."

"All right, Koda."

"Do it now!"

Moya disappeared behind me. A few moments later, the tracks along the ground flashed orange from the fireball that devoured Kōtenbō's desperation. The screaming of birds filled the air. Hundreds of shrill voices flapping and melting into the slow roar of a distant bonfire. I stood in a field near Kusaka Station and watched the flutters of fire that spun up into the dark sky and then plummeted back to earth. The air was sweet and sickening. The smoke drifted up like funeral incense.

"Everything dies," I whispered to no one.

29

NOTEBOOK/FUJIWARA, <u>AIKO</u>

DATE: 2006年9月4日

A black bird followed me home today. He stood on a stump and watched me walk into my house. When I went upstairs to my room, he was at my windowsill. I opened the window, but he wouldn't come inside. Father walked in and the black bird flew away. Father asked if Mother had called. I told him no. He said the three-legged crow would bring her home. He says that a lot. The black bird didn't return. Nothing stays around this place for very long.

Moya and I walked along the banks of Kusaka River. The sky was night above us, but we pushed through the cattails and the river grass. We dropped down embankments of slippery rock and jumped over the mud and water and fallen logs.

I held Yori's goggles in my pocket. They were cold from

the trauma, but I was so focused on revenge that even the pictures stayed away. "Can you kill him, Moya?"

She looked back at me. "I can stop him," she said.

"No. I don't want him stopped. Not like the Seven Noble Families or blowing up a shrine. He has to stay dead this time. Can you do that?"

"I'll try."

"Can you *do* that?" I shouted.

"Yes," she whispered.

"Thank you."

My face was flushed and red. I removed Yori's goggles from my pocket and slipped them over my head. They hung around my neck like a pendant. The goggles were cold and dark and full of pictures of trains and body parts, but hating Kōtenbō made it so much easier to control. Moya watched me silently.

"Do you feel it?" she asked.

"Feel what?" I shot back.

"The Tengu Road, Koda. It's beginning to push in on you."

"Nothing's pushing in on me. I just want to find the *tengu*. I want to find him and tear out his soul. I want to replace everything he's ever known with smoke and ash and fire. I can break him, Moya. I can find him and I can break his mind and stomp on it until nothing is left but a black hole."

Moya lunged forward and hugged me. I pushed back, but she held on. I struggled, but she wouldn't let go. Slowly the anger and the emptiness and hatred chipped apart and started to drain.

"No one I care about is safe," I said into her shoulder.

"No one in this town is safe. Not until Kōtenbō is gone. We can stop him, Koda. We can stop him together."

"Winning isn't really winning if you lose everyone along the way," I said.

Moya kissed me on the cheek. "You won't lose everyone. I promise." She let me go and looked out to the river. "C'mon, little thief, let's find Taiki's truck."

I nodded and wiped my face as we walked off through the cattails.

Forty meters behind Taiki's house, we caught sight of the abandoned truck from my cold dream. Shimmering moonlight from the water cast an eerie glow on the banks of Kusaka River.

"Which barberry bush was it?" Moya asked.

"That one," I said, pointing. "I think."

We walked over an old footbridge and stood to the side of the thorny bush.

"It doesn't look like the entrance to a *kappa* den, does it?" Moya said.

I shrugged because I didn't know what a *kappa* den entrance was supposed to look like.

Moya stepped up to the prickly branches. "Shibaten!" she called out. "Show yourself, you ugly little river troll. I've brought a *suri*. We're hunting the *tengu*."

The barberry bush stayed deathly still. Moya looked up at me.

"That's it?" I asked.

"You want to take a turn?"

"I've never summoned a *kappa* before," I said.

"Neither have I."

"Maybe there's a magic word."

"Do you know a magic *kappa* word?" Moya said. She motioned for me to step up to the bush. I walked forward a bit and shouted into the branches.

"O Shibaten! My name is Koda. Um . . . of the Okita clan. We are a mushroom-growing people." I looked over at Moya.

"Oh, keep going," she said with an eyebrow raised. "You're doing great."

I ignored her and turned back. "I have arrived here on the banks of the mighty Kusaka River to seek your wisdom, O Shibaten."

"Dear gods and goddesses," Moya whispered.

"My companion and I, we are hunting the ancient *tengu* known to you as Kōtenbō. I am a human. My companion is a fox. We would like to slice the *tengu* many times. I will cut his face and also his body. I will wear his feet as boots and his hands as gloves. And we will give you the heart, O Shibaten, for you to bite, or just have, or whatever." I stepped back. Nothing. "Hmm, thought that would work."

"Bite his heart?" Moya said. "Gods, how did you think that was going to work?"

Deep below the barberry bush came a loud sucking noise. The branches and the leaves shuddered as the earth caved in, pulling the barberry into a yawning black pit. From the mouth of the hole drifted a stench so powerful that Moya and I stumbled backward.

"What is that?" I said, coughing and covering my face.

"That is Shibaten."

"Did he die in there?"

"Why don't you ask him yourself?"

From the darkness, a child's arm reached up and clutched the soil.

"Whoa!" I yelled, backing up against the river.

The *kappa* dragged his rotting carcass from the underground lair. He was the size of a young boy, covered in damp scales from the nails of his feet to the mud-soaked ring of hair on the top of his head. He had a chipped and peeling beak where his mouth and nose should have been. His wiry legs, webbed at the toes, barely seemed able to support the weight of the filthy shell hanging from his back. On top of Shibaten's head sat a cavity of water marked up with dings and dents. His right eye was dead and gray, and even in the fading light it was easy to see the arrow scars dotting his chest and abdomen. Shibaten looked to the left and then to the right.

"That was a dramatic entrance," Moya said.

Shibaten stared at me.

"Oh, right, sorry." I started to clap. Because that's what you're supposed do for dramatic entrances, right?

Moya closed her eyes and shook her head so I stopped.

Shibaten looked back at her and blew air through the holes in his beak.

"He's a *suri*," Moya answered. "Not a genius."

"Did he just talk to you?" I said. "Was that his talking?"

Shibaten growled.

"Shibaten says you talk like a squirrel with rocks in its mouth," Moya said.

"What? I do not. Wait, do I sound like that to you?"

"No," Moya said. "Most of the time, no. But sometimes, yes."

"Hey."

"Can we just get on with this?" she asked.

Shibaten sat back on his sinewy haunches and watched us.

"We want the eyes," Moya said.

"I'm sorry, the what?" I said.

Shibaten growled and scratched at his chest.

"We know they're yours, but we need Kōtenbō's eyes. It's the only way to find him."

Shibaten looked down at the ground. The water in the indent on his head sloshed from side to side, but didn't spill. His chest vibrated softly.

Moya took a few steps forward. "The eyes are yours, we understand that, but our deal is simple. Hand them over, and we will kill Kōtenbō. Everyone profits, everyone gains. Unless you want to hide from his crows like a rat in the mud for another two centuries."

Shibaten looked up at Moya and grunted.

"No," she answered.

"What is it?" I asked.

"He wants us to buy the eyes from him."

"Okay, I'm going to look past the fact we're trying to purchase eyeballs from a *kappa* and I'm just going to ask what he wants."

Shibaten's throat began to click. It got louder until he stood on his feet, chest heaving, bellowing from the pit of his stomach that echoed out across the river. Then the night fell silent again.

"What. In the hell. Was that?" I said.

"Shibaten's price."

"It sounded expensive."

"It was." She looked down at Shibaten. "No. Give us the eyes."

"What does he want?" I asked.

"It doesn't matter—we're not going to pay it."

"Just tell me."

"No."

"Say it."

"Fine. He wants Nobu Ikeda."

"My gym teacher?"

"Yep."

"Why?"

"So he can kill him," Moya said in an exasperated tone. "That'd be my guess."

Shibaten snarled.

"I'm sorry," Moya said. "He would like to pulverize his bones and siphon off his life-energy. Which I think would also kill him . . . so, yes, kill him."

"Why kill Ikeda-*sensei*?" I asked.

"Really? I thought you had this figured out. It was the Ikeda clan that betrayed Shibaten. Yes, that was your fault, Shibaten. What did you think they were going to do? Let you skip along the river eating their children as you please? Of course they shot you full of arrows. *I'd* shoot you full of arrows, you little monster. Now, give us Kōtenbō's eyes or the *tengu* will kill us all."

Shibaten pounded the ground with his foot.

"You can't hide from him forever," she said. "The Seven Noble Families are almost wiped out. What do you think he'll do next? Just forget about the river troll that stole his eyes? Do you think he won't poison the river? Or dry it up entirely to find you? Kōtenbō will never stop. He cannot be reasoned or bargained with. Every human and magical creature in this valley will be consumed if we don't stop him." She paused, then said again, "Give us the eyes."

Shibaten scratched his knees and looked at the ground.

"Don't be stupid, *kappa*. Give us Kōtenbō's eyes!"

Shibaten turned his face away. Smoke drifted up from Moya's shoulders.

"You won't survive the darkness that is coming, troll. How can you be so blind?"

"Tell him we agree," I said.

Moya looked over at me. The smoke disappeared. "What did you say?"

"Tell him we agree to his price."

Shibaten's good eye fixed on me.

"Why?" Moya asked. "Why would you say that?"

I stared at the old *kappa*.

"You will have Ikeda," I said. "Is my squirrel babble clear enough for you? *I* will give him to you, but not for the eyes. Giving us the eyes will save your life. That's not something we're going to buy. I will bring you Nobu Ikeda, Shibaten, but in exchange I want a trick."

Shibaten glanced over at Moya.

"Don't look at her, look at me," I said. "That's what you do, isn't it? Tricks and pranks? I want to buy a prank."

Shibaten growled.

"What kind of prank?" Moya asked.

"A complicated one. There's an eighteen-year-old boy. His name is Haru. He lives down the street from my house and used to work at the Lawson's convenience store. I want you to trick him into believing he is me."

"Why?" Moya asked.

"Then you must trick my parents," I said. "Make them believe that Haru is their son and they want to take him away from here. Far away. To some place like Tōkyō. Until Kōtenbō is dead. They must drive away in their truck and not return until the *tengu* has been killed. If the *tengu* doesn't die, they must never return. Ever. Do you understand? Play this trick for me and I will bring you Ikeda."

"This is a very bad idea," Moya said.

Shibaten stood. His chest vibrated and he stomped the ground.

He is afraid of the crows, my brain said. *He is afraid they will tell the* tengu *where he is hiding. Tell him they will not.*

"The crows won't bother you," I said. "Not while you do this thing for me."

"How could you know that?" Moya asked.

Look into the kappa's *eye and assure him that he will be safe.*

I looked straight at Shibaten. "Because I know."

The *kappa* turned to Moya. She shrugged. He looked back at me and blew air out of his nostrils.

"Good," I said. "Then it's a deal."

NOTEBOOK/FUJIWARA, <u>AIKO</u>

DATE: 2006年9月13日

i sit with the black birds. only they listen. only they stay.
i ask them if the three-legged one will bring my mother
home. it makes them sad. they say no one can find her.
they want to stop hurting me, but the monster wont let
them. they want the three-legged crow to save them, but
they cant find him either. i tell them my family worshipped
Yatagarasu at a temple near our home so he will help us.
they don't know where the three-legged crow is or why
he is taking so long. i dont want the black birds to leave.
even with the crying i dont want to be alone again.

                      Not   not   not   not

        again

we leave together.

       Fly

black birds

fly

I walked into my house sometime after midnight. *"Tadaima,"* I said, kicking off my shoes in the *genkan*, even though I knew no one would call *"Okaeri"* back.

"Come into the kitchen, Koda," my mother would have said. "I made your favorite soup for dinner—*shiitake.*"

"No time, *kā-san,*" I'd reply if I were a normal kid and we were a normal family. "I have homework to do. And then I want to watch TV."

If my life were normal.

I walked upstairs to my parents' room and slid the door back just a bit. They were both asleep on their *futon.* My father was snoring.

I slid the door open wider. Maybe Haru would be a better son than me. Maybe he'd tell my mother how much he liked her soup. Maybe—

"Aah!" my father screamed. "Who is that? Who's there? Mother, Koda's come to murder us!"

"It's just me, *tō-san*, I didn't mean to—"

But then my father was snoring again. Was he sleep-talking? And also, does my father think I'm going to murder him in the middle of the night? How often does he wake up like that? My poor mother.

I really was the most dangerous thing that could have happened to them. Maybe in the space between awake and asleep, my father sensed that and resented me for it. I closed the door and walked down to my bedroom. I folded my *futon* and dragged it back along the hall to my parents' room. I unfolded the mattress, and that's where I slept my last night with them, listening to my mother's breathing and my father's terrified snoring through the door.

30

NOTEBOOK/FUJIWARA, <u>AIKO</u>
DATE: 2006年9月10日

There's something strange about the black birds. They follow me. Not just one now. Brothers and sisters and cousins. they all follow me. they know I'm looking for the three-legged one. they know my father and I have been searching for Yatagarasu since my mother left. the three-legged one will know what to do. the three-legged one will bring her home. maybe Yatagarasu can help these black birds, too. I hear their crying. inside they're crying, but outside they're watching.

i talk to *them* now. ask *them* questions. i tell them i am waiting. *they* tell me they are crying. someone is making *them* act this way. someone is tttttttttrapping *them* here. The black birds don't want to hurt *me*, but they have no choice.

he is making *them*.

I woke up to the sound of banging in the kitchen and stumbled down the stairs.

"Isn't it wonderful?" my mother cried when she saw me. She stood at the counter chopping her way through a stack of cucumbers.

"What are you doing?" I asked, rubbing the sleep out of my eyes.

"Your father put his meat hands in the front of the auto-carriage and now it's operational again!" she said with a smile that looked like someone was holding up the corners of her mouth.

"Are you talking about the truck?"

"Yes, that's it," she said, returning to her vigorous chopping. "The auto-truck! For transporting humans!"

My father slid back the front door and marched into the kitchen wearing the largest, most awkward smile I'd ever seen.

"Eat your breakfast, boy. We have a long day of rolling forward in a metal box before we reach the capital city of Kyōtō, where the other monkey people live!"

First of all, Kyōtō was the capital of Japan, like, two hundred years ago. And second, that smile is way too big for a human face. Though now I see where I get my terrible bullfrog grin.

My mother dropped a plate of poorly diced cucumbers onto the table in front of me. "Put these in your talking hole, Koda. They are delicious and very desirable."

"That's just a hill of cucumbers."

"They are delightful to the tongue," my mother said, trying to match my father's grin.

"So . . . no *shiitake?*" I asked.

"Of course not!" my mother said. "Mushrooms are filthy molds that grow on trees and should not be eaten by humans or any other creatures."

I looked around for Shibaten. My father dropped to his knees in front of the low table and shoveled cucumber pieces into his mouth.

"See?" my mother said. "This older person loves to eat the cucumbers, and so can you!"

"They are happy to eat," my father said, dribbling juice down his chin.

Cucumbers are a favorite snack of *kappa*. They may like cucumbers even more than sucking the life-energy out of river victims. Any doubts about Shibaten keeping his end of the bargain had vanished. The *kappa's* trick had started.

"Join us, Koda," my mother said, tearing into a particularly ripe cucumber.

So they'll be all right on this diet for just a few days, I hoped. *Cucumbers have, like, nutrients and stuff, right?*

"Actually, I think I'm going to go check on Haru . . . before we leave," I said.

I slipped into my coat and shoes and walked out the front door.

"Hurry," my parents called from the *genkan*. "And remember, you are our youngling and we feel a fondness for you!"

I dropped my helmet into the bicycle basket and looked

back. My father had his arm around my mother's waist. They were smiling and waving. Sure, they had cucumber juice running down the front of their clothes, but I'd never seen them so happy.

I ran back up to our entrance and kissed them each on the cheek. "I will hurry," I whispered to them.

For just a moment my mother's eyes changed. She touched my face. And then the vacant, happy look returned. I turned around and ran to my bike.

"Osu!" I called out to Haru as I turned the corner to Lawson's. Or what was left of it. "I thought I'd find you here."

"Don't have anywhere else to go," Haru said, kicking a chunk of loose cement with his cast.

I stopped my bike and walked over to the curb where Haru was sitting. His crutches were propped up against the sheets of plywood that covered the gaping holes in the side of the store. I really doubted Lawson's would reopen. No one had even bothered to sweep the glass and cement chunks out of the parking lot. Haru lit a cigarette.

"Huh," I said. "Didn't your time in the hospital teach you about the dangers of smoking?"

"Nope." Haru blew out a lungful of cancerous smoke. "If anything, I learned I should smoke more." He tapped the cigarette on the curb. "Nobody guesses they'll be offed by a van driving through a front window, you know?"

"Yeah, I guess so."

"Maybe an airplane will drop out of the sky on my way home. Maybe a motorcycle will fall down a flight of stairs. Maybe my uncle will finally cross the line and they'll find my body in the backyard thirty years from now." He coughed into his hand, then spit on the ground. "You never know, man, you never know. So smoke on."

Haru ground his cigarette into the parking lot. "Let's talk about something else."

"Fine," I said, looking around for Shibaten.

The cars in front of us roared down Route 33. "Thanks a lot for not coming by yesterday."

"I'm sorry," I said. "Something came up."

"Yeah," Haru said. "Something always comes up in this town. And not in a good way."

"Okay. So why haven't you left?"

Haru leaned back against the curb. "It's hard to explain to you, Koda, since you're just a kid and all, but . . . I loved my job."

"The job you used to have? At Lawson's?"

"Yep. Loved it. Couldn't get enough of it."

"You might want to seek alternative employment," I said, tossing a shard of glass into the lot. "Since this place doesn't look like it's bouncing back anytime soon."

Haru motioned over his shoulder. "Remember the girl who used to work here?"

"Sure. It was a week ago."

"Her name was Emi."

"Nope. It was Natsuki."

"Emi and I are in love."

"Also incorrect. I was there."

"And soon we're going to get married. We'll get a nice little apartment in that stained concrete building at the north of town. We'll have a boy and a girl. She'll stay home and take care of them while I hop on the train to my salaryman job. I'll have a love affair with my secretary, but Emi will be too polite to say anything—"

"It's Natsuki."

"I'll yell at the kids and drink *sake* at night, and when I finally drag myself into our *futon* we'll lie next to each other, hating each other in the dark, refusing to say anything because that would bring shame upon our families. You know, the perfect Japanese life."

"I don't think that's right."

"That's just my point, Koda. There's a difference between fantasy and real life. Sure, who wouldn't want to fly around the world in a Zero-*sen* fighter plane? Hell, I would. But that's not real life, is it? Real life is working at a convenience store in the middle of nowhere. Real life is walking to work each day because you can't afford a car. Real life is going home each night because you have nowhere else to go. That's real life, Koda."

I looked around again. This would be a good time for Shibaten's little happy trick.

Haru lit another cigarette. "Most people are stuck in the

life they fell into," he said, "and they never find the strength to crawl out of it."

"We should talk like this more often, Haru. Why don't we do that?"

"Then they lose all hope."

"That's why."

"Do you know what happens to those kinds of people, Koda? The kind who lose hope?"

"Surprise birthday party? Really keeping my fingers crossed for surprise birthday party."

"Nothing happens to them. Absolutely nothing ever happens. They live a meaningless life and eighty years later they die a meaningless death."

"There was no birthday party anywhere in that story."

I heard rustling in the grass across the lot.

"Ugh, my breath tastes weird," Haru said. "These are your smoke sticks, aren't they? Gross! I don't want your smoke sticks."

"What?"

Haru tossed the cigarette onto the asphalt. Like *I* would do if I suddenly realized I was smoking cigarettes.

"Gods, did I put that into my talking hole?" Haru squealed. "Disgusting! I wish I had a cucumber instead."

He picked up a chunk of cement. "I'm going to rub this rock on my tongue now to make the smoke taste disappear."

"Okay, don't do that," I said, snatching the rock away from him. "Very funny, Shibaten. Can we just get on with this?"

The rustling in the grass didn't answer.

"Well," Haru said, leaping to his one good foot, "I am a weak human boy and I have to go to Kyōtō now."

"I'm not that weak."

"I'm so weak that I must protect my skull with this enormous head covering and ride on top of these pink metal tubes until I reach my home with the older humans."

"They're red metal tubes!" Stupid *kappa*.

Haru limped over to my bike and undid my helmet, but it didn't fit him at all. *"Kso, kso, kso,"* Haru swore, pounding on the top of my helmet. Finally he just gave up and let the straps hang down over his face.

Haru swung his cast over the side of my bicycle frame and dropped it onto the pedal. He turned and gave me the most frightening smile I'd ever seen. Haru didn't wear his happiness so convincingly.

"Sayōnara, Haru," Haru said.

"See you around," I said.

Haru fought to keep his balance on my bike, tripping over the gears and slamming his cast onto the asphalt until he disappeared down the nearby back roads. Under any other circumstance this would have been a pretty funny prank, but I knew that by the time I walked home, the people I cared about most in Kusaka would be gone.

I pushed up from the curb and brushed the dust from Lawson's off my pants.

"Koda, may I speak with you?"

"Whoa!" I flipped around. Shimizu-*sensei* was standing just a meter away.

"Where did you come from?" I said.

My homeroom teacher looked nervous. His weird eye shot from one corner of the parking lot to the next.

"Koda, I need your help," he said.

Shimizu-*sensei* took a step forward. "You can see them, can't you?"

I took a step back.

"What are you talking about?" I asked.

"The ghosts, Koda. They're all around us. That old one. The little girl over there. The hag standing behind her. I think she's a great-aunt or something. I can't remember. You are a hag!" Shimizu-*sensei* shouted at a parked car and then turned back to me. "Don't listen to her. She's a hag."

"Okay." Was this part of Shibaten's trick?

"The *tengu* is holding us," Shimizu-*sensei* said. "Kōgubu is keeping us prisoner."

"You mean, Kōtenbō?"

This was not a trick.

"Yes, we know about Kōgubu." He turned around. "Kōtenbō? Right, Kōtenbō," he said, turning back. "You see that *rōnin* standing in the road? The so-called master swordsman?"

"I see a parked car." And a crow. Perched on the hood.

"Well, he's the one who lost Kōtenbō. It was his job to hunt down the *tengu* and end this all. But he failed. He's the reason none of us can ever leave this place."

Shimizu-*sensei* turned to the parked car.

"*Damare!*" he screamed. "You just shut your mouth! You don't get to talk! Not after what you did."

The crow flapped into the air and landed back on the hood.

"Maybe I should leave you and your friends to sort this one out," I said, backing away.

Shimizu-*sensei* spun around to face me, his one light eye moving slower than the rest of his face. "They aren't my friends, Koda. They're ancestors. Dead ancestors."

"Right."

"We need your help. I need your help. To get rid of them. Of course, to get rid of you," he shouted over his shoulder. "I don't care where you go. Just get away from me."

"I really don't know how I can help," I said.

Shimizu-*sensei* ran his fingers through his hair, hands shaking.

"We'll never be free, Koda. Do you understand? He is keeping us here in this cursed town. We can never leave until the *tengu* gives us permission. But you can find him. You can find Kōgubu."

"Kōtenbō."

"Yes. And when you do, we want to fight by your side."

"You want to fight Kōtenbō?"

"Yes. With you. And the fox girl."

"You know about Moya?"

"Yes. Moya. Of course. We see many things," Shimizu-*sensei* said. "When you find the *tengu*, let us know. We can help you defeat him."

A white fox emerged from the grass and snuck up behind my homeroom teacher.

I slowly shook my head at Moya. *Don't worry. I've got this.* "I want to help you, Shimizu-*sensei*," I said. "This isn't your fault. We'll work together and return this town to the way it used to be."

A smile crept across my teacher's face. "That is wonderful, Koda. Why don't we go to the school to discuss our schemes and make our plans. Together. Like you said."

"That's a little strange, since no one's there right now and it's dark and isolated. But sure, let's go. You lead the way."

"No. You go first. I insist."

The shadow of the fox grew to the size of a fifteen-year-old girl.

"Wait!"

"What?" Shimizu-*sensei* said.

"We have to shake on it. Hurry."

"Shake on it?"

I had about five seconds to trap him before Moya intervened. "Like we're making a business deal," I said, extending my hand. "You know—schemes and plans and all that stuff."

Shaking hands is not really something we do in Japan, but maybe Shimizu-*sensei* would be too confused to see the snare tightening around him.

Moya was standing right behind my homeroom teacher when he finally held out his hand. I grabbed hold of it and whispered, "I see you, Kōtenbō."

Before the world turned to ice, though, Moya picked up a chunk of concrete and slammed it into Shimizu-*sensei*'s head.

31

In my cold dream I was standing in front of a sign at the western edge of Kusaka.

ようこそ佐川へ
WELCOME TO SAKAWA TOWN

On top of the sign perched a brood of crows, black and shiny as ink. The air that filled the gaps between them was as cold and still as space.

Shimizu-*sensei* walked up from behind me. He wasn't alone.

Fathers. Mothers. Sisters. Grandparents. Aunts. Uncles. Brothers. Children. A crowd of Shimizus surrounded my homeroom teacher on every side. Some were dressed in suits and fine clothing. Some wore *kimono*; others wore *samurai* armor.

It will never work, the crowd said. *Best to turn back and go home. It's our curse.*

"But if I can leave, then so can you," Shimizu-*sensei* answered them. "Isn't that what you want?"

One man in the crowd started to laugh. The others looked at him and joined in. Soon the border between Kusaka and Sakawa rang with coarse laughter.

Go, my son, a man in a business suit said. *We have all tried. We have all failed.*

Shimizu-*sensei* walked away from the crowd. He lifted his foot and set it next to the sign. *Easy enough,* he thought. He took another step along the road. *No problem.*

The next step pushed the wind out of his lungs. Shimizu-*sensei* stopped and took a deep breath. A woman behind him smiled.

Another step and another step. It was difficult to keep breathing. Every time he set his foot down on the asphalt, his lungs locked up like he'd just run a race. He began to feel light-headed. His movements were slow and groggy. He felt like he was pushing his way through a torrent of water.

How much more can he take? a man from the crowd asked.

I bet he makes it to the other side, a woman said.

Muri da, grumbled the *rōnin.*

The world around Shimizu-*sensei* was moving fast. Cars on Route 33 shot by. Birds darted in and out of trees. Insects zipped around like machine-gun fire. *I just need to get across,* he thought. *I'll be safe there. I just need to touch the other side.*

He leaned against the swirling dizziness and fought to keep his body moving. He felt heavy, like invisible arms were yanking his shoulders, pulling him back. His head dropped forward and he looked at his shirt. *That must be it,* he thought. *My shirt. I'm wearing a shirt made of pure steel. How did I not no-*

tice that before I left the house? Who would make a steel shirt? Why would I ever buy something like that?

Shimizu-*sensei* struggled to undo the buttons.

Oh, he won't make it, a boy from the crowd said.

Shimizu-*sensei* shrugged his shoulders and the shirt slipped off, fluttering to the ground. *There,* he thought. *Now I'll be fine. The weight is gone. I feel lighter already.*

Shimizu-*sensei* pressed on for the same reason a rock climber reaches up for the next ledge. Backing down is not an option. Staying still is not a choice. *If I don't take the next step, I will fall and die.*

His shoes felt like two massive stones around his feet. He stepped down on the back of one and pulled. With a little jerking, he was able to step up and out of his rocky footwear. Now the next one. *There. But I still feel so heavy. Is it my skin? Oh gods, yes, that's it. My skin is holding me back.*

Maybe we should do something, a woman said.

Do what? a teenager answered. *We can't hold him down.*

This is sad, another woman said. *He won't listen.*

By the time Shimizu-*sensei* forced his way to the bordering line of Sakawa Town, he had no shirt and no shoes, and his breath came in shallow bursts.

A truck pulled over to the side of the road. A man in a straw hat opened his door and asked Shimizu-*sensei* if he was all right.

"Ehhhhhhhhtoooooo," was the only word that came out of Shimizu-*sensei*'s mouth.

"Do you need help?" the farmer asked.

Shimizu-*sensei* closed his mouth and tried to picture the words. They were in his brain, all scattered and floating around. He pretended his eyes had arms and they were grabbing at the words, trying to collect them and hold them down into proper sentences, but every time a word was caught, another wriggled away.

"You're the schoolteacher, right? Shimizu-*sensei*? Do you need a ride somewhere?"

Hai. One word. Two little syllables: *ha* and *i*. Easy to make. Where did the letters go? There they are. Up in the corner. Grab them. Okay. Hold on. Move them both down to my mouth. Yes. I need a ride. I need to leave this place. Please. *Hai.*

But as Shimizu-*sensei* opened his mouth to let those two tiny letters out, his jaw came unhinged. The left side popped like a warm carrot snapping. He stood there in front of the farmer, half naked, half jawed, the word *Hai* hanging out of his mouth like a string of drool.

Well, he almost made it, someone from the crowd said.

I wouldn't call that almost.

He made it farther than I ever did.

Me too.

The farmer stepped out of the cab and took Shimizu-*sensei* by the arm. He helped him into the truck and ran back to scoop up the clothes that were scattered like a trail of bread crumbs. The unseen crowd waited behind, some smiling, others shaking their ghostly heads.

"Why would you do this to me?" Shimizu-*sensei* mumbled. "Why won't you let me go?"

It isn't us, my son, the man in the business suit said. *It is the demon. He's the one keeping us here. There is no escape without appeasing the* tengu.

As the truck pulled away and drove into Kusaka Town, the flock of crows lifted off the sign and disappeared.

I jumped to my feet. Shimizu-*sensei* was lying faceup in the Lawson's parking lot.

"Moya?" I yelled. "Did you hit him with that chunk of cement? I was trying to steal his memory. I had it under control!"

Moya rolled Shimizu-*sensei* over with her foot. "Take a look," she said.

My homeroom teacher was still clutching a kitchen knife in his fist.

"What is going on here?"

"I'd say Shimizu-*sensei* made a deal with someone else," Moya said.

"He was going to stab me?"

"Or make you a home-cooked meal," Moya said. "But considering that his grip on this knife is more aggressive and less *teriyaki,* I'm gonna go with the first one."

I stepped back. "Gods, Moya, that was cutting it a bit close, don't you think?"

"I'd say my timing was right on. I had to hang back so I

could be sure, but I think Kōtenbō promised to release your teacher from Kusaka Town."

"If he murdered me? He'd be arrested! How did he think that was going to end for him?"

"Kōtenbō was inside his mind," Moya said. "Your teacher only cared about getting off the Road. How he got off it didn't matter at all."

"Gods, Moya, did you have to kill him?"

"What?" she said. "He's not dead. He'll wish he was dead without some *kampō* herbs for his headache, though." Moya rolled him back over with her foot.

"Shouldn't we call someone?" I said. "Or at least not be kicking people who have obvious head injuries?"

"He'll live," Moya said, picking up the knife and tossing it into the grass. "The bigger problem is your teacher waking up. The *tengu* had his claws so deep into Shimizu-*sensei*'s mind that he barely knew what he was doing. Kōtenbō will not be happy about this failure."

"So we're just going to leave him here?" I said.

"The best thing we can do for him is find and stop Kōtenbō." She turned and walked toward the exit of the parking lot. "We don't have a lot of time. Let's go get your gym teacher and feed him to a *kappa*."

I looked around for Shibaten and then ran to catch up with my totally-not-scary girlfriend.

SHIBATEN, SHIBATEN:
a child's rhyme

by Akemi Sato

Kōchi Press © 1919

Shibaten, Shibaten
Hiding in a water den
River boy with turtle skin
Shibaten, Shibaten

In the rivers, on the sand
Shibaten will grab your hand
Drag you down into the wet
Trap you in a *kappa* net
Shibaten, Shibaten
Hiding in a water den

Don't go near the river side
That is where the *kappa* hide
Snap your bones and suck you dry
Shibaten, Shibaten

If you wander much too near
In a flash you'll disappear
Cracking bones is all you'll hear
Shibaten, Shibaten

Kappa steal your energy
Drink it down like morning tea
Break your body, suck it dry
Make you scream and make you cry
Under water, there you'll die
Shibaten, Shibaten

Is there something you can do
If a *kappa* corners you?
There's a way that's tried and true
Shibaten, Shibaten

Spill the water from his head
He'll fall down just like he's dead
It's not hard if you know how
Face the *kappa*, smile, and bow
They are mean and full of fight
But a *kappa* is polite

When he bows, run away
He'll be weak, he'll have to stay
Don't return to laugh and play

Shibaten, Shibaten
Hiding in a water den
River boy with turtle skin
Shibaten, Shibaten

33

With a final jerk of my arm, the saw blade slipped free. The top half of a baseball bat dropped to the ground.

"I'm a little confused as to what this whole thing is," Moya said, making a circular motion with her hand.

"I have to get close enough to Shibaten to hit him, right?"

"Um, no. That's a terrible thing to do."

I tied one end of a string to the handle and the other to my wrist.

"So let me get this clear," she said. "We're not feeding your gym teacher to a *kappa*?"

"Gods, Moya, that was never the plan."

I gave my sawed-off bat a little test, dropping it down my coat sleeve and catching the handle.

Moya watched and then said, "Well, it sounds like you've thought this through. Hitting a *kappa* in the face probably won't make him mad, or make him fold you in half like a lady's purse."

"I'm not just going to hit him," I said. "Haven't you heard that nursery rhyme? 'Spill the water from his head. He'll fall down just like he's dead.' A *kappa* draws its energy from a cavity of water on the top of its head."

"So you created the new plan with the help of a children's nursery rhyme?"

"All I have to do is spill that water on Shibaten's head and he'll become as weak as a box of kittens."

"What is it with you and kittens?"

"They are totally harmless! Cute and harmless. Like Shibaten will be."

"I dislike your definition of cute."

I zipped up my jacket. "If I can get the jump on Shibaten, I'll drain his energy and make him swear an oath to never leave the river again."

Moya clapped dryly. "Brilliant," she said. "Absolutely nothing could go wrong with a plan like this. And I should know—I have experience setting traps for creatures that totally don't work at all."

I balanced the bat handle on the palm of my hand. "How do I look?"

"Like you have no idea what you're getting into."

"No different from how I look any other day, I guess. Let's go."

We walked out into the street and turned toward Kusaka River. The sun was just reaching its highest point, and as we walked I started sweating through my winter coat.

"So," I said, pulling down the front zipper to let in a little air. "Why his eyes?"

"What?"

"Why did Shibaten steal Kōtenbō's eyes?"

"That was the trick," Moya said. "The *tengu* never trusted the peace agreement with the founding families, and they knew it. Every night, Kōtenbō would turn into a giant vulture and patrol the skies, spying on the humans below. The humans knew that without his eyes, the *tengu* leader would be harmless. You know, like a kitten when you pop out its eyes and toss it into the air."

"Okay, leave the kitten analogies to me, please."

"Shibaten stole Kōtenbō's eyes, but the *tengu* escaped the massacre that followed. Over the next century or so, Kōtenbō hid somewhere here in Kusaka. He seethed alone in the darkness, searching out the Tengu Road and drawing from its dark power."

We stepped off the street and into the reeds that lined Kusaka River.

"By the time he murdered Seimei's parents," she said, "Kōtenbō had learned how to use the crows as his eyes."

"Is that what happened at the shrine?" I asked.

Moya stopped.

"I mean, Kōtenbō wasn't really blind," I said. "He probably had a hundred eyes wherever he went. Is that how he escaped your trap in Ōmura Shrine?"

She turned to me and poked her finger at my coat. "He didn't escape."

"I'm pretty sure he did."

"I exploded him through a wooden wall that was half a

meter thick, Koda. He didn't escape. He . . . survived." Moya turned and continued walking.

"You think he went back to the same hiding place," I said. "He let the whole Tengu Road thing simmer for another seventy years and when it was done, he'd learned how to use the crows to break into people's minds."

"That's my theory," Moya said.

We reached the banks of the river.

"Well, the attempted barbecue at the shrine must have messed him up," I said. "If Kōtenbō has to send crows out to hack people's brains now, he can't be doing too well with the walking and the moving and the decapitating people in front of their families."

"I'm definitely counting on that," Moya said. She looked around for the abandoned truck. "All right. We're here."

We jumped across the rocks in the river and walked up to the barberry bush.

"O Shibaten!" I called out.

"He knows we're here," Moya said.

A sudden chill ran up my spine. I pulled my winter coat tighter around my body. Maybe the temperature had dropped. Or maybe I was starting to doubt my nursery rhyme plan. "We have returned, O Shibaten! With your tribute!"

"Gods, Koda. Are you trying to alert every crow in Kusaka Town?"

Deep beneath the barberry came a loud sucking noise, followed by the stomach-churning stench of the *kappa* Shibaten.

"That is potent," Moya said, covering her face. "I'm just going to step off to the side here and vomit all over my hands."

"Wait, don't leave me."

"Do the best you can," she said, and then disappeared into the cattails.

When I turned back around, Shibaten was standing in front of me. "Aaah!" I cried out. "You scared me. And you look bigger. Have you gotten bigger? I didn't remember that you had all those . . . muscles. Gods, even your fingers are ripped."

Shibaten rotated his head in curiosity. The water in the dent on his head sloshed gently. I stepped back.

"Do you have the eyes?" I said.

Shibaten looked from side to side.

"Ikeda-*sensei* is coming. Soon."

Shibaten raised his arm, clutching a crude wooden box.

"Are they inside?" I asked. "I can just take them now, if . . ."

Shibaten lowered his arm and sniffed at the air.

"Or you could hold on to them for a while. I do have to actually touch them in order to start a cold dream, but hey, it's not like finding Kōtenbō's secret lair and stopping him before he kills everyone in this valley is a time-sensitive issue, right?"

Shibaten grunted.

"Well, I guess we do this the hard way," I said, slipping my hand up into my sleeve and gripping the sawed-off baseball bat. "Ikeda-*sensei* will be walking along this path over here. We can hide beneath the bridge, and then you can eat him— or whatever you plan on doing. Follow me."

I took a few steps and looked behind me. The *kappa* blew

air out of the holes in his beak but crept forward to follow me. As we got close to the bridge there was this awkward silence, so I thought I'd try to make small talk. With a *kappa*.

"So . . . you like cucumbers, huh?" I asked.

Shibaten clicked his beak and smacked his chest with the box of eyes. Which is probably *kappa* for *Shut your squirrel mouth—it's annoying my ear holes.*

Fine. Awkward silence it is. Your choice.

When we reached the bridge I turned around and said, "Let's hide down there. I'll take the eyes so you can hold Ikeda-*sensei* down and break his bones. Or suck the life-energy out of his anus. Which is totally not the grossest thing I've ever heard. You're probably used to it, though—why would it be gross to you?"

Shibaten stomped his foot and walked past me. He didn't offer Kōtenbō's eyes.

So when is the best time to jump a *kappa* and smash him in the head with a sawed-off baseball bat? When his back is turned, I guess. I'd never done it before, but that seemed as good a time as any. I let the bat slip from the palm of my hand and caught the handle. Without a word, I stepped up behind Shibaten and cracked him in the back of the skull.

The *kappa* pitched forward, dropping the box as he reached out to steady himself. The water in his head rippled against the edges of his hair, but almost nothing dribbled out. I took another step, swung my arm up, and caught the *kappa* on the side of his head with a dull wooden *thunk!*

Shibaten rolled facedown into the dirt. A little water spilled out, but before I could run forward, he shoved himself up to his feet. The tremor from his throat became a bone-jarring roar and his pale blue eye fixed like stone onto my face. The element of surprise was entirely gone.

"*Kso,*" I whispered.

From the reeds, a white fox tore between us, snatching the thin box from the ground. *It's about time,* I thought. *I can't actually fight a* kappa. I'd hit him twice, and from what I could tell, he might have a headache later on. Moya was right, this was an awful idea— *Oh gods, he's running right at me! Moya, where did you go?*

I swung my bat again. Shibaten caught it in the air and squeezed. The wood exploded into a shower of splinters.

"Betrayal!" Shibaten roared.

What? He knows actual words? Shibaten yanked the shattered bat from my arm, snapping the string and flipping it into the reeds behind us. He kicked me in the chest, and I slammed into the footbridge hard enough to jumble my insides.

Shibaten leaped at me. He pulled me up from the ground and threw me through the air. The ground raced up and punched me in the brain. Shibaten landed on my arm and shattered it. Light shot in and out of focus. The sounds of Kusaka River fell away. I could feel the end coming. I looked up in the sky and saw the *kappa's* foot hovering right above my face.

"Betrayal," Shibaten growled.

I was going to die, but the fact that in two hundred years *betrayal* was the one word Shibaten had learned from his interactions with the human race was actually pretty sad.

The *kappa* didn't stomp down, though. Moya shot out from the reeds and sank her fox teeth deep into Shibaten's leg. With her jaw locked like a steel trap, she rolled her body, loudly popping the *kappa*'s bones from ankle to knee.

"Betrayal!" the *kappa* cried.

Moya dropped to the ground at my feet, growling and snarling and smoking. Shibaten's leg hung loosely on the ground. He hopped back, still facing the *kitsune*, hissing and grunting and trying to keep his balance. Never taking his eyes from hers, Shibaten roared but slowly disappeared beneath the barberry bush.

I looked to the side as the world shook in and out of focus. The *kitsune* was gone. Two hands grasped my shoulders and began to drag me.

"Moya?" I could see her face floating above me. "I'm not doing very well."

"I know, you stupid, stupid, little thief."

"It hurts so much."

Moya stopped to lean over me. "Look into my eyes, Koda. I give you permission this time. To escape the pain."

I looked up and tried to smile my appreciation as the world slipped easily into ice.

"Seimei," the whisper said. "Seimei, open your eyes."

The boy obeyed and the park burned all around him.

"You are safe. I am with you."

When Seimei looked up he saw a girl in a long silver *kimono* covering him, shielding him from the flames. She smiled, just centimeters from his face.

"Who are you?" he asked.

"Who do I look like to you?" she replied.

"A girl. In a gray *kimono.*"

"Then that is who I will be."

"No!" Moya yelled out.

The cold dream vanished like smoke. I turned my head painfully to the side. We were at the edge of the bamboo forest looking in at the *kaki* tree. Only the *kaki* tree wasn't there anymore. Moya was screaming. I tried to shift, but ribbons of fire seared up my arm. The *kaki* tree was in pieces on the ground, an ax thrown hastily to the side. Was I still cold-dreaming?

Moya's face appeared above mine. Dark trails of ash ran down her cheeks. "It isn't safe here," she cried. "Oh gods, Koda, it isn't safe here anymore." She grabbed me by my coat and yanked hard. The world, and my pain, disappeared into ice again.

"No!" Moya screamed.

Kōtenbō moved like lightning, sinking his sword so deep into Seimei's chest that the blade wedged itself into the smoking shrine wall. Kōtenbō grabbed the boy's face in his enormous red hand and yanked the sword free. Seimei's body hung limp in the *tengu*'s grip until Kōtenbō dropped him like a bag of rotten fish.

Moya rushed forward and cradled the boy's head in her lap.

Kōtenbō turned and suddenly ran for the exit. When he pulled the handles, the doors stayed shut.

"Seimei," Moya cried.

Fire swept along the walls. The crows stormed around the door and Kōtenbō yanked until wood popped and hinges whined, but the chain on the outside of the shrine held true.

Moya didn't look up. Her silver *kimono* covered Seimei's legs. Her light hair fell over his empty eyes. Sulfuric tears ran down her neck. "No, no, no," she whispered. "Please, Inari, no."

Kōtenbō banged his massive fist on the door again and again. Moya saw nothing. Where her eyes should have been, embers burned brightly. Moya opened her mouth and screamed light, and Ōmura Shrine exploded in a hurricane of fire. Kōtenbō's broken body sizzled as he was flung through the tops of the trees and into the valley below.

"Seimei," the flames wept, "I am so sorry."

34

Shimizu-*sensei* sat alone in a train car. The doors would be closing soon. In just a few minutes there would be no escape.

He'd woken up in an empty parking lot, his head throbbing. The spirits were watching and waiting. They mocked him for letting a young boy and a silly girl make such a mess of him.

The demon will never let us go now, they said. *You are too stupid for him to keep alive.*

Shimizu-*sensei* had pushed up to his feet and stumbled to keep his balance.

There is still a way, a young girl told him.

"I failed and he will kill me," Shimizu-*sensei* shot back. "He will trap me here forever."

A woman in a black dress stepped forward and placed her hand on his cheek. *Would that be so bad, my son? To stay with your mother forever?*

"I hate you," Shimizu-*sensei* whispered. "I hate every last one of you."

Yowamushi, the *rōnin* at the back of the crowd grunted.

"I am not a weakling. You make me do terrible things!"

A man in a business suit pushed to the front. *We can still escape this. Look over there. Do you see the ax? Pick it up, my son. Pick up the ax.*

Shimizu-*sensei* looked across the street at a pile of logs. A silent crow perched on the handle.

"He won't let us go," my homeroom teacher said. "No matter what we do. He will always keep us here."

We have to try, the spirit in the suit said. *Pick up the ax.*

"I can't kill the boy," said my teacher. "I don't think I ever could."

You won't have to. Pick up the ax.

Even sitting on the train, Shimizu-*sensei* couldn't force the sounds out of his mind. The *kaki* tree had whined and creaked under the force of the heavy blade. It was crazy, he knew, but as he tore at the trunk, he'd heard something on the air, floating along the breeze. A scream. No. Lighter than that. Like remembering a scream that wasn't really there. When the tree was mauled and dead, the screaming breeze drifted away. Shimizu-*sensei* dropped the ax and ran from the bamboo grove.

Now there were only a few moments before the train doors would shut and Shimizu-*sensei*'s fate would be sealed. The spirits around him hadn't left at all—they'd only gotten louder. The ghosts shouted and ordered and begged him to get off the train, but Shimizu-*sensei* wouldn't listen.

The crows are calling us back, a small boy screamed. *He wants us to return to him.*

If we help him this last time, his mother pleaded, *then the* tengu *will let us go. We can move on from this place. We promise this time.*

But Shimizu-*sensei* pulled his jacket close around his body and tried to shut them out.

You will die if you do this, said a man in a bowler hat. *You will become like the rest of us, trapped forever in Kusaka Town. No one will be left to free us.*

"If I go to the *tengu,* he will make a murderer out of me," Shimizu-*sensei* whispered.

If you don't go, he will kill your soul.

"The boy is innocent," Shimizu-*sensei* said.

The world is full of innocent people.

"No, this is our fault. Our clan. Our betrayal. Our consequences."

We were just trying to find a way out.

"Desperate people always are," Shimizu-*sensei* said. "But that doesn't make it right."

You will never be free, said the man in the bowler hat.

"We were never free anyway."

The conductor's announcement blared out over the speakers. Next stop: Sakawa-*chō.* The doors rattled closed and the voices around Shimizu-*sensei* fell silent. The train lurched forward and started down the tracks. If other people had been in that car, they wouldn't have seen a man surrounded by two hundred years of ancestors. They would have seen my homeroom teacher with a lump on his head, gripping the front of his jacket, staring straight into the face of a crow perched on the opposite seat.

The 11:00 p.m. train to Sakawa blasted over the border, but Shimizu-*sensei* was screaming long before it reached that point. Once he left Kusaka, the sound of his voice only traveled backward, as if sucked behind him into that cursed town.

Microscopic bits of Shimizu-*sensei* were pulled toward Kusaka. The scraps flaked away and escaped the car through open windows and slots in the metal. The deeper the train barreled into the next town, the longer Shimizu-*sensei*'s cometlike tail became. He was a meteor flying straight into the sun. The cosmic particles broke free and, while he screamed in silence, Shimizu-*sensei*'s body unzipped at the smallest level.

Kusaka Town was embedded so deeply inside the Shimizu clan that it tore them all to dust. Ghosts, humans, even the crow perched in the seat couldn't escape the pull. In a final flash of light, the Shimizu clan ceased to exist.

Their funeral ash hung in the air for several moments before siphoning out of the cracks in the train.

I opened my eyes and looked up at the flickering green ceiling of my bedroom. I smiled. My body felt light. Sure, a *kappa* had just tried to tear my arms off, but I couldn't feel any of that. I could barely remember it. The world felt warm. And shappy. That's a whole new word—shining and happy. I just made it up. Because I'm awesome.

"Well, you're grinning like an idiot," Moya said, a sad smile on her face. "Those herbs must be working—otherwise you'd be screaming."

I dropped my head to the side and smiled extra wide for Moya. A handful of leaves and grass dribbled out of my mouth.

"Can I sit up?" I mumbled.

"I don't know. Try."

I rolled over and pushed up from the floor with my good arm. The broken one hung limp at my side.

"Not bad," she said.

I spit out the last of the leaves and wiggled my arm. It flopped like a wet noodle. "But not good, either," I said.

"Your bone is like *konyaku* jelly right now. I think the feeling will come back soon."

"You think?"

"Well, not if you keep shaking it around like that."

"How did you fix the bone?"

"Just a little *kitsune* power," she said. "It was either that or gnaw your arm off. As a fox, I'm not picky."

I lifted my wrist and let my arm fall again. "Well, you definitely made the right choice. Dragging my butt around while you're fighting a *tengu* could make things a little harder."

Moya didn't say anything. She pulled her knees up to her chest and stared into the green flames of the spectral fireball floating in my room.

"That's not going to burn the house down, right?" I said, dropping next to her. "It's cool, but my parents have a strict no-burning-down-the-house policy. Probably."

"I can't do this," she whispered.

I looked over at her.

"I'm a protector spirit that can't protect anyone."

"Don't say that."

"It's true."

"Seriously, though, you're the only protector spirit I've got."

Moya burst into tears. The sulfuric streaks ran down her face and sizzled holes into my *tatami* mat floor.

"You're scaring me, Moya."

"You should be scared. Kōtenbō is a horror! He doesn't care if the innocent suffer. He murdered Seimei. He murdered the last *kaki* tree. And he will murder us if he gets the chance."

"The *kaki* tree is really dead?" I whispered. "I thought it was just a cold dream."

"Kōtenbō must have sent his puppets to chop it down while we were distracted with Shibaten. She was dead by the time we got back."

"I'm sorry, Moya." I tried to put my arm around her, but it just flopped against her back. I reached across with my good arm and awkwardly patted her shoulder. "He knows we're close. Remember that. He's desperate."

"This was more than desperation," Moya said. "This was his plan all along. Every time I think I've trapped him, I realize he was trapping me the whole time. We can't fight this. He's going to win, Koda. There's nothing we can do."

"You can stop him," I said.

Moya looked over at me.

"I believe in you, Moya. You're one of the good ones, right?"

Her eyes fell back to the floor. "I don't know anymore," she whispered.

"I do."

She stared into the flames for a long time. "The shrine was Seimei's idea," she finally said. "I didn't want to use him as bait. I told him not to do it. I told him he should hide in a temple to Inari until Kōtenbō was dead, but he said we had to find the *tengu* fast. He said that other people would die and he couldn't live with that."

"I understand the feeling," I said.

"The shrine was Seimei's idea, but I was supposed to protect him. Instead, I just chained him inside with a monster." She wiped her cheeks with her fingers. "When I walked out of the shadows, Kōtenbō didn't lunge at me. He didn't hack at the door or kick through the walls. He turned and drove his sword straight through Seimei's heart. The poor boy was dead before I could even reach him."

The floating fire shrank and burned a deeper shade of green.

"I can't protect anyone," she whispered. "Kōtenbō killed Seimei. He killed the *kaki* tree. And he is going to kill you."

"You did your best," I said.

"Yeah, well, sometimes doing your best isn't good enough."

"But if we put our bests together," I said, "then maybe it will be good enough."

She looked at me. "And maybe it won't. My partner is a kid

who hurts himself at sporting events. I think you're overestimating your value to the team."

"First," I said, "that's rude. Second, I may not be able to fight a *tengu*, but I'm the only person who can find one. Where are the bastard's eyes?"

Moya pointed to the open wooden box next to the wall.

I scooted over and picked it up. "These are eyes?" I said.

"They used to be."

"Gods, that is disgusting. I'm literally going to throw up every time I see a yellow raisin from now on."

Moya shrugged.

"They're too gross," I said. "Will you put them in my numb hand for me?"

Moya crawled over and pushed my head back onto the floor. "This is the kid who was going to cut out Kōtenbō's heart and give it to a *kappa*?"

"I don't remember saying that."

"You did."

"I say things I don't mean, then."

"Obviously."

Moya turned the box over onto my floppy hand.

"Did you do it? Is it working?" I asked.

Moya rolled my fingers into a fist. "Do you feel anything?" she said.

"I don't know! There are eyes in my hand, Moya. Eyes! I'm freaking out here!"

"Calm down and concentrate."

"Okay, my arm definitely feels cold."

"Is that a good thing?"

"Yes."

"I'll be here when you wake up," Moya said.

"I feel it now."

"*Ja mata*," Moya said.

"Thank you," I told her, and fell back into my world of ice.

35

Before Kusaka was a town or a village or anything at all, Kōtenbō soared high above the trees, peering down at the fires dotting the valley. If he flew long enough, the humans would see him crossing the moon and the stars, but he didn't care. He circled the mountain one more time and swooped down toward the *tengu* camp. Humans were loud and carried fire wherever they went, so Kōtenbō wasn't afraid of an ambush. He just wanted them to know he was always watching.

The giant vulture hit the ground and shook its head. It stepped left and right to gain its balance, then folded its colossal wings. The neck twisted and cracked, receding back into the tuft of white at the top of its body. The face of the vulture disappeared down the emerging throat of a *tengu* whose nose and long teeth rose from the feathers. The talons expanded into toes. The scaly legs became thick and red. The wings and tail shrank into arms and a sword scabbard at the waist. Kōtenbō stretched and brushed away the feathers that didn't pull completely into his pores. He stroked the long white hairs of his chin and lay down with a sigh next to his favorite tree.

Kōtenbō closed his eyes. He hadn't dreamed since he was human. That was so long ago he'd lost count of the years. Stealing memories felt like dreaming, but that was as close as he got. Sometimes he missed regular dreaming. People dream for a reason, and that reason was missing from Kōtenbō now.

A twig snapped. The *tengu* opened his eyes to see Shibaten standing over him, a broken twig in hand. Normally, Kōtenbō would have run his sword through the river troll for sneaking up on him like that, but something stopped him. The world didn't feel real. Kōtenbō felt drunk on invisible fumes. It was kind of like a dream. Or a vision. Or a trick.

Of course, the *tengu* thought, *a prank. A spoof. A lark. A bit of tomfoolery. Kappa* were trickster spirits. Full of mischief and obscenity. Kōtenbō didn't know what it was doing so far from the river, but he would ask the troll after he pinned it to a tree with his sword.

The *tengu* shook off the intoxication and sat up against the tree. Shibaten held a thin wooden box up to his face.

"Move away from me, *kappa*," Kōtenbō growled. "Your trickery has no power here."

But Kōtenbō was wrong. In an instant he found that he was looking back at himself from the inside of the wooden box.

"What is this?" he watched himself say, only this time with two vacant holes where his eyes should have been. Shibaten snapped the box shut.

Through the icy air I watched the *kappa* turn and run. I watched Kōtenbō stumble to his giant feet and roar so loudly that leaves fell from branches. I watched swords and spears and armor break through the trees and fall onto the unsuspecting *tengu* camp.

Kōtenbō knew that without his eyes he would be cut down by the humans and their treachery. He had to transform. Had to escape. Somehow he must find his way back to Sarutadō Cave. He crashed through the forest and rolled down a hill, smacking into tree trunks along the way. The *tengu* strained to transform, beating his giant wings in the direction of the abandoned cave on the east side of town.

The cold dream should have ended there—the scarring memory trapped within Kōtenbō's eyes was spent. But instead of evaporating, the air and the earth shifted to the banks of Kusaka River. Shibaten held out the wooden box to a huge man decorated with *samurai* armor and demon blood.

The man who looked remarkably like my gym teacher looked down at the *kappa* and laughed. "We weren't sure you would accomplish the trick. You have our thanks, troll. You contributed significantly to the *tengu* defeat."

Shibaten blew air through his nose and tapped the box.

"Ah, yes. Your reward."

Archers rushed through the bushes and took aim. Shibaten stepped back toward the river.

"Hanare!" the man cried.

Shibaten's body recoiled from fifteen arrows striking him in the chest and stomach. The *kappa* fell back into the river with a splash. The wooden box floated away and lodged itself downstream in the reeds.

After the men and their laughter left the banks of Kusaka
River, a small hand wrapped in turtle skin rose up from the
icy water to grasp the box.

I shot straight up against the wall of my bedroom.

"Whoa!" Moya shouted, still nursing her green fireball.
"No warning at all. Just, *pop*, and out you come."

I looked over at Moya and smiled.

"Do you know where Kōtenbō is hiding?" she asked,
scooping the demon's dry eyes into their wooden box.

"I'm a mind-thief, aren't I?"

"More like a misery thief, but sure, you can say it that way
if it makes you feel better."

"It does. After Shibaten stole Kōtenbō's eyes, he flew to
Sarutadō Cave."

"Good job, Koda," Moya said with a smile that was stretched
a little too thin. She stood up and looked out through my dark
window. "We'll go in the morning."

I rolled over and grabbed a pillow from my closet.

"What's that for?" she asked, turning around.

"I thought we should get some sleep before, you know,
killing a mountain demon together."

"You still want to kill a mountain demon with me? Even
after everything you've seen?"

"I'd kill a mountain demon with you anytime, Moya."

"That's so sweet," she said. "How am I your first girlfriend?"

"I knew it! You *are* my girlfriend."

Moya laughed.

I unfolded my *futon* with one arm and laid it out on the floor.

"Yipes," she said. "I think this relationship is moving a little too fast."

"What?"

"Save a boy from a bloodthirsty *kappa* just one time, and he thinks he can invite you to sleep in his room. So typical."

"What? Gods, Moya, no—that's not what I was doing. I'll sleep over here. Way over here. On the other side of the room, I swear." I ran over to the opposite end of the room all floppy-armed and dropped onto the *tatami* mats. "See, it's really comfortable all the way over here by myself on this hard floor. It feels great."

No, it didn't. I should have grabbed a blanket.

Moya crawled across the room and sat next to me. After a few moments she asked, "Can you choose what you see?"

"What?" I said, turning to her.

"Can you choose what memories to steal from a person?"

"I honestly don't know."

"What if the person helped?"

Moya put out her hand.

"What do you want me to see?" I asked.

"A trauma," she said, closing her eyes.

I reached out and held her hand in mine. She smiled at me. The world turned to ice.

Moya and Seimei were standing in the same park where his parents had died just a few weeks before. Moya wore a silver *kimono* that fluttered softly at the hems. Seimei wore his brown school uniform, washed but still snagged and torn from his first encounter with Kōtenbō. I walked through the park gate and noticed for the first time how eerily Seimei looked like me.

"You cannot defeat him," I heard Moya say.

"But *you* can, Kemuri," he said, looking down at the ground.

Kemuri? Did Moya change her name when she met me?

Moya lifted Seimei's chin until their eyes met. "Run away from this village, Seimei. Go to the shrine of Inari. The goddess will protect you."

"You will protect me, Kemuri."

"I am only one, Seimei. And the *tengu* is one. I cannot tell you what the end will be."

In that moment, Seimei seemed small and powerless. He was no *suri* or supernatural creature or great swordsman. But Kōtenbō was all of those things.

"Running is death," Seimei said. "If not to me, then to the others whose blood is also cursed."

Seimei knelt down and drew Ōmura Shrine in the dirt with his finger. He explained his plan to use himself as bait to lure Kōtenbō in. Moya slowly shook her head when he instructed her to chain the doors from the outside.

"The *tengu* is a cunning demon," Moya said. "You will not be safe in the shrine."

"Because he is cunning he will not enter without me there."

Moya must have known he was right, because her only reply was a single drop of sulfur that smudged her porcelain cheek.

Seimei stood and took her hand. "We will win, Kemuri. We are the good ones. We have to win."

But I knew what Seimei did not—deserving to win and winning are not the same thing. Moya suddenly turned and looked in my direction, as if, for a moment, she sensed someone there in the cold and the ice.

"We will win," she whispered to Seimei. "Somehow and somewhere we'll bring the *tengu* down."

I was lying on my *tatami* mat when I opened my eyes. Moya was curled into a ball behind me, her forehead against my back. We lay on my floor together staring out into the darkness, knowing that tomorrow morning Sarutadō Cave would be our shrine.

"You *are* one of the good ones," I whispered to her.

Moya slowly squeezed my hand.

36

NOTEBOOK/FUJIWARA, <u>AIKO</u>
DATE: 2006年9月22日

T   R   A   P   P   ED
inside.
how does the monster make the screaming inside. the
black birds are in me now. can you be released. Can
yyyyyyyyyyou be released. find the door. find the way. you
cant belong here. you cant belong inside. i can hear it. i can
hear it. i can hear it. i can hear it. i can hear it. i can hear it.
i can hear it. i can hear it. i can hear it. i can hear it. i can
hear it. i can hear it. i can hear it. i can hear it. i can hear it.
i can hear it. i can hear it. i can hear it. i can hear it. i can
hear it. i can hear it. i can hear it. i can hear it. i can hear it.
i can hear it. i can hear it. i can hear it. get out. be free. i
can hear them hearing me. i will do it. i will drink it and
you will be free. open my mouth and free the black birds.
the three-legged one is not coming. hhhhhhhhhheee
is nnnnnnotttttttttt here. drink the potion. drink the

potionpoisonpotionpoisonpotion. free the black birds trapped inside. drink the key. open the door. flyyyyyyyy away with them. fffffffffffflllllllllllllllllllllllllllllllyyyyyy yyyyyyyyyyy away. we are alone. but we will not be travelers lost on this road.

The next morning Moya and I walked out to the last *kaki* tree. Or the twisted mass of branches and chopped-up trunk that used to be the last *kaki* tree. We stood there for a long time.

"We can beat him," I told her, massaging my now-unbroken arm. It was still a little tender.

"I'm sorry, my dear," Moya whispered as she walked slowly toward the shattered tree. She knelt down and touched the gnarled trunk. "Koda, I want you to stay here with the tree," she said without looking back.

"No." I slipped Yori's goggles over my neck.

She stood and turned around. "Kōtenbō killed Seimei. He killed the *kaki* tree. And if you go with me to Sarutadō, he will kill you, too."

"He also killed Yori and Aiko and Ichiro and Taiki. I can help you defeat him."

"It's too dangerous."

"I can help you."

"You're just a silly human kid."

"You need me, Moya."

"I don't need you!" she cried back.

Moya wiped at her cheek.

"If you go in there alone, you might not come back," I said.

"If you come with me, *you* might not come back," she said. "How can you be so foolish, Koda? I tried to show you that Seimei thought the same thing." Moya slowly sat down on the grass. "You could run. You could run far from Kusaka Town and become a priest at a shrine to Inari. She would protect you from everything."

"I couldn't live with myself," I said, walking up to her.

"Why doesn't anyone like my priest idea?"

"Because it sounds really boring."

She looked up at me.

"And the whole abandoning-our-town-to-a-murderous-*tengu* idea," I said. "There's that, too."

I sat down next to Moya. "Besides, hiding me is what Kōtenbō thinks you'll do. Who in their right mind would take a teenage kid and lock them in a room with a murderous mountain demon? Twice?"

"Certainly not a sane person."

"Exactly."

"You're not helping your argument at all here."

"That's just my point. The reasonable thing to do is keep me away from that cave at all costs."

"Right."

"Maybe leave me at my house or in this grove. But if Kōtenbō reached the *kaki* tree, he can reach me. I don't think I'd last long against an ax-wielding tree killer. And if I have the choice, I'd rather face my threats standing by your side."

"You know just what to say to make a girl swoon, Koda."

"We can bring down Kōtenbō," I said. "This time is differ-ent from any other time because you have a secret weapon."

"What would that be?" she said.

I pointed at my face and whispered.

"What?" she said.

I whispered really softly again.

"I can't hear you."

"My brain, Moya! My brain."

"Your brain is our secret weapon?"

"Yes," I said, snapping Yori's goggles to my forehead. "I am a *suri* and Kōtenbō is scared to death of me."

"Gods," she breathed, "I wouldn't say he's scared to death."

"He is very scared of me."

"A little nervous, maybe."

"Petrified."

"Anxious, at best."

"The point is, he doesn't know everything in the whole world, Moya! He can't see inside my mind. He doesn't know what we're thinking. What we're planning. Hell, I don't even know what we're planning!"

Moya thought for a moment. "It would be a shame for your homeroom teacher to chop you into bits while I'm gone."

Moya stood and pulled a long broken shard from the core of the *kaki* tree. A small flame stood up from her finger. It whipped in the wind, searing the outside of the wood.

"What are you doing?" I asked.

"Making you a spear," Moya said. She blew on the singed

bark and then scraped the end on a rock, turning it over and over in her hands to sharpen the point.

"Wait, do *kaki* trees kill *tengu*?" I said, squatting next to Moya. "Is that why Kōtenbō was killing them off? It makes perfect sense now."

"Nope. It's just a regular wooden spear."

"But if I throw it hard enough, it should tear through him like it would tear through rice paper, right?"

Moya tested the point with her finger. "I don't think any law of nature would allow for that to happen."

"Then what am I supposed to do with it?"

She held the spear up in front of her face and lit the whole thing in green flame. The wood crackled and pulled together, shrinking and shining like polished stone.

"You're going to do what you do best—distract people."

She blew out the flame and handed me the spear. It was warm to the touch.

"So you need me to wound him?" I asked.

"You just have to hit him. Or throw it near him. Just get it somewhere in his general vicinity."

I looked down at my spear, which had seemed so awesome when it was on fire. "This isn't going to hurt him at all, is it?"

"Like throwing a toothpick at a bullet train. But you just have to give me time to grab his sword."

"Wait, you can grab swords?" I said. "That's, like, a thing you can do?"

"Sure. Or melt it. Whatever. We'll figure it out when we get there."

"Figure it out? Dear gods and goddesses, I take back what I said. This plan I didn't know is actually freaking terrible."

Moya shrugged.

"We are so screwed," I said.

"The most important thing, Koda, is getting that sword out of his hands. Every person Kōtenbō personally murdered was stabbed in the chest. We have to get the sword out of his hands before he can use it."

"And again, this hinges on me hitting a *tengu* with a sharpened stick?"

"Yep," she said, walking away from me. "Master your weapon, my little *samurai*. We'll leave when I've paid my last respects to the *kaki* tree."

"Just like that? No demonstration? No words of advice?"

"Pick something," she said. "Throw your spear at it. Do that a bunch of times until you don't miss."

Oh, we are so screwed.

37

NOTEBOOK/FUJIWARA, <u>AIKO</u>

DATE: 2006年9月20日

i can free you. he hates me but the monster showed me
how. i cannot see you be free. but i can make you be free.
if i had his eyes i could wish you away from here. if I had
his thieving eyes I could steal you for myself.

F
R
E
E

t
h
e

B
L
A
C
K

B
I
R
D
S

猿田洞

Sarutadō.

Monkey Field Cave.

Which is a weird name to give this cave system, since I've never seen a monkey in Kusaka. Fields? We've got plenty of those. Caves? Sure, I guess. But monkeys? Nope, never. Maybe they were running all over the place before humans got here. Or maybe *monkey* actually refers to humans. Considering how many magical creatures probably live in these mountains, that seems obvious to me now.

Back when *samurai* and warrior clans ruled Kōchi (or Tōsa, as it was called then), Monkey Field Cave was famous for its *ninja* assassins. That's right. *Ninja*. From Kusaka. How cool is that? The caverns of Sarutadō twist and turn, dropping into pools of ice water, then climbing high into the mountain. At the very top, they open up into a man-sized hole in the ground. It was through this hole that *ninja* escaped after stabbing some unsuspecting *samurai* or *shōgun* or whatever. And if assassins can disappear and reappear unseen from Sarutadō, so too can a murder of crows.

There was a time when schoolchildren used to tour the caverns. Were we secretly training *ninja* elementary school students? No. That would be the most awesome field trip ever, but no. Instead it was just boring old tours full of history and junk.

Lights had been strung up, ladders and walkways nailed into the rock, but eventually the water inside Sarutadō stopped people from coming around. The metal in the ladders rusted away, bats chewed through the electrical wires, plants grew over the entrance, and before long Sarutadō returned to its quiet *ninja* ways—dark, mysterious, full of legends and whispers. The perfect place for a mountain demon to hide.

Moya and I jumped over the small stream running in front of the cave's entrance. Miniature *shintō* statues guarded the rocky mouth, which was cool, and stale.

"Are you afraid?" Moya asked.

"Nope," I scoffed, zipping up my jacket. "*Terrified.* That's a better word."

I adjusted Yori's goggles on my head. In some tiny way, the Desert Punk was going to have his revenge today.

"Listen, Koda, we need to talk."

"Really? You sure it's not a bit late for a we-need-to-talk moment?"

"If something should go wrong in there," she said, "you need to get out as fast as you can."

"So you don't want me to avenge your death with my fake spear?"

"Avenge my . . . Gods, no. No, no, no. I will shield you from Kōtenbō, but if something happens to me, you have to get out. As fast as you can. Get away from these caves. Then get out of this town."

"I have a feeling Kōtenbō won't let me leave so easily."

"There are worse things in these caves than Kōtenbō."

"What's worse than a giant *tengu* that wants to rip out my skeleton?" I asked.

"The darkness in this cave is not natural. Skeletons can be put back inside bodies. Minds, however, cannot."

"How exactly do you think the human body works, Moya? Having your skeleton on the outside is pretty freaking bad."

"And things could end even worse than that."

"We really need to work on our pep talks here."

"The important thing is that you get out, Koda. Forget about me. Leave me here and don't stop running until you find a shrine to Inari."

"I feel like our relationship has taught me so much about being a responsible boyfriend. Thank you for that."

"Kōtenbō is a demon. He's a walking nightmare, but he's still just the crest on a much larger wave. Do not let the Road take you, Koda. Do not let that darkness slip into your soul. Run away from it. As fast and as far as you can."

Moya stepped up to me and unclipped the silver barrette from her hair. She put it in my hand and closed my fingers.

"Always remember the good in this life," she said. "Remember Aiko. Remember Ichiro and Taiki and Yori. Remember me."

I turned the barrette over and over in my hand.

"Do you know what an *akai ito* is?" she asked.

"A red string?"

"When you love someone, you are never really lost to them," she said. "A red string reaches from one end of the sky to the next. From the moon to the oceans to the highest mountains. No matter what happens in life, focus on that instead of the sadness or the pain. I will be with you, Koda. Remember that. I will be watching. And our *akai ito* will always help me find you again."

Moya looked up and kissed me. Like she had done at the Kusaka Festival under the lights and the glow of the booths and the statues looking down on us. My heart had been bleeding that night, but something in her kiss had made me forget my fears. They melted away and disappeared and made me never want to leave her side again.

Even though Sarutadō stood open in front of us, waiting to swallow us whole, her kiss pushed out the despair and the fear once more. Kōtenbō may have killed the *kaki* tree, but part of it survived in Moya. And for just a few seconds, I felt its light inside her. The Tengu Road fills the vast spaces of the universe, but for those brief moments I felt like it could never touch me. Like I could simply walk away from it all.

I smiled when she stepped back.

"Let's go inside," she said. "Let's stop Kōtenbō." She took

my hand and we walked up to the mouth of the cave. "That last part fixed the pep talk, right?" she said.

"Sure," I said.

She smiled. "Little thief."

Together we entered Sarutadō.

38

The deeper Moya and I walked into the caverns, the darker and colder it became. Moya rolled her hands and created a little green flame to lead the way.

"Do you know where we're going?" I asked.

"To the very heart of Sarutadō Mountain," she said in an ominous voice. "I can sense it with my fox powers. Nah, just kidding, I'm following the bird poop."

I looked down. The floor was wet and slippery.

"With that many crows," Moya continued, "we just have to follow this smelly highway straight back to Kōtenbō's lair."

"Gross."

"Eh," Moya said. "It's fitting that Kōtenbō would be knee-deep in bird shit."

We waded through icy pools of water, over molding wooden planks, up crumbling, slippery ladder rungs loosely bolted to the rock. We followed Moya's flame and a wide trail of bird droppings deep into the roots of Sarutadō.

"This is probably it," she said, standing over a dark drop-off. "I don't think it goes any farther."

I looked over the edge into blackness.

"Should we wait for him to come out?" I asked.

Moya sat down on the grime of the edge and scooted off into the darkness.

"Really? We're not even going to talk about this?" I called after her.

I heard her hit the ground below.

"Are you dead, Moya?"

She didn't say anything back. But she was standing. I could see the green flame.

"If I break my leg," I said, kneeling next to the edge, "you are totally fixing it."

I twisted and let go, hitting the ground, and slipping in dung.

"Oh gross, gross, gross," I squealed, frantically wiping my hands on my pants. I pushed Yori's goggles back onto the top of my head. "And it got on the spear, too. I'm going to throw up."

Moya stood in the main cave chamber, staring off into a darkened corner.

"Moya?" I said.

I heard something rustle above me. I looked up. From the reflection of her light, I could see them. Feathers. Shiny. Black. Hundreds of thousands of them, covering the ceiling like living armor. Writhing. Shards of pale gray beaks and claws.

Vacant eyes. A rippling shield of crows staring down at us from all sides.

"Moya," I whispered again, "I think they know we're here."

"Gods above and below," came a deep voice from the corner of the chamber, "I could hear you tramping through the cave from the moment you entered it. I hope your plan wasn't to sneak up on me. That would have been a very bad plan, *kitsune*, considering your human can't walk down the street without falling on his face."

"That's why I wear a helmet sometimes!" I shouted.

"Maybe let me handle this," Moya said.

She reached out and lit a bunch of old torches that had been placed around the main chamber.

"Thank you," Kōtenbō said. "Saved an old *tengu* the trouble of having to get up. Not that it makes much difference, though. The world is always dark when you have no eyes."

"That hasn't prevented you from murdering people, *tengu*," Moya said.

"Thank you. I'll take that as a compliment."

Kōtenbō was kneeling *seiza*-style on the cave floor with a sword scabbard at his side. If I'd ever wondered why this enormous demon hadn't just run around Kusaka killing people, I now understood. Kōtenbō was huge, but he looked like he'd run face-first into a harvester. His limbs were knotted and crooked and stiff. Thick cords of scar tissue snaked over his entire body. Even his long, red nose, the pride of any *tengu*, sat bent above his lip like that of a boxer who'd taken too many punches. He didn't look like much of a threat to anyone anymore. Getting exploded out of a shrine really messes you up. Even if you are a mountain demon.

Kōtenbō pushed up on his good leg and set his mangled one on the cave floor. He leaned on the sword scabbard and stroked his patchy white beard with a gnarled hand.

"At first I was furious that your mind was locked down, man-child," Kōtenbō said. "No poisoning or leaping off school roofs for Koda Okita. Koda the *suri*. Koda the pickpocket. Koda the mind-thief. But then I realized something."

He hobbled forward a bit. Moya stepped in front of me.

"I had actually been wrong this entire time," Kōtenbō said. "You aren't powerful at all. You are just a weak, narcoleptic child who is too stupid and too fragile to be controlled.

"That is why I had such a hard time breaking you, Koda. I was trying too hard! You are a walking imbecile. A danger to yourself and everyone you have ever known. I should have just ignored you. You would have killed yourself eventually. Fallen off a bamboo mast. Walked in front of a van. Stabbed yourself with your teacher's kitchen knife."

"You did all of that!" I shouted.

"Maybe I did. Maybe I didn't. The important thing is that the famous Koda Okita did not die."

"Wait, I'm famous?"

"He mustered up the courage in his puny, little heart and hunted down the monster in his lair. And your prize will be a warrior's death, courtesy of a real *samurai* blade." Kōtenbō placed his hand on the sword handle. "What more could a Japanese boy desire?"

"I could think of, like, a hundred things I'd rather have."

"Get back, Koda!" Moya shouted.

Now? Wait, I know what to do! I fumbled the *kaki* spear up to my shoulder and threw it with all my might. It flew like an arrow from a master bowman, slicing through the air, sparkling in the light of the torches that surrounded us.

Kōtenbō tried to shield his face with his hands, but not before the spear struck him squarely in the chest.

"I did it!" I screamed.

The spear bounced off Kōtenbō and clattered noisily on the floor.

"That was a little premature," Moya said.

"You told me to throw it!"

"I said to get back."

"Well, now I've lost my spear."

"Um, it's okay, Koda. I'll think of something."

The *tengu* faced us, mouth still open. "What was that?" He laughed. "Was that your plan? To throw a stick at me?" He grabbed his belly and roared with laughter.

Moya raised her arms high above her head. The air swirled around the cave and grew warm. Her fingernails glowed. Her eyes shifted from hazel to deep orange to searing green. She reached out to Kōtenbō, flames licking the tops of her fingertips. I stepped back against the wall because we really hadn't discussed this part of the plan.

"Are you watching, *tengu*? I want you to see me taking your eyes for the second time." She looked up and the birds above squirmed to get clear. Smoke poured from her hands and legs and shoulders.

"Moya, wait," I said, reaching out to her. "Don't burn them."

The smoke stopped.

"They're his eyes, Koda." She looked over at Kōtenbō, who gave her a broken grin. "Let's see how well he wields his sword when he's truly blind." The smoke lifted up again and the feathered ceiling clawed to get away.

"They're hurting," I said. "They're screaming inside. Don't burn them, Moya. It's not their fault."

"Gods," the *tengu* snickered. "Such a squishy heart for a *suri*. You read her diary, didn't you? Of all the things to focus on, Aiko latched on to the crows. Well, you can't predict what the Road will do once it's inside you."

Kōtenbō steadied himself on the rock wall. "She was right, just so you know," he said. "The 'black birds' didn't want to hurt her. Which made everything easier. Why would she think sipping on poison could release my crows? It really was absurd. And hilarious to watch. Especially when she was kicking out her last on the gymnasium floor."

"Don't burn the crows, Moya," I seethed. "But do burn their master to ash."

"Wait!" Kōtenbō cried. "At least let an old *tengu* die with his sword in his hand."

"As you wish, demon," Moya said. "Let's see if you can get past me a second time."

Kōtenbō gripped the handle at his side. Moya's hands burst into hot light.

The *tengu* yanked his sword from the scabbard. Except there was no blade attached. Kōtenbō guffawed and threw the wooden handle onto the cave floor at Moya's feet.

"What is this?" she said.

"Silly me," the *tengu* said. "I'm blind and I must have misplaced my weapon. Oh, wait, now I remember where it is. Nobu, save your father."

Moya turned as a huge shadow emerged from a side chamber.

"Ikeda-*sensei*?" I said.

My ex-*sumō* gym teacher drove a jade-handled *samurai* sword into Moya's breast. The hilt slammed against her chest, nailing her to the rock wall.

"Moya!" I screamed.

Kōtenbō steadied himself on his good leg. He hobbled forward a few paces, laughing. I ran toward Moya, but Ikeda-*sensei* hit me with an open palm and sent me flying to the floor.

"You didn't think I'd repeat my mistake from last time?" Kōtenbō shouted with glee.

Moya struggled against the wall.

"Look at this place," the *tengu* said, knocking on the cave. "There's nowhere to be blown out of. If you pulled the same shenanigans you did at the shrine, you'd bring the whole mountain down on top of us. So, really, I just saved us all."

The *tengu* steadied himself and stroked his beard. "You'd

think a fox would be cunning enough to anticipate something like this. I mean, the human is clearly a moron, but a *kitsune*? I expected more from you, vixen."

Moya coughed orange, sizzling blood onto the ground. Kōtenbō shook his head.

"I'm sorry, Father," Ikeda-*sensei* whined. "I didn't see the monsters come into our house. Now they're making a mess on the floor."

"Yes, they are. But it's all right, son." Kōtenbō looked down at me. "Your gym teacher may be the dumbest of you all. Daddy issues are some of the easiest to piggyback. Nobu!"

"Yes, Father?"

"Bring me my sword. I need to stab your heart with it."

"Yes, Father," Ikeda-*sensei* said. "Did I make you proud?"

"Yes, son. I will let you go to your mother now."

"Thank you, Father, thank you."

"Stop! Please!" I shouted, but the blind *tengu* just grinned with broken teeth.

Ikeda-*sensei* grabbed the jade handle as Moya kicked her feet against the floor.

"Rest, dog-girl," Kōtenbō said. "Your journey of pain is coming to an end."

Moya dropped her head and clutched the jade hilt. Ikeda-*sensei* tugged, but Moya locked her fingers onto my teacher's arm. From the wound in her chest, Moya bled. Bright, boiling orange lava blood.

"What is she doing? Stop her, Nobu!" Kōtenbō yelled.

Ikeda-*sensei* grabbed Moya's hair and yanked on the sword

again and again. The blood popped and crackled on the metal of the blade.

"No!" Kōtenbō cried, hobbling forward. "Bring me my sword!"

Moya looked up at the *tengu*, and as blood flowed stronger from the corner of her mouth, she coughed and smiled. The sword bent under her weight, stretching from the heat. With a flat *click*, the blade snapped and Moya slid off the metal. She crumbled to the ground, leaking molten blood over her stomach and legs.

"No!" Kōtenbō cried.

"Run, little thief," Moya whispered to me.

"I'm sorry, Father," Ikeda-*sensei* mumbled. "I tried to pull the sword, but the monster broke it."

"I was going to kill you quickly," Kōtenbō said, turning on me. "But you've cost me a sword. A very old and very dear sword."

"Moya," I whispered back to her.

Run, she mouthed.

"Death will not come easy to you, man-child. Or to you, Nobu, you great, giant fool. Bring me the *suri* and then beat your own head in with a rock."

"Yes, Father." Ikeda-*sensei* ran over and grabbed me by the throat. He lifted me into the air and squeezed until I couldn't feel my legs anymore.

"Bring him to me," the *tengu* barked from far away. "Be careful, he is truly the weakest thing alive."

But Ikeda-*sensei* froze in place.

"Nobu?"

The giant *sumō* wouldn't move. Or rather, couldn't move.

Open your eyes, Koda, my brain said.

"I can't," I gasped.

Yes, you can.

I forced my eyes open. My gym teacher held me above the ground but stood as still as stone.

Moya is dying. Like Aiko and Ichiro and Taiki and Yori before her. But the fox's fate is not sealed. You can stop the tengu. You can save Moya. You just have to let me in.

"How can I let you in? You're my brain."

Open your mind, Koda. Embrace me.

"Who are you?"

Not a who.

"What are you?"

Something that has been inside you for a very long time.

"The Tengu Road."

The voice inside your head whispering that you can be so much more than you are.

"You want to destroy me."

Not destroy, Koda. Return. I want to return everything to its proper place. To its peaceful, cold silence.

"I don't believe you."

Look at the universe, young one. The light you see is a disease. It is turmoil and burning, violent energy disturbing the tranquility of the darkness. Rest, Koda. Open your heart and embrace the peace of the void that surrounds you. A dark road holds no fear when you know you're the only one on it.

"I won't let you in."

You're saying that because you know you will. It is the only way to save her.

And the voice inside my brain was right. I had stood by and done nothing while Kōtenbō murdered so many people I cared about, but for the first time I felt like I could actually do something to stop him. Me. Alone. I could stop him. It would be so simple. I just had to step back and let the universe in.

Everything I had ever known paled in comparison to the power waiting for me. The Tengu Road was long and empty, but it was also quiet and glorious. Kōtenbō was nothing. I could see him now as the Road saw him.

A blind and broken sparrow.

I could break him for what he did to Moya. I could embrace the Road and shatter his pathetic body with a single thought.

My sleeping was no longer weakness and my body was no longer frail. My cold dreams had been just the surface of an ocean a million fathoms deep. *The Road was the true power.* Its world of smoke swirled around me, cold and silent as the middle of space. This was a power I could control. *I would own the Tengu Road. I would be its master. The Road would serve me for all eternity in beautiful, empty darkness.*

I easily spotted Kōtenbō's control over my gym teacher. Three threads of smoke ran from Ikeda-*sensei*'s eyes and mouth to the *tengu*'s skull across the cave. I reached out and grasped Ikeda-*sensei*'s face. I tore the threads away and shattered his glasses. My gym teacher dropped me to the floor.

"Nobu, bring the man-child to me!" Kōtenbō ordered.

The air froze my skin, but I knew I wasn't sleeping. The vacuum of the universe filled every corner of my mind.

You will rise . . .

". . . above all of them."

I could feel Ikeda-*sensei*'s consciousness pulling toward me. I adjusted Yori's goggles slightly on my forehead.

"Run," I said to Ikeda-*sensei*.

"What is this?" Kōtenbō cried.

My gym teacher broke into a sprint. I smiled at the broken *tengu* across the cave, but having just been released from the demon's hold, and being legally blind, Ikeda-*sensei* had no idea where he was or where he should be running. With a dull *thud* he dashed straight into a cave wall and knocked himself out. Kōtenbō's amazement turned to laughter.

"It isn't so easy placing thoughts, is it? You can't just yell something out, you dimwit. You have to create the memory. Make them believe that what you want is their only choice. There's an art to controlling people, you brain-dead clod. Something you will never have a chance to master."

Kōtenbō reached his gnarled hand above his head. "Bring him to me."

The cave ceiling erupted in feathers and talons and sharp cries. The crows descended on me like a swarm of bees, swirling and snapping and pushing me forward. But just like Ikeda-*sensei*, I could feel their pull. Each crow was a star in the vast cosmos and I was a black hole, yawning, drawing them in.

FREE the BLACK BIRDS. Aiko had seen something that

no one else had, but when I opened my eyes in the hurricane of feathers around me, I saw it, too. Tiny sulfuric threads from every eye. Twisting. Floating. Leading back to the source—an ancient monster, now crippled and weak. I punched through the storm and snapped the threads. The crows dropped like stringless marionettes. Dazed and confused, they stumbled up from the floor and fled Sarutadō Cave in a single, furious cloud.

"Oh, I am definitely going to eat your brain now," Kōtenbō said. "Those were my favorite eyes!"

"Your time is done, Kōtenbō," I said. "I am the Tengu Road now."

Kōtenbō laughed again. "You don't even realize what a simpleton you are. No one controls the Road. The Road controls you. You have eyes. Open them! You are just a miserable pickpocket, not a god. And I don't need magic to break the body of a fifteen-year-old thief!"

Kōtenbō threw his sword scabbard on the ground, balancing on his one good leg. "I am still a *tengu*, and I will tear out your heart and eat it in front of you."

"I thought you were going to eat my brain," I said with a smile.

"I'll eat them both!" Kōtenbō cried.

He hobbled toward me, but only a few steps. Without his eyes, he never saw Ikeda-*sensei* coming. With a cry, my ex-*sumō* gym teacher rushed Kōtenbō, lifting his twisted frame into the air and slamming it with skull-shattering force into the rock wall behind them.

The *tengu* screeched in pain as Ikeda-*sensei* wrapped his arms around the monster and squeezed with all his might. Bones popped under Kōtenbō's thin red skin. His mangled leg flopped desperately against the floor. Ikeda-*sensei* roared, crushing the blind *tengu* in his iron grip until black tar spurted from the monster's long nose. With his arms pinned to his sides, dying breathlessly was the only thing Kōtenbō had left to do.

Or he could transform into a giant vulture. There was always that.

Kōtenbō opened his silent mouth, allowing a massive beak to push free. White feathers strained through his neck and face. His legs shriveled into scales.

Kōtenbō slammed his giant beak into Ikeda-*sensei's* face. Again and again and again the vulture struck the *sumō*, barking and hissing. When Ikeda-*sensei* loosened his grip, Kōtenbō's talons tore at his calves. Ikeda-*sensei* dropped the giant bird, which reared up, flapping its enormous wings and hurling itself at the *sumō* over and over. Ikeda-*sensei* fell against a wall and Kōtenbō leaped on him, slamming his beak into my gym teacher's face and head and neck.

The vulture snapped around and stared at me with empty avian eyes.

"Gods," I said, smiling, never taking my gaze from Kōtenbō. "Death by vulture head-butt. That seems like a particularly nasty way to go."

Ikeda-*sensei* groaned on the ground. Kōtenbō puffed his wings and screeched and charged me.

Now!

A thread of smoke shot from my forehead, puncturing the vulture's skull. The bird froze, wings high, neck stretched, staring blankly into the void.

Suri cannot break into other *suri* minds. That's what they say. Until it happens.

Koda Okita can't kill a giant *tengu*. That's what they say. Until he's standing in front of one with a fist-sized rock in his hand.

This is the easy part, my brain said.

"He is weak," I answered.

A fragile mask sits behind that beak. With all the threats and all the rage, Kōtenbō could never escape his thin frame of bone and brain. This is the easiest part, Koda. Stop the monster. Stop him forever.

The rock shook in my hand. I stepped forward.

Shatter the demon's soul like glass. Take his place and keep the world for yourself. Rule the Tengu Road!

Nothingness swirled in my chest. What would life be like without pain? Without sadness or disappointment or anger? There would just be nothing. An eternal numbness. A safe, eternal, night.

And a road and a wanderer who is lost.

But a dark road is the safest kind of road when the only monster you will ever meet is you.

I raised the rock high above my head.

Moya shot across the cave in a flash of white and sank her teeth into the vulture's neck. Locking her jaw like a steel trap, she spun her *kitsune* body, spraying molten blood across the wall and snapping Kōtenbō's neck with a single, fleshy *crack!*

The massive vulture shuddered once, then crashed to the ground.

"Moya?" I cried out from the void.

My threads of smoke disappeared, leaving Kōtenbō's eyes staring off into nothing. The small fox next to it, however, breathed furiously in a crumpled pile. Each time her ribs rose, blood and light leaked out.

"Moya!" I yelled again.

The despair and the hate and the fear inside me began to burn away. I dropped the rock and knelt down next to her. The Tengu Road broke apart beneath my feet, crumbling into smoke and dust on the cave floor.

"I'm sorry, Moya. I should have run. I know that, but I thought I could stop him. I thought I could save you."

The fox pulled its tongue into its mouth for a moment and then let it fall out again, panting faster and faster.

"But, Moya, we won," I said, breathing out the last of the smoke inside my soul. "No one else needs to die. We can leave together now."

The fox's breath changed. It became shallow. Uneven. The heat from her wound grew cold and gray.

"Moya, what are you doing? Don't leave me here."

The dimming blood hardened to rock on her pelt. She turned her eyes up and looked into mine.

"But we won, Moya," I whispered. "We won."

39

There was no bright light or Shintō god that entered Sarutadō to take Moya home. She lay there in the dirt, watching over me until her eyes could watch no more. With a final breath, she followed Aiko and Ichiro and Taiki and Yori. The most magical creatures I'd ever known. I hoped that wherever they were, they had found happiness. I hoped Yori was battling Rain Spider somewhere, and that Ichiro was a famous baseball player, and that Taiki was a friendly giant. I hoped Aiko knew that the black birds were finally free and that the three-legged crow would bring her family together again.

I wrapped Moya in my jacket and carried her small body out of Sarutadō. We walked through the cattails and the camphor trees for the last time. Moya was my protector spirit. The Tengu Road had almost taken me, but she had saved me. From myself—the most dangerous thing in that cave.

At times I still feel the Road, pulling at the edges of my mind like a hole in space, but then I remember Moya. I remember the festival, and the *kaki* tree, and the kiss in front of the cave. It helps me breathe the numbness out and let the light back in.

A week and a half later I returned to school. The students ran back and forth, totally unaware of the other lives this town had claimed. With Kōtenbō's illusion broken, Shimizu-*sensei* woke up unharmed in the last car of the 9:00 a.m. train to Sakawa. He never returned to the high school. Or to the town he risked everything to escape.

I wish I could say Ikeda-*sensei* walked out of Sarutadō and became a famous *sumō* wrestler. Or a well-known baseball coach. Or even a functioning human being. He survived the vulture attack, which was good. But his brain was so scrambled he barely remembered the past year. Which was not so good.

After returning from the hospital, Nobu Ikeda spent most of his days sitting on the front steps of his house, staring out over the rice fields that had long since turned brown and dry. He doesn't answer when I ride by. He doesn't even look up.

The school told everyone Ikeda-*sensei* fell while exploring the abandoned caverns. Which didn't make sense to anyone. Spelunking *sumō* wrestlers is not a thing. I think Ikeda-*sensei* is just trying to unwind the damage Kōtenbō did to his mind. Maybe he'll work it out and return to school. Or maybe he'll just watch rice fields, happy that he's finally free from his father's control.

My first day back to school was like any other day before this all started. The first-years chased each other through the halls, the third-years talked about movies and TV games and J-pop stars. Toriyama-*sensei* gave us composition homework. Kenji attacked his lunch like a wood chipper attacks a tree.

"Slow down there, kid," I said. "That salmon didn't do anything to you."

"Did you call me 'kid'? *Baka.* I'm bigger than you. And where's your helmet, anyway?"

"In a trash can somewhere, probably. I don't know. Besides, I don't need it anymore."

"Why not?"

"Because sometimes people get better, Kenji. With the help of good friends, they get better."

"What in the hell are you talking about?"

"I'm talking about being a pilot. I'm going to be a stunt pilot and fly all over Japan."

"Yeah, well, stunt pilots still wear helmets, genius."

"Shut up, Kenji," I said, picking up my salmon with a smile.

It was a totally normal, uneventful, fantastic day. And just like I always had, I rode out to Lawson's to meet Haru after school.

"Hey, Fly-Boy," Haru said.

"Thank you! I knew it would catch on. And I appreciate that *you* are saying it and not some voice in my head."

"Gods, you are weird," Haru said.

I thought Shibaten might be a little peeved about the whole

smashing him in the head with a baseball bat. But the day after Kōtenbō's defeat, my parents returned home, refreshed from their Kyōtō vacation. I guess Shibaten had to admit things turned out pretty well for him. Even if a fox almost bit his leg off.

"Are we going to the tree?" Haru asked.

"Let's do it," I said.

Haru jumped on the back of my bike, still dressed in a fine black suit. The cast on his leg wasn't slowing him down. He looked better than he had in a long time.

"How did the interview go?" I asked as we rode along.

"Hard to tell, you know. But I was really enthusiastic."

Haru had decided Kusaka Town wasn't that bad after all and applied for the vacant position in the town hall accounting office. He had no qualifications whatsoever, but it was a better plan than sitting around in a parking lot all day.

"Well, enthusiasm counts for something," I said. "It doesn't really outweigh, you know, job experience or a college degree or basic competence, but it counts for something."

"*Baka*," he said.

"I'm glad you're back," I told him.

"I didn't go anywhere," he said.

I smiled and pedaled faster.

I'd buried Moya Okita under the fallen branches of the *kaki* tree.

Okita.

No one should leave this life without a last name, right? Without a family name? Moya was part of my family now, so I thought she should have mine.

I looked at the broken trunk surrounded by new shoots of green. One day there would be a forest of *kaki* trees in this place. A persimmon tree is a very strange kind of tree. It looks so weak on the outside. So fragile. So odd. But there is great power in a *kaki* tree. Moya sensed it. And for some crazy reason, she sensed it in me, too.

In a dark cave beneath Kusaka Town, Moya pushed me off the Tengu Road. She helped me see the world as it actually is. A place of pain, but also a place of hope. Of despair, but also joy. Of fear, but unforgettable love.

I turned her silver barrette over and over in my hand. It was our *akai ito*, our red string reaching from one end of the sky to the next. From the moon to the oceans to the highest mountains. "When you love someone, you are never really lost to them," she had told me. "No matter what happens in life, focus on that instead of the sadness or the pain. I will be with you, Koda. I will be watching. Our *akai ito* will always help me find you again."

It's something I hope for every day.

Haru hobbled up beside me and reached into his pocket. He pulled out a cucumber, took a bite, and offered it to me.

"I'm good, thanks."

"I can't get enough of these stupid things," he said, chomping into it again. "It's kind of freaking me out."

I guess Shibaten hadn't completely forgiven me for the baseball bat.

Haru looked over at me and said, "Girls, am I right? They'll kiss you one day and then run off to Tōkyō to . . . Why did you say Moya left?"

"To be a scientist."

"Yesterday it was a model."

"To be a scientist *and* a model," I said.

"Before that it was deep-sea diving."

"A scientist *and* a model *and* a diver. She can do all three. She can do anything."

Haru took a loud bite of his cucumber and wiped his mouth on his sleeve. "It's okay, man. Everyone gets their heart broken. But it'll all work out in the end."

I slipped the silver barrette back into my pocket.

"Yeah," I said. "I know it will."

I bowed to Moya's resting place and then walked away from the last *kaki* trees in Kusaka Town.

Acknowledgments

I would like to thank the village of Hidaka for graciously hosting me—while characters and events have been fictionalized, the locations and charm of this village have not. I'd like to thank the Japanese Exchange and Teaching (JET) Programme for creating a valuable bridge of cultural exposure; my insightful editor, Angie Chen; my agent, Michelle Brower; my *akai ito* and first editor in everything I write, Rebecca; my children, Elliott and Anson, the most affectionate obstacles a writer could have; my mother, who read (and praised) anything I put in front of her; Michiru Imanishi, Chieko Bramhall, Chisa Nagoshi Enyeart, and, most important, Fumi Okita, for checking my Japanese and keeping me connected; and, last of all, the crows—who, never flitting, still are sitting, *still* are sitting.